THE MISSING MOTHER

BOOKS BY CASEY KELLEHER

THE MISSING MOTHER

CASEY KELLEHER

bookouture

Published by Bookouture in 2024

An imprint of Storyfire Ltd.
Carmelite House
50 Victoria Embankment
London EC4Y 0DZ

www.bookouture.com

ISBN: 978-1-83790-714-4
eBook ISBN: 978-1-83790-713-7

The first book I've had to finish writing without you by my side. This one is for you, my little Sassy-girl.

1

EVIE

The blaring chaos of noise erupts all around me, jolting me out of the trance like state.

I'm daydreaming again. Standing concealed under a blanket of darkness, lingering aimlessly like a ghost on the corner of this bleak and freezing cold street, for what feels like hours.

Has it been hours?

Metal shutters from across the road drag against the concrete road beneath them with the high-pitch intensity of a serrated knife, screeching its way across a china plate. Sirens blare their distinctive urgent warning, wailing like a chorus inside my ears, almost deafeningly so.

I flinch. Closing my eyes tightly to shield myself from the sudden glare of blue lights that illuminate the street as three fire engines roar past me.

Their light seeps inside regardless.

The pulsating flashing rhythm matching my pounding heart.

Thud-thud. Thud-thud. Thud-thud.

When I finally open my eyes again, the rear lights of the

engines have grown as small as the sound. They are almost out of sight, fading into the distance at the end of the road.

The street is silent once more. Eerie now.

I hook my hand across the bulge beneath my woollen coat, the buttons almost bursting from where the material has stretched across the mound that I have concealed there.

I can no longer feel my fingers. The prickling sensation of needling pain from my freezing flesh has seeped down into my very bones. I am completely numb now. Immune to the cold. Void of all pain. Part of me is grateful for it. For the numbness and the nothingness that has spread through me like a rapidly growing cancer.

The less I can feel, the less this will hurt. Right?

Yeah, right.

I stare over to the vast space between the open fire station doors, where the bright white light pours out onto the street, like a beacon.

Guiding me towards it like a symbol of hope, willing me to step forward and do what I came here to do.

Only still, I hesitate. Aware that despite the chaos just seconds earlier, the station might not be completely deserted, there may be staff inside, remaining behind to man the station.

If I do this, I'll need to be quick.

My feet leave the kerb, the movement delayed, disjointed almost. As if somehow I'm outside of my body. A vague wishful hope floats from somewhere at the back of my mind.

What if this is all just a bad dream that I can't wake up from?

It isn't a dream though.

It's my worst living nightmare.

Soon, I tell myself. *Soon I will wake up! Soon I'll be free again.*

My pace slows as I reach the wall by the fire station's

entrance. My eyes fix on the box that has been built into the wall especially.

It looks just how it looked online.

I dare myself, peering out from the oversized hood of my coat, which I've been using as a shield to hide my face from the world, to scan both ends of the street and make sure there's no one out here watching.

Waiting.

That this isn't some kind of a trick. A trap.

No... No. I'm just being paranoid.

Further up, the road is mostly clear. I see a temporary flash of yellow headlights before a car turns off into a side road. A cluster of people linger in a shop doorway. Some kebab or burger place. The name of the takeaway restaurant is too far away for me to see from here. Their faces blurred.

There is no chance that they will see mine.

Do it. Do it now before you lose your bottle.

Guilt swirls turbulently in the pit of my stomach like a dark storm brewing, and a surge of adrenaline floods my system at the thought of what I am about to do. If I stand here much longer, I might faint. My brain throbs inside my skull, a loud whooshing inside my ears.

I bring my eyes back to the box.

The bold yellow lettering screaming out at me like a warning.

DO NOT OPEN UNLESS YOU NEED OUR
SERVICES. A SILENT ALARM WILL ACTIVATE.

My hands shake as I reach out and pull down the handle.

Too late to change my mind, too late to go back.

One last look. I will allow myself that much, at least.

Tugging at my coat, I peer down to where the tiny baby is nestled against the warmth of my body. Her long, thick lashes rest on the edges of the chubby bulges of her pink cheeks. Tufts of wispy hair poke out from where the blanket is wrapped around the top of her head.

Sleeping soundly now, oblivious of her fate.

Her tiny doll-like features no longer twisted with rage and frustration at being pushed out into the world by the detached, frantic woman she'd been born to.

Lifting her to my face, I breathe in the sweet smell of her, a combination of soap and freshly baked bread, before pressing my lips to the warmth of her forehead. A single tear escapes my eye as I register that this, my first kiss, is also to be my last, before we say goodbye.

I feel as if my heart is breaking in two as I place her inside the box. Careful to lie her gently in the plastic crib there, lined with a mattress and blanket of its own.

She'll be warm here. Safe.

I notice the envelope, the bold letters printed on the front.

PLEASE TAKE THIS

Such a pitiful swap.

My child, my own flesh and blood given in exchange for a piece of paper inside of an envelope. A life that grew inside of me, traded for empty words of advice and reassurance and a charity phone number that I know I won't call.

'I'm sorry. I'm so sorry. Please forgive me...' I start, except my voice cracks under the enormity of the words as they leave my mouth. The finality of what I am about to do hits me and I start to sob. I think of the silent alarm. How it would have been activated.

How someone will be coming for the baby.

I think about the alternative and why I know I have to do this.

The threats that he'd made. The things that I have no doubt

he is capable of doing to me. Of what would happen to my baby if I didn't go through with this.

'I'm sorry. I'm so sorry. But this is the right thing to do. For both of us. I must keep you safe!'

I move. Quickly. Fast on my feet. Back towards my car that I've abandoned much further up the road.

I don't look back.

2

JENNA

No bag. No bag!? Shit! No fucking keys.

Jenna stares at the windows of her ground floor flat, knowing that they are all locked from the inside and, without her keys, now that the Uber has driven off, she's stuck out here.

Shit!

Her head is pounding. A sharp jolt of pain radiates from her temples as if she is being repeatedly jabbed there.

Is that why her thoughts are so fuzzy and sporadic, and she can no longer think straight?

Did she hit her head? She thinks that maybe she did, but she can't quite remember. She isn't sure entirely what happened tonight, but she feels it, something bad lingering on the perimeter of her subconscious. A vague memory of something dreadful.

But what?

Urgh! She needs to get inside her house.

Now.

Wrapping the soft material of her cream scarf tightly around her clenched fist, once. Twice. Three times for luck.

How had she managed to keep hold of her scarf but not her handbag?

Curling her fingers into a tight fist, she draws her arm back, instinctively closing her eyes, to protect them from any rogue shards of glass as she punches the window.

'Fuck!' The word explodes from her mouth with the same vigour as the hot, searing pain that ricochets up her arm. Loud enough, she hopes, to drown out the sound of the glass pane as it shatters into a million pieces.

Her scream isn't the worst of it, she finds, looking down to where her scarf has slipped. The material twisted up her arm along with the quick reflex of her movement. To where a long, jagged slither of glass protrudes from her exposed flesh.

Blood, there is so much blood.

The sight of it, running down her arm, dripping onto the ground, makes her feel dizzy and weightless, and her legs threaten to buckle beneath her, and she is forced to grip so tightly to the window's ledge that her knuckles, drained of blood, turn a bright white.

She stands firm. Refusing to fall, refusing to faint.

Of all the things that could have brought her to her knees tonight, she won't allow this to be one of them. If she can just get inside her house, she'll be all right, she thinks.

She looks at the wound again, ignoring the waves of nausea that threaten. The familiar burn of the tequila now, too, that she'd stupidly guzzled earlier this evening, as it shoots back up her throat at the sight of the blood spurting from the wound, thick and pooling.

Tequila mixed with bile, hotter now, even more potent. Scorching the inside of her mouth.

Jenna swallows it back down. She will not be sick. Not here. Not now.

She stares over towards the neighbouring houses through tear-blurred eyes, feeling sorry for herself as she examines the windows. Scanning for any signs of movement behind each tightly drawn curtain. A faint glow from a bedroom lamp, a twitch of the material.

Nothing.

There are no tell-tale signs of anyone watching, and she is grateful for that.

That no one will come for her.

No one will call the police.

She couldn't cope with that. Not now. Not tonight. Not on top of everything else.

Biting down hard on her lip, she twists her face into a distorted, ugly grimace as she grips the slither of glass between her thumb and her finger and prises it out from her flesh. The gaping gouge will leave a nasty scar, she thinks, wincing. A permanent reminder of her fucked-up night etched into her skin, forevermore.

She'd promised herself she wouldn't get into such a state tonight.

'Go easy, Jenna!'

The memory of Kirsten's words echo inside her head, taunting her now, though she knows that her friend had only meant well. Kirsten had spoken lightly, as she had softly placed her hand on Jenna's arm, disguising the nagging edge behind them.

'Please don't let me drink too much and do something crazy...'

Her own words.

Sober Jenna. Sensible Jenna.

Jenna, before she'd left her flat tonight and allowed herself to be persuaded by the sweet promise of nothingness that she knew tequila would so generously bring to her.

She'd only had a few shots, but maybe that was the problem. She wasn't used to the potency of alcohol any more. She'd left the days of getting black-out drunk long behind her.

Tonight, she'd been purposely careful, because she knew how her work's alcohol-fuelled celebrations went normally. How her boss, Liam, would treat them with endless drinks, commemorating all the hard work they'd done by getting the team absolutely wasted.

Tonight, Jenna was the reason for the newspaper's celebrations. It was Jenna who the chief-editor and the rest of her colleagues had been raising their endless champagne glasses to. Jenna's continual praises they'd all sung in union, for the sensational public takedown of a well-known MP.

Following allegations of stalking and sexual harassment made by the MP's Personal Assistant, Jenna had worked tirelessly on the piece, going undercover and putting her all into the investigation, until she'd not only gathered enough concrete proof for the allegations made against the MP for the young PA to press charges, but she'd also uncovered damning evidence of the MP violating several other unsuspecting victims too.

Jenna had gone on to identify the MP as an active member of one of the UK's biggest incel sites, where the man had boldly shared the lewd, graphic video footage of his female colleagues that he'd secretly recorded on a hidden camera, which he'd planted in the ladies toilet cubicles at his offices.

Jenna's front page exclusive in the *Islington Gazette* today had stated how it would only be a matter of time now until the former MP would be facing a lengthy prison term. Though, of course, Liam insisted that Jenna's reporting would be printed under a pseudonym, to protect her from any unwanted abuse from the MP's no doubt disturbingly dangerous counterparts – and that suited Jenna just fine. Reporters were usually on their own when it came to trolls or backlash from their news stories, but Liam always looked out for his team as best as he could. Liam could be a lot of things but he was a good boss, and the safety of his team was paramount to him.

Jenna didn't care for all the fuss and had never needed to

take the glory for any of her writing. She did it for the sake of the story. For getting the truth out there into the hands of the readers. To right all the wrong doings that went on in the world.

Of which, there were so, so many.

The stress of this investigation had got to her this time though. So tonight, against her better judgement, she'd succumbed to a couple of shots of tequila to help relieve a bit of the tension that had built this week. Her much-needed bit of respite from the sickening revelations that had come to light while she'd been immersed in the investigations.

Going undercover and interacting with some of the most troubled members of society on the incel site, pretending to be one of them, had come at a price it seemed.

Costly to her. Because she knew better now, didn't she?

Just because she'd managed to bring one predatory public figure down spectacularly didn't deny the fact that there were hundreds more men just like him out there. Thousands, in fact.

The thought terrified Jenna.

How they all walked amongst them. Pretending to the watching world that they were decent people before gathering anonymously, in the darkest corners of the web, to share their sick, depraved thoughts and fantasies with each other.

Jenna had read it all. The detailed accounts of all the things these sick individuals had done to women or would like to do to women just like her.

Tonight, she'd only wanted a couple of drinks to numb the feeling of foreboding, to settle the nerves that had seemed to fire up within her. Two at the most, she'd promised herself. Assuring herself that she wouldn't cross the invisible line and get drunk tonight.

She had only had a couple of drinks, hadn't she?

She had a flashback of standing at Kirsten's side at the bar, while ignoring the concerned look on her friend's face, before she'd ordered yet another round of shots. Kirsten had refused to drink hers when the barman placed it down in front of them, but Jenna had tipped her head back and drunk them both down as if to prove a point.

'Honestly, you have no idea how much I need this,' Jenna had reasoned with Kirsten, wincing as the hot, stinging liquid slid down the back of her throat, before dismissively waving at her friend with an easy flick of her hand, letting her know that she wasn't going back on her earlier promise.

'I'm only having a couple. Besides, Liam is footing the bill.' Jenna had nodded her head in the direction of the cluttered table that sat in the long bay window at the front of the bar, as the rest of their colleagues crowded around the chaos of half-full glasses, clearly happy to take full advantage of their boss's generosity. 'We should make the most of that!'

She'd grinned playfully, hoping to play down the fact that she really needed this.

She'd just have the one. Okay then, two. Oh, may as well make it three. Cheers!

Once the tequila had started flowing through her veins, along with that familiar warmth of nothingness, Jenna had actually started to believe it too. That a few drinks really wouldn't hurt. That she wouldn't succumb to drinking again after tonight, for that constant craving for oblivion that she once desperately, purposely used to seek out.

It was different this time. She was an adult; she knew what she was doing. Tonight was just a blip, a release of sorts. She could handle it.

Only as it turned out, Kirsten must know her better than she knows herself, because she clearly couldn't handle it at all.

The rest of the night is a blur.

'Please don't let me drink too much and do or say something crazy...'

Ha! Something crazy. *Famous last words, Jenna!* she thinks

as she watches blood trickle down her arm and drip onto the mosaic of shiny, splintered glass scattered at her feet.

Placing her hands on either side of the wooden window frame, she hoists herself upwards. Teetering on the ledge, unbalanced just for a few seconds.

She falls.

Landing with a thud on the cold kitchen floor. Her body crumples and it's only then that she realises how exhausted she feels. Unable to keep her eyes open a moment longer, she curls her body into the foetal position, shivering violently at the cool jet of air from the broken window that sweeps into the room above her.

Closing her eyes tightly to stop the tears that had already formed there, from sliding down her cheeks.

Stupid girl.

What was she thinking, getting herself into such a state?

That's her last coherent thought before she takes a long, slow, deep breath and finally, finally, allows herself to give into darkness.

3

JENNA

The harsh glare of sunlight that pours into Jenna's eyes when she opens them is blinding. Quickly, she shuts them, squeezing her eyelids tightly, in a bid to block the light out. She waits a few seconds before opening them again; such a small slight movement yet it seems to be the catalyst that makes her head start to pound like a drum.

Disorientated, she stares up at the window above her as she tries to work out where she is, because she is not in her bed, she realises. She is lying on the cold tiles of the kitchen floor. The pane of glass is missing, she notices. A gaping hole surrounded by a wooden frame, bordered with shattered edges of the fragmented glass that look like delicate jagged remnants of lace.

Did she climb in through that?

The shrill, urgent buzz of her phone vibrates from somewhere nearby, and she turns her head towards the noise, wondering if that's what woke her. Pulling herself upright so that she is sitting now, so that she can try and locate where the sound is coming from, she winces as the pain in her head intensifies with the sudden jolt of the movement. The almighty thudding inside her skull becoming so intense that it feels as if her brain is being repeatedly hit with a hammer.

The urge to be sick overcomes her. She moves, placing her hands down at her side, ignoring the sharpness that jabs at her skin as splintered shards of glass crunch beneath her palms. Scrambling quickly to her feet, she only just makes it to the bathroom in time before vomit explodes from her mouth. She retches over and over again, until her stomach is empty. Then, wiping a long, thin string of bile that hangs down from her dry, cracked lips, with the back of her hand, she sees it: a thick trail of dried blood smeared up her arm marking out a newly formed, jagged cut.

A fleeting memory of her, standing at the bar, drinking a shot of tequila. Later, much later, her fist punching through glass.

The spaces between them empty. Her memory as fragmented as her broken kitchen window.

This is all her fault, she resolves to herself tightly.

This almighty, debilitating hangover, that feels as if it might be capable of ending her, is her much-deserved punishment for stupidly allowing herself to get into such a state last night.

Black-out drunk had been a skill of hers once, one of her specialities. Drinking until she blocked out whatever unwanted feelings festered inside of her. Drinking until she simply blacked out.

Disappeared.

Old Jenna, Jenna before.

She hadn't drunk like that for years though. That wasn't her life any more. She wasn't that person.

Blood on her arm. The stench of sick filling the small bathroom. Broken shards of glass at her feet. Who are you kidding Jenna! Look at yourself! You're still in there!

Making her way over to the sink, she splashes some cold water on her face in the hope of feeling more human. But it doesn't help. She still feels dirty and disgusting and exhausted.

She thinks about sinking into the warmth of her bed, of pulling the covers up around her and shutting the world out, only the sound of her phone comes again, the incessant caller forcing her to go back in the kitchen and search for her handbag.

Her bag is not there.

Her phone lies on the floor, face down, on the other side of the kitchen, as if it's been thrown there. Another image flashing inside her mind of her standing outside in the dark, staring at the locked windows. Then falling in through it. Passing out.

Bending down she picks up her phone and sees 'No Caller ID'. She eyes the time with apprehension, wondering who would be calling her at four in the morning.

She's had a few calls like this, this week. Answering her phone only to the sound of heavy breathing. A silent caller on the end of the phone line who wouldn't speak or answer her.

She wonders if it's another one of those.

There was only one way to find out, she thinks as she presses the button and answers it. The voice at the other end of the line is urgent and unapologetic. Startling her.

'You need to come now. You need to see this.'

His next sentence floors her.

'A baby has been left.'

Jenna tells the caller that she is on her way before ending the call and looking down to the floor. Unsteady again, as if she is outside of her body. Unsure if it's her head that is spinning now or the room that she's standing in. She thinks of what the caller has just told her. The urgency she heard there. The words swim inside her head, and her chest tightens as she closes her eyes and fixates on the image of a tiny baby tucked inside a cardboard box: an image that has haunted her for most of her life.

She looks down at her mobile phone, which she still holds,

loosely, in her hand. Wondering for a second if she is still drunk? If the alcohol she'd consumed last night was still surging through the blood in her veins, keeping her reality confused and distorted.

She must be hallucinating. Hearing and seeing things that aren't really there. But as she looks down at the call log, and sees the call time, she has her confirmation that she hasn't just imagined the short, urgent voice at the other end of the line.

It was real.

She is not drunk now, she can't be, she knows that because the alcohol is no longer working, she no longer feels numb.

Right now, she can feel every single emotion firing up inside of her, all at once.

Her hands shake and her head pounds.

Not now, Jenna. Not now!

Pulling on her coat over the clothes she wore last night, because there is no time to change, she stares at her sallow, sickly-looking reflection in the hallway mirror, wiping the black smear of smudged mascara from under her eyes as she tells herself silently that this isn't about her.

You're a big girl now, Jenna, you said you could handle this career and all it entails.

Well, handle it then!

4

JENNA

'Wow, she's tiny. How old do you reckon she is?' Jenna asks, unable to hide the shock in her voice as she stares down at the infant nestled in the firefighter's arms. 'She looks like a newborn.'

'Oh, I'd say she's a few hours old. A day maybe at the very most. I've been calling her Holly, after my sister. Hate to think of the little mite without a name.'

The last time Jenna met Chris had been here at the station. This time, though, he seemed sombre; this time his voice crackled with emotion.

That must be Holly's doing, Jenna thought. How incredible that something so tiny can have such a colossal, significant affect.

'Beautiful little thing, isn't she?' Chris says as he leads Jenna through Islington Fire Station's main lounge area, before making his way towards the back room to where he told her that he discovered the baby.

'It's just so hard to get my head around the fact that someone could do this. That they could give up such a tiny, helpless baby like this. Hey, are you all right?' Chris asks, focusing his attention back to Jenna.

Standing beneath the harsh white strip lights of the station there was no hiding how dishevelled and sick she must look right now, and she is acutely self-conscious. Reaching a hand up, she drags her fingers through the flattened patch of short blonde hair, squashed at the nape of her neck. Wishing she'd at least taken the time to run a brush through it. Severely hungover and convinced that she stinks of a mixture of vomit and tequila. She washed her face before she left the house, but she's almost certain that she still has the remnants of dried black make-up smudged underneath her eyes that she'd tried to wipe off, which no doubt makes her look ghoulish against her already deathly pale complexion.

As awful as she knows she must look right now, it's nowhere near as bad as she actually feels.

'I'm fine. I'm just tired,' she lies, hoping that the firefighter won't be able to tell the difference between someone suffering from the mother of all hangovers and being woken up in the middle of the night, and dragged from sleep for a breaking news story.

The only small mercy she has right now is that she no longer feels the urge to throw up any more. There's nothing left inside of her to bring back up, and the cool icy blast of air that had swept over her as she had raced across Islington to get to the fire station in record time had been just the tonic she'd needed to clear her head.

'I just don't understand how her mother could just give her away. I mean, look at her. She's so small and so defenceless.'

Jenna homes back in, realising that the firefighter is still talking, saying the same thoughts that she is thinking.

'The poor little thing has no idea what's going on.'

Jenna nods. Making a conscious effort to stay focused. Stay present. To not allow her thoughts to drift to the dark recesses at the back of her mind that she doesn't have the time nor mental capacity to deal with right now. She needs to get this story and get out of here as quickly as she can.

'Did anyone happen to get a look at the mother? Did you see her? The woman who left her?'

'No. We've just had a major incident go out. All three fire engines and the rest of the crew have all gone on a call-out to a huge warehouse fire over on Roman Way Industrial Estate. It's looking like a bad one. So, I'm here on my own, manning the station, but I'm guessing maybe that's what the mother had intentionally waited for. For a job to go out, so that there were less people here and less chance of her being seen.' He shrugs as if that's only just occurred to him.

'How did Holly seem when you found her?'

'She seemed fine. She was placed inside the cot. To be fair it looks cosy enough in there.'

Jenna watches as the firefighter walks over to the secure-looking box that has been built into the wall and opens the chunky metal door. It looks like a safe but once it's open, Jenna sees the tiny crib inside lined with a mattress and blanket.

Warm and safe and secure.

She sees the flash of an image then. A tiny baby shoved into a tatty box made of thin cardboard dumped in a communal stairway. The child blue with cold, wrapped in a grubby blanket. Her umbilical cord still attached.

Jenna shakes her head, as if shaking the image out.

'She was inside that?'

'You not heard of these before?' the fireman says, clearly reading Jenna's dazed expression as shock. 'It's part of a scheme by a non-profit charity called Safe Place Baby Boxes. We had this one fitted a few weeks back. The boxes are installed in the wall and there's a door at either side.'

'Christ! How long had she been left in there, do you know?' Jenna interrupts, trying her hardest to gather herself now.

This was the first story she'd covered in her career about an abandoned baby, and she'd always told herself that if it happened, when it happened, she would be ready for it. She would stay professional and not let her emotions get in the way of getting the story.

'Not long. A few minutes at the very most. The idea is that a new mother can place her newborn baby inside of the box, and as soon as they securely lock the door again, a silent alarm is triggered, alerting us that the baby is in there. So, I'm going to say she wasn't alone for any more than two minutes. Maybe three at the most by the time I got to her. And there were no signs of the mother. I looked, you know, just in case she'd had a change of heart or was in distress of some sort. But my guess is that she would have been long gone by then.'

'And you've notified all the relevant organisations?' Jenna asks. 'Social Services or the charity themselves. Are they on their way?' She is unable to hide the confusion on her face at why the press seemed to be the first here at the fire station.

'I've called them too. But I called you first,' Chris admits. 'I just wanted to delay them for a few minutes that's all, nothing more than that. Because I was hoping you would get here first...'

'Why? You want me to launch a public appeal in the newspaper for the mother to come forward? To reunite her with her baby? I take it the charity won't be keen on that?' Jenna asks uncertainly. She has a feeling that this firefighter has another agenda for calling her this morning because he's acting coy now.

She watches as his eyes keep anxiously going to the main doors like he's on edge about something. Or someone turning up.

'There won't be an appeal for the missing mother.' The firefighter shakes his head. 'By using the box, the mother has technically safely surrendered Holly. Which means the mother hasn't committed any kind of a crime, and it also means that she'll be granted full anonymity. The scheme guarantees her that. No one will be looking for the mother, nor will anyone want to...'

'But? You think, what? That they should be?'

'Well, according to my superiors, what I think doesn't come into it! The bosses want us all on board with this. The charity gives us a big annual pay-out for being involved and housing the box here at the station. So even though it's still technically on trial, the bosses have already approved of the scheme, and they want us all to be seen as actively encouraging it. The last thing they'd want is one of the crew who doesn't agree with it, speaking out to a member of the press.'

'But here you are, speaking to the press anyway?' Jenna raises an eyebrow.

'Like I say, the mother is protected, she can surrender her child and simply walk away, no questions asked.' The firefighter shrugs before getting to his point. 'And that's the bit I have an issue with. It doesn't sit right with me. What if we *should* be asking questions? What if the kid has been snatched or the mother is being trafficked? What if the mother didn't have a say in the baby being left here? And no one knows what mental state she must be in to think that leaving her baby in a box in a wall is her only option. I mean, she obviously cared enough to bring her baby here. She obviously wanted her baby to be safe. To be found and looked after.'

The firefighter shrugs again before looking Jenna in the eye intently, as if sussing out whether or not he can trust her.

'Look, I'm going to level with you here. I can't be seen to go on the record with this one, so I'm really not sure if there is anything you can actually do. But I remembered you from the story you covered on our strikes last year, and how well you put our point across about the pay increases. You got us a lot of positive attention. And well, I figured if anyone could get this story out there and get people to actually listen, it would be you.'

Jenna nods, recognising the opportunity that is being placed in front of her, not only for the newspaper but for the baby and her mother too.

What if she could really make a difference here?

'Only there is something else,' Chris adds, his voice full of caution as if he's still deliberating whether or not he should tell Jenna this next bit. 'There's something I haven't shown you.'

Taking the letter that he has carefully concealed in his pocket, Chris hands the piece of paper to Jenna.

She's in danger. Please keep her safe.

'The mother left this note with the baby. My guess is that the charity and social services still won't go public with this. They won't want this getting out and putting any negativity on the trial. Because like I said, the mother has a right to anonymity. She can give her baby up, no questions asked. No one will be looking for her. But perhaps they should be, because if the baby is in danger, then doesn't that mean the mother might be too?

'But you said that you've already rung the charity, and social services? That they're on their way?'

'As much as I'd have loved to hold them off, I had to.' He nods. 'They'll be able to work out what time the baby was left due to what time the alarm went off. They'd be suspicious if I didn't call them straight away. They'll be here any minute.'

Jenna is quiet as she tries to work out how they can do this without any suspicion coming back on the firefighter for tipping her off.

'Okay, let's make this quick,' Jenna says, looking around for her work satchel with her camera inside and realising that she didn't pick it up in her haste to get here. That she'd been so out of it, she'd left it hanging on the coat hook behind her front door.

Grabbing her mobile phone from her pocket instead, she points the lens at Holly.

'Don't look at the camera. Look at Holly. As if you're not aware that I'm taking any photos. Do you know how long they are planning on doing the trials for?' Jenna asks, as she takes a few candid shots, only to be interrupted by an abrupt voice that booms from the doorway behind her.

'Er, excuse me, can I ask who you are and what you're doing here? Why are you taking a photograph of that baby?'

Jenna turns towards the thin older woman, before shoving her phone and the note quickly inside her coat pocket, ready to make a fast exit.

'I'm sorry, I was just checking that she was okay,' she says, stalling for time as she takes in the casually dressed woman's appearance. How she too is devoid of make-up or having brushed her hair, yet she still looks ever the professional, despite clearly being woken at this early hour of the morning. Unlike Jenna.

She is also wearing her official ID lanyard around her neck to let anyone interested know who she is. The ID stating clearly that she's a social worker from Children's Services.

'She's such a tiny, little thing,' Jenna continues, keeping her response vague. Her words neutral. She had learned that a long time ago. Never to give direct information or answers to anyone, if you didn't have to. Especially when you were somewhere that you shouldn't be.

Jenna turns to Chris and says in a small voice: 'I'm so sorry! I lied to you. I'm not from social services. I had a tip off that someone intended to use the scheme tonight. That a baby would be left here.'

'You what?' Chris says, playing along, a thunderous look on his face that could rival any fully seasoned actor. 'You tricked your way in here under a false pretence. What are you, a bloody journalist?'

When Jenna doesn't answer, Chris runs his fingers through his hair, giving the impression of being flustered. His other arm still holding on to baby Holly, protectively now.

'You shouldn't be here,' he says, as if he's unable to hide his anger.

The social worker intervenes. 'He's right. You shouldn't be here, and you certainly shouldn't be taking unauthorised photographs of that baby. The charity will take legal action if you publish…'

Jenna isn't listening now. Walking fast, she is squeezing past the woman as she stands in the doorway, without giving her a chance to lecture her further.

'The audacity of people like you disgusts me. Using innocent babies to up your newspaper ratings and further your career. You should be ashamed of yourself.'

The woman's loaded words fall on deaf ears. Jenna isn't listening. Nothing she says is anything new and it certainly doesn't faze her. The truth of the matter is, that the woman isn't far wrong. It's all part of the job. Lying and manipulating her way in to places any way she needs to in order to get her news story.

The woman was wrong about her motivations though. She didn't become a journalist to gain ratings or notoriety; she did this job because she desperately wanted to make a difference in the world. Because every story that she feeds back to the world is laced with facts and unbiased truths.

This morning's efforts aren't about the newspaper's ratings or furthering Jenna's career; this morning's story is only about that poor abandoned baby and a mother who might possibly be in danger, and if there is any chance that she could actually make a real difference here, then she is prepared to do whatever is necessary to get her story out there.

If that means playing the bad guy, then so be it.

She's said and done a lot worse in her time to ensure she got her story.

It will be more than worth it.

More than worth all the stories that came before this one combined.

Because this time, this story feels personal.

5

JENNA

NIGHT AT THE BAR

'Oh, come on, Jenna. I know Bar Magic is a bit of a hole, but we'll make it a laugh. You don't have to stay long, just have one more drink, what do you say?' Liam pleads with her as the rest of their colleagues pile out from the crowded bar, onto the busy London street.

Jenna eyes them through the main bay window at the front of the bar.

'Fresh air,' one of them had said, and she had laughed at that. Fresh air in central London is plumes of black car exhaust emissions, cigarette smoke and vapes, while they all stand outside freezing, waiting to move on to someplace just as crowded and claustrophobic as this.

At least there is an atmosphere here and decent music. A real vibe, Liam said, when he had suggested going on to somewhere better than in here.

Though Jenna wasn't entirely convinced that that was what Bar Magic was at all, and she couldn't be persuaded. The nightclub was a notorious dive that people only suffered because the drinks were dirt cheap and the overly handsy bouncers always allowed young girls in. The ones wearing too much make-up and minuscule clothing in a desperate attempt to make themselves appear older.

Which never worked.

The harder they tried, the more they stood out, and Jenna could spot them a mile off. As did the men that went there in their droves for exactly that.

Underage girls had always been seen as 'easy pickings'. A meat market, that's how the locals referred to the place.

'I'm good. Really. Go on without me. Besides, I'm not sure I can even manage this one.' Jenna nods down to the drink that Liam had placed down in front of her just minutes ago. Tequila with a splash of soda. Classier than shots, but still just as lethal.

'I really don't think I can drink another drop.'

Lies.

Even Liam raises his eyes at that one.

She wasn't there yet not nearly. The only real sign of the alcohol even mildly affecting her was when the odd word slipped out, slightly delayed and slurry as it left her lips, but Jenna hid it well like a pro that she was, doing her best to disguise it.

She wasn't like that anymore.

Drinking until her thoughts became blurred into nothingness. Until she passed out.

Drinking until she reached oblivion.

Tonight, Jenna only had a few glasses to help relax her, to help take the edge off a difficult week.

Liam was way ahead of her.

Swaying slightly on his feet, back and forth, back and forth, completely out of time with the beat of the music, which she isn't even sure he can actually hear any more. Grinning at her like a demented Cheshire Cat, with a strange gleam in his eyes.

His hands gripping the bar stool on which she is perched as if to steady himself.

If anyone looked worse for wear, it was Liam.

'Course you can manage another one! Come on, down it! We can dance it off. Show the kids in Bar Magic how it's really done,' Liam slurs, swinging his arms wildly above his head, as if to give her a demo of what he thinks is an offer that Jenna won't be able to refuse.

She laughs again, despite herself, at the rare glimpse of Liam outside of work. Away from the stress and chaos of the newsroom.

A lighter, more playful side of him that isn't stressed out and manic.

'Wow! Those kids aren't going to know what's hit them, Liam. Literally! You'll end up doing some poor sod an injury if you keep busting out moves like that. Or yourself if you're not careful!' She smiles, flattered, because she can tell that Liam isn't just being nice to her or treating her like an afterthought. He's not just saying it to be polite.

He really wants her to go to the club with them all.

It's the alcohol, she thinks, noting the hopeful look on his face. Not just that she will join them, but that for once she might actually let her guard down and have some fun for a change. With him.

Liam isn't her idea of fun, though. Not in that way anyway.

'I can't. I've got to get back,' she says politely.

Adamant that she will never even so much as entertain his constant advances no matter how persuasive he can be, because he dated her friend first. The fact that Kirsten dated him once, years ago, long before Duncan, means that Liam is officially out of bounds. It doesn't matter that they only saw each other for just over a month, Jenna knows that the relationship had affected Kirsten. She refused to talk about it at first, pushing it down as if to make it seem like it had been nothing, which only magnified to Jenna that it must have hurt Kirsten more than she ever disclosed.

Now, Jenna won't even reciprocate his flirting: it was the unspoken girl code that Jenna would never, ever break.

'Honestly, it's not my scene. But you go! Have fun!' she says gently, not wanting to hurt his feelings. 'Besides, I've already ordered an Uber.' She pulls her phone out and waves it vaguely in Liam's direction, as if to make her point, hoping that Liam doesn't look too closely at the app and spot that she hasn't yet booked her ride.

'Says it's less than five minutes away.' She shrugs and shoves her phone back in her pocket, before pushing her unfinished drink away, relieved that it seems to be enough of the deterrent she needs as, finally, Liam gives in.

'Okay, okay, but don't be jealous in the morning when we tell you about all the fun you missed out on,' he says, before flashing her one last grin.

* * *

She should have gone, she thinks now, not even five whole minutes later. After Liam and the rest of the team have gone. Questioning her decision to stay in a packed bar, full of people, alone.

Alone doesn't normally bother her. She always enjoys her own company, prefers it on some occasions. On lots of occasions, in fact. Growing up in care had made her used to that from early on, taught her from just a young child how to fend for herself.

Later, as an adult, it was a pattern repeated. A habit of a lifetime, taking herself to see the latest movie that she fancied watching. Eating alone in fancy restaurants without intimidation. Losing herself in her favourite books in quaint little coffee shops.

She never felt alone in those moments.

And she doesn't now.

People watching as she soaks up her surroundings, drinking in the atmosphere along with the odd sip of tequila, as the people around her all speak animatedly to one another, raising their voices to be heard over the thrum of music and the constant chatter and laughter. The sound so loud that it vibrates up through the metal legs of the stool, before pulsating through her body like electricity.

It is at times like this when she feels most alive. When her adrenaline is pumping and she is doing something spontaneous, something out of the ordinary, with only herself to fall back on if anything goes wrong.

She waits a beat before turning.

Glancing over to the table nearby, pleased that the man sitting with just a pint of beer for company is still there.

The man sitting alone, just like her, in a room full of people. Still and quiet amongst the chaos of people huddled around tables and standing in clusters around the room. Which is probably why she noticed him at all, because everything about him looks average. His build, his height, his nondescript facial features. Plain looking, the kind of man who would normally melt into the background.

But not tonight.

Tonight, out of the hordes, he stands out.

Allowing her gaze to linger expertly for just a few seconds longer than she knows that she should, Jenna forces herself to look away. Not wanting to appear too obvious, too needy. Too desperate when he finally meets her eye.

He isn't her usual type. This thought makes her smile to herself. *Ha! Who is she kidding?*

Like she has a usual type. Unless you count the randoms that she's met in bars, that she always ends up going home with. The countless strangers' beds she'd woken up in over the years.

The vague recollection of things being done to her body while she hadn't been in control of herself. While she hadn't been inside of her body at all.

Passed out, drunk. Dead to the world.

Some men like that, don't they? Having complete control over women, being the ones to hold all that power.

Jenna likes it too.

No complications, just straight sex without any commitment.

A means to an end.

She thinks about the incel site that she's been ploughing through the past few weeks. What the men in there would make of that.

They'd call her a slag. And perhaps she is.

Or was.

So what? There's no shame in that and besides, she's not like that anymore, or at least, that's what she tells herself.

She shifts in her seat, realising that lost in her thoughts she hasn't looked away in time and now he is staring straight at her.

Shit!

She holds his gaze. Tries her hardest to catch whatever unspoken words pass between them.

And it's there.

The glimmer of something forbidden staring back at her. Something dark and intense and dangerous that she recognises simmering there.

Look away.

Only it's too late for her to try and attempt to play the game and pretend she hasn't noticed him staring over. She is firmly on his radar now. She can feel his eyes on her. The burn of his stare singeing the tiny, downy hairs that stand on the back of her neck. Burning right through her.

Until a group of lads move in, huddling directly behind her chair as they make for the bar, blocking the man's view. This amuses her immensely, how she isn't even the one trying to play hard to get, but here she is anyway. It takes what feels like an age until they finally have drinks in their hands, and they move away and, by then, his table sits empty.

She feels a tiny flicker of disappointment, at the missed opportunity.

A fleeting feeling of relief too. That in hindsight, maybe him leaving was fate. The best outcome.

The safest thing.

What are you doing, Jenna!

She is about to leave too. To go home and sink into the warmth of her bed. But just as she decides to leave, she feels the warmth of a body press against hers. She turns her head and is startled to see that it's him. Standing right next to her, at the bar. Holding a crisp twenty-pound note in his hand as he nods to the barman to get him another pint.

He looks at her then, shy perhaps, coy. Unsure.

So, Jenna immediately smiles back.

'How about you? Can I get you a drink?' he asks.

Braver.

A hunter moving in on his prey.

'I'd love one! Tequila and soda. Thanks!' Offering the man a wide smile, Jenna holds out her hand and introduces herself. Ignoring the alarm bells that ring loudly inside her head, that maybe she shouldn't be doing this.

She is doing it though.

She picks up the unfinished drink that has sat discarded on the table next to her since Liam and the others left, and she drinks a big, greedy mouthful down.

Dutch courage.

For what might be coming next.

6

JENNA

'Christ, Jenna! Wow, no offence, but you look bloody awful! How are you feeling? Is everything all right? Are you all right?'

'I'm fine.' Jenna nods, relieved to hear the genuine concern in her boss's tone as she makes her way across the open-plan newsroom, past the last of the skeleton crew of the night shift, towards Liam's office. Glad that she no longer has to do the graveyard shift, as it had been aptly nicknamed, because to her they always felt so void of the loud buzz of creativity that she thrives on in the dayshifts, her energy always higher when the office is full of its usual noise and chaos. The phones constantly ringing, the conversations around them becoming louder and more exaggerated.

She'd been expecting mildly disguised irritation from Liam at being summoned into the office at ridiculous o'clock in the morning, after such a heavy night out last night, but instead she got nothing. Which in all honestly was even more unnerving. Stepping inside his office, she closes the door behind them. Shutting the rest of the office out of their conversation for now.

'Are you sure?' he presses. 'Only you really don't look it and, well, you said it was urgent? Has something happened?'

'I'm fine, really. It's just a hangover, nothing I can't handle,' Jenna says, hoping she sounds convincing as she silently curses the beaded film of perspiration that she feels prickle across her brow. The watery sickly feeling is back with a vengeance, and she is starting to feel like death warmed up. And going by the rare sympathetic look on her boss's face, she clearly must look like death too.

Liam rarely shows any form of empathy towards his staff. Especially if technically, he is to blame for being the one to pour all the alcohol down their throats.

Sympathy is the last thing she'd expected or need right now.

'But you're right, the reason that I asked you here is urgent.' Jenna nods. Forcing herself to stay professional, to stay focused, having called Liam the second she'd left the fire station, straight after she'd called Kirsten, knowing that a story like this one was too big to sit on.

He interrupts her train of thought again.

'Is it about last night? Because that was quite a state you got yourself into. Do you remember what happened? Do you remember getting home?'

'Of course, I do!' she lies, unable to hide the defensive tone to her voice, not willing to admit that her memory of the evening is fragmented and blurred and there are huge chunks of time missing. Does she remember getting home? She does remember the vague recollection of a car door slamming, and two bright orange lights disappearing off into the distance at the end of her street. Leaving her standing unbalanced on her feet, outside her flat.

No bag. No bag. Shit! No fucking keys.

She lowers her eyes, unable to hold Liam's steely gaze in case she falls apart under his scrutiny. In case he somehow has the power to reach inside her mind and pick apart her private thoughts. In case he knows that she was in a much worse state than she is letting on.

Black-out drunk, just like old times.

'I did offer to help get you home, but you didn't want me to take you, you were quite adamant about that. But you did at least allow me to call you an Uber. Don't you remember any of it?'

'I guess that tequila was stronger than I realised,' she says with a shrug, not wanting to admit to him that before last night it was well over a year since a single drop of alcohol had touched her lips. That she'd gone completely T-total and, last night, those few drinks had been all it had taken to throw her straight back there. Right over the edge.

Ruining all the hard work she'd done to get herself sober.

'Do you remember hurting yourself? It looked pretty nasty.'

'I thought you didn't take me home?' Jenna narrows her eyes, speaking with caution. Pushing down the violent swirl of nausea that intensifies in her stomach at the image of her punching her window, and then later sprawled out on her kitchen floor, shards of smashed glass all around her.

She thinks about the thin strip of bandage that she wrapped around her arm in haste before she made her way to the fire station early this morning. How it's hidden beneath her jumper and coat, and there's no possible way that he can know it is there, unless he was there when she got home last night?

'I didn't?' Liam says, looking confused before giving a small laugh. 'God, you really don't remember any of it, do you? Wow, you really were out of it.' He pauses, to let her catch up before he clarifies what happened last night.

'You fell. Outside the bar. Landed with a real bang. I was across the road having a fag with Brendan from Finance. I saw your fall and ran over to try to help you up.' He shakes his head disbelievingly at the blank expression on her face.

'I fell?' Jenna shakes her head. Mortified that she can't quite capture the memory of being outside the bar and falling over. Of her own boss scraping her up off the floor like an incapacitated drunk. A million questions spin inside her head, but she tries her hardest not to give away the flurry of panic that is erupting there: she has no memory of any of it.

'Was anyone else there?' She pauses now, looking thoughtful as an awful recognition only just occurs to her. 'When you found me outside the bar. Was I with someone?'

'Someone?' His eyes twinkle mischievously, a smirk dancing on the edge of his lips. 'What, you mean you pulled?'

Jenna is unsure if she can hear a tiny hint of jealousy in his tone as he teases her. If there is, he plays it down, throwing her a playful look so that she knows he's only messing with her. He's enjoying winding her up and watching her squirm.

'Kirsten and Duncan left, and we all went to Bar Magic, and you insisted you were going home. Alone. Said you'd ordered yourself an Uber. Only you must have hung around for a bit after all. Got a better offer huh?'

'It wasn't like that. I was... just talking to someone.' She starts to protest, only the smug grin on his face grows wider with every word, so she stops herself, knowing the more that she tries to deny it, the guiltier she sounds.

'I remember Duncan offering me a lift before he and Kirsten left,' she says, trying to gauge when it all started going downhill for her. 'But it all goes a little blurry after that. Later. After you'd all gone.'

'Blurred lines. Always convenient I find. Especially when it comes to new relationships. He must have scarpered because I don't remember seeing anyone else helping you up when you fell. But then I was a little worse for wear myself last night. What was he married?' Liam asks, giving Jenna a conspiratorial wink as if she'd just let him in on her little sordid secret.

'It wasn't like that,' she replies crossly. 'Being unfaithful – and encouraging anyone else to be unfaithful – isn't my style,' she bites, purposely insinuating that it was his though.

Everyone in the office knows that Liam is notorious for never staying in a relationship for more than five minutes, and how often those relationships 'overlapped'. He never took any of them seriously.

No one ever mentioned his very brief encounter with Kirsten when she'd first started here at the newspaper. Years ago, before he had been promoted to Chief Editor.

Though the relationship had been brief, a month at the most, he'd cheated on Kirsten back then too. The worst part for poor Kirsten had been that the whole workplace had known about it. Liam had boasted about his newest conquest and treated her heartbreak like a joke.

Kirsten had done her utmost to save face and pretend it didn't bother her after that. And Jenna wasn't sure when it started to feel as if it really didn't, because she moved on with Duncan very soon after, whom she'd been with ever since.

Two point four children and a white picket fence later and the rest, as they say, is history.

'Woah!' Liam says, a feigned wounded look on his face that she thinks isn't genuine. 'Hey, I tried to help you last night. I'm on your side here.'

'Shit! I'm sorry,' she says quickly, recognising her low blow. 'I'm hungover and tired and I shouldn't have said that.' She feels awful at making such an unprovoked, personal attack against someone, someone who last night had only done their very best to help her.

'Hey, I probably deserve it! You're right, I'm no angel, I can admit that.' Liam grins playfully, while holding up his hands apologetically as he steps closer. 'But you're right, that isn't your style. I should learn to keep my nose out of things huh! Maybe if I did that then, well...'

It's only then, when he touches his cheek, that Jenna sees a red scratch mark that is clawed down one side of his face.

'Oh my god! Please tell me that *I* didn't do that?' she asks, instantly dreading his reply, because even before he opens his mouth to speak, she knows the answer.

The gouged-out scratch that snakes its way across his face was caused by her.

'You didn't do it on purpose.' He shrugs it off like it's no big deal. 'You just got a fright that's all. You were out of it, and you didn't realise that it was me who was trying to help you. Probably mistook me for some chancer trying it on and putting his hands on you. Christ knows there's enough of that kind about.' He raises his brows in understanding and then offers Jenna a small smile to let her know that it really is okay.

'To be honest, after the week you've had with that MP, and that horrible incel group, you've had some heavy shit to wade through. And hey, if it's any consolation I was actually impressed at your self-defence skills. At least I don't have to worry about you being able to look after yourself. You could probably give Jackie Chan a run for his money.'

'Christ! I'm so sorry, Liam! I had no idea. I really didn't mean—'

'It's nothing. seriously. Forget it—' he starts, though he's quickly cut off.

'Oh, well this all looks very cosy.' Kirsten's voice booms from behind them both, silencing Jenna mid-sentence as she turns and watches Kirsten make her way towards them across the newsroom.

'Whatever you've got had better be worthy of my 5 a.m. wake-up call.'

Kirsten does a double take, her disapproving gaze sweeping the length of Jenna's body. Stopping on the coat Jenna threw over the top of the outfit she wore last night. 'Oh Jenna, you look awful. Don't tell me you pulled an all-nighter? Have you not been home?'

Jenna sees the way that Kirsten's eyes go to Liam then, as if she is trying to work out if he is dressed in last night's clothes too.

If the pair of them are as dishevelled and hungover as each other.

If neither of them have been home. If they'd both come back here together.

And it's only then that Jenna realises that Liam has managed to change into a tracksuit, and he doesn't look anywhere near as hungover as she does.

'I called Kirsten in too,' she explains, filling Liam in before she shoots Kirsten a small sarcastic smile. 'Fancied a bit of an ego boost. You know how she's always showering me with compliments,' she quips, knowing full well that Kirsten is only speaking the truth. The contrast between how Liam looks tired but the complete dishevelled state she is in, is not lost on her.

'For your information I did manage to get home and get some sleep as it happens,' she says resolutely, and she isn't lying. Passing out on the kitchen floor must count as sleep, surely. 'I got woken up with a tip off, so trust me, your wake-up call is most definitely worth it. I wanted you both here for this. It's a big story and you're going to want to break it as soon as possible.' She fights to hide the tremor in her voice as she takes a seat in front of Liam's desk, facing them both.

'Before another journalist gets their grubby mitts on it you mean?' Liam pipes up. Not missing a beat.

'Well, for now, we've got ourselves an exclusive.'

'Oh, I'm intrigued!' Kirsten says, pulling up a chair and getting herself comfortable.

Jenna smiles then.

Glad that Kirsten is here, and they can finally change the subject. So that she can do what she does best.

Focus on other people's stories instead of her own.

'You might want to sit down for this one too.' She nods over to Liam.

'I got a tip off that a newborn baby was abandoned at Islington Fire Station in the early hours of this morning. There was a note left with the child. The mother sounds as if she might be in some kind of danger.'

7

JENNA

'An abandoned baby? A mother in danger?! Shit!' Liam clasps his hands together in pure delight. Not bothering to hide the excitement in his tone at Jenna's promise of another front page exclusive. 'What a week it's been for us!'

'Not such a great one for the poor baby and its mother, though!' Kirsten says, her words prickled with sarcasm at Liam's heartlessness before being quickly replaced with concern. 'Wait, is the baby, okay?'

'Yeah, the baby seems fine. Tiny, but okay.' Jenna nods. 'They're going to give her a health examination, but at first look she seemed happy and healthy, and she's in very safe hands thanks to the firefighter who found her. He's named her Holly.'

'Oh, hang on, Islington Fire Station. Aren't they the ones taking part in that charity scheme? They're trialling one of those baby box thingies, aren't they?' Kirsten says, before pulling out her phone and tapping at the screen so that she can get confirmation of the details for that.

'Yes, that's right. The Safe Place Baby Box Scheme. It was actually the firefighter who found the baby who tipped me off, but that information doesn't go outside of this room, okay? He did me a massive favour.' Jenna continues to explain. 'Do you remember that piece we ran a few months ago, about the brigade gearing up for their first national strike in twenty years. Chris was the firefighter who I interviewed back then. Let's just say that he's not overly keen on the new scheme. He feels that the mothers who use the scheme won't be getting the mental support that they might need. That they might be open to coercion by others. Only he isn't supposed to voice any of that.'

'Well, the bloke has a point!' Liam chimes in, nodding his head in agreement. 'Sounds properly messed up if you ask me. What sort of woman dumps their own baby in a box in the wall?'

'Desperate women!' Kirsten retorts, her voice full of irritation at Liam's lack of compassion and understanding. 'Women who don't have any other choice! Women who leave notes begging whoever finds her child to "keep her safe".' Kirsten tries again, but already Liam isn't listening.

'*From flames to family. Baby abandoned at Islington Fire Station.*' Liam practically sings the newspaper's headline, as if they are the lyrics from his most favourite song.

'Er, I'm sorry to piss all over your headline, Liam, but you can't claim that the baby was "abandoned",' Kirsten casually corrects Liam while tapping her pen against her notepad repeatedly.

'Yeah, Kirsten is right. She wasn't abandoned. Technically, it's called a "Safe Surrender",' Jenna intervenes.

'A safe surrender? Oh, please! These people can dress it up however they want, but it doesn't change the fact that women are still dumping their kids in a hole in the wall like those tatty, unwanted books in those neighbourhood free-library boxes.'

'Christ, Liam! It isn't as simple as that.' Kirsten shakes her head. 'I'm going to take a wild guess and say that for the woman who carried that child inside of her body for the past nine months, before physically giving birth to her, a decision like this wouldn't have been made lightly. We don't know what the missing mother's circumstances are, but I'll be prepared to put my whole year's wages on it being complex and messy and brutal, because no woman wants to give up her child willingly, not if she doesn't have to. She left a note saying the child is in danger. There's clearly more to this than meets the eye. Have a little heart!'

'Heart?' Liam laughs before rolling his eyes. 'I'm not the one who shoved my kid in a box in the wall. And since when did heart sell the papers or pay any of our wages, Kirsten? You know as well as I do, that it's the cold, hard facts that do that. Besides, this story does have heart. A tiny baby thrown away like rubbish by its own mother is the kind of story that our readers will be invested in.'

'Great! So, is that the angle you're going with on this then? Instead of helping this poor woman and her baby, you just want to create some kind of villain in order to shift more copies of your newspaper? Make out that this woman is a monster when you don't actually know a single thing about her.'

'Hey, I don't think we need to make this woman out as anything. We can let the members of the public be the judge of that.'

'But that's the point. She doesn't have to come forward. The child has been placed in the care of the scheme. And if the public are judging her – condemning her – well, that's hardly an incentive for her to come forward, is it? A public appeal might have the opposite effect. Especially once this story breaks. I'm sure the last thing the mother will want is all the media attention if she fears for the safety of her baby. She might be in danger too. If anything, an appeal for the mother could end up forcing her further underground.'

'Jesus! Do you two ever stop arguing!'

'Perhaps we should have made a proper go of it. This is marriage material right here,' Liam says, chuckling to himself, thinking that he is hilarious and then looking over to Jenna as she presses her knuckles into the dip of her temples, before moving them in slow, circular movements.

'Hey! Are you feeling all right, Jenna? You look a bit pale? You want me to grab you a coffee or something? Maybe some water?' Kirsten says, ignoring Liam's cutting comment and throwing Jenna an apologetic look on behalf of their boss and his blatant insensitivity of the subject matter.

'My head's banging actually. I'm going to open the window, it's a bit hot in here.' Jenna gets up too fast and feels herself wobble on her feet. She grabs on to the table's edge to steady herself.

The pain in her head is not a complete lie.

Her head is thumping, but so is her chest.

Fuelled by the anxiety that surges through her at Liam's words, which feel as though they have been aimed right at her. Magnified before being slammed so hard into her stomach that she feels momentarily winded by them.

The baby was thrown away like rubbish.

Worthless. Like it was nothing.

Shit!

How had she spent her entire lifetime working so hard to push down all the hurtful, complex feelings that swirl inside of her, only to find in moments like this that they are still there.

Her demons. Buried just beneath the surface, waiting to rear their ugly heads at the first opportunity they got. All those wasted hours she's spent in therapy, dissecting the jumble of questions that are tangled inside her head.

Only she never found any answers. No real answers anyway.

Was this really all it took to bring her to her knees again, all these years later?

Another abandoned baby.

One thoughtless, flippant comment from Liam.

Hold it together, Jenna! You can do this!

'Here,' Kirsten says, retrieving a packet of paracetamol from her bag and throwing them over to her.

Thank you! Jenna mouths the words gratefully, fighting to hide the tremble of her hands as she takes the tablets from the foil and swallows them down. without water.

It's only then that Jenna realises that Liam is staring at her with narrowed eyes, a strange, puzzled expression fixed to his face.

'What?' she asks defensively.

'You do look bloody awful!' Liam shrugs before adding. 'It was just booze last night, wasn't it? You didn't take anything else, did you?'

'Drugs?' It takes Jenna a second to realise what Liam is implying and when she speaks again, her voice is full of indignation at his allegation. 'No, of course not, Liam. They're not my thing. You know that.'

'Hey, no judgement here. Each to their own.' He holds his hands up in the air in front of him, now that he can see he's clearly offended her.

Cocaine was consumed with the casualness of passing around sweets with the younger members of this newsroom. And it is no secret that Liam dabbles in it himself from time to time.

A social crux, he'd say on those odd occasions he took it on a night out. A much-needed pick-me-up.

'I'm only asking because you did seem really out of it last night. Like, there was no one there behind your eyes. And you don't seem entirely yourself now either. I just wondered if maybe you took something, that's all. There's so much dodgy shit knocking about out there now, cut with all sorts, it could have had a weird effect on you,' he adds, eyeing her curiously.

'I'm not on drugs!' Jenna is offended.

'Okay, okay! Forget I even mentioned it.'

Easier said than done, Jenna thinks. Aware suddenly of how stifling and airless the room feels as the rush of heat prickles at her skin, beads of perspiration forming along her forehead again. A wave of nausea as she stares at the scratch that twists its way down his face.

The vague memory of feeling the urge to get out of that bar last night. A feeling lingering, of being in real, sudden danger.

When she'd woken this morning, alcohol had been the first and most obvious assumption.

Because old habits die hard, and Jenna's worst nightmare was that she'd somehow, stupidly spiralled right back there. Black-out drunk.

Drugs hadn't even factored into her thinking because they were never anything that Jenna had never considered doing.

Sure, she smoked a few joints while at secondary school. Huddled with her best mates on the playing fields behind the football pitch at lunch times, but weed has always left her feeling light-headed and sick.

She got no real buzz from it.

Drugs. No. Rule those out.

Only now that Liam suggested it, it's the only explanation that would make any real sense of how she'd rapidly spiralled downhill last night.

A few shots of tequila, no matter how potent or un-used to drinking Jenna was any more, could never have been responsible for affecting her the way they had. Attacking Liam. No memory of how she got home. Just because she hadn't willingly taken anything last night, didn't mean that a toxic substance hadn't somehow got into her system.

Fuck!

'I'm sorry. Can you both excuse me for a minute,' she says, moving now, unsure how she is staying upright as the room tilts violently beneath her jelly-like legs. The walls of the room rapidly closing in on her, and she fixes her gaze on the door. Her only escape route.

'Jenna? Are you okay?' Kirsten's voice melts into the background, drowned out by the loud whooshing noise that fills her ears.

All she can do is nod.

She needs to get out.

'Yeah, I'm fine. I just feel a bit sick.'

8

EVIE

I slam the front door and lock it, before pressing the entire weight of my body up against it.

Shutting the world beyond it out, just as I have done for the past nine months.

I am home now. Safe now.

Only I don't feel any of those things, not really.

Instead, all I feel is empty and disjointed. As if a part of me is physically missing.

Part of you is missing, Evie!

She is missing.

It wasn't supposed to feel like this, I think as I stare around the empty lounge in despair at the chaos I created only hours earlier, as the almighty waves of agonising childbirth had taken over. My eyes staring beyond all of that to the open bathroom door, and the carnage that awaits me in there. How the warm-water-filled bath that I'd sat in to give birth to my child just hours earlier would be freezing cold now.

I wince at the memory of the excruciating, burning agony I'd felt seconds before I reached down between my legs and felt the wiggling, squirming flesh of a small child there.

My child.

How I pulled her towards me and placed her on my chest.

I'd felt it instantly. An intense rush of emotions that were completely indescribable. Something close to euphoria I would guess.

Quickly replaced with fear and dread and panic as I realised that I couldn't keep her.

Not if I wanted to keep us both safe.

Not if I wanted to keep *her* safe.

And she is safe now.

That's all that matters.

So why don't I believe it?

The absence of noise is almost deafening this morning. The bitter silence only magnifying the feeling of being completely and utterly alone.

I don't want to be here. In this flat. I want to escape, but even if I could, where would I go?

Who would I turn to?

I have nothing and no one to help me. No real friends or family. No work colleagues that I can talk to.

What have I done? What have I done!

I push all thoughts of her out of my mind.

Stop it! Carry on as normal.

Normal.

I think about the endless, monotonous nightshifts, of spending hours anonymously mopping floors and cleaning shelves in a local supermarket.

I'd called in sick last night.

Sick. That's one way of describing being ripped in two, the contents inside physically expelled from my body.

Now, all that remains is a gaping void.

I picture her perfect, doll-like face. Those thick, long lashes, those chubby, pink cheeks.

His baby.

Stop! Stop thinking about her now. I will myself.

Only I can't.

She is the only thing that I can think about.

Because she is my child too. *My* baby.

And now she's lying alone, inside a box in a wall. Waiting to be discovered by a stranger. Waiting for her new life to begin.

A life without me, her mother.

Gone forever.

9

JENNA

Jenna's fingers tremble as she bolts the toilet cubicle's door and leans up against it as a wave of burning heat creeps its way up the entire length of her body. Her chest tightens and, greedily, she sucks down a huge lungful of air in a bid to fend off the familiar onslaught of the panic attack that is threatening.

Breathe!

Closing her eyes, she pushes all thoughts of baby Holly and her missing mother from her mind so that she can try and summon a memory of what actually happened to her last night.

She knows now. She's sure of it.

Someone slipped something into her drink last night.

Someone drugged her.

It's the only thing that makes any sense.

She'd been so caught up in feeling mortified at her actions last night, so consumed by the humiliation of the state that *she* had managed to get herself into, that any other alternative to her getting so stupidly, recklessly, black-out drunk hadn't even entered her mind.

But all the tell-tale signs are there, aren't they?

She didn't drink enough alcohol to be that drunk. She remembers feeling so hot and dizzy. How there are parts of her memory that are lost to her. Parts she knows now where she behaved so irrationally. Physically attacking her boss.

She feels awful about that as she tries to at least imagine it. To conjure up an image of that. Of Liam. That potent smell of whisky on his breath, that boyish stupid grin he'd thrown her hours earlier. Leaning over her, selflessly offering his hand before she claws wildly at his face, like a woman possessed.

So drunk and disorientated that she'd had no idea that he was one of the good guys, that he'd actually only been trying to help her.

Then she'd tried breaking into her own flat.

Any sane, normal, *sober* person would have made a call for help once they realised that they were locked out of their home. She could have done that, couldn't she? Despite losing her bag and keys, she'd had her mobile phone on her.

She could have called Kirsten and Duncan. Duncan had said before he left, if she needed anything to call him. That he would come and pick her up, if she wanted. Make sure she got home safely. Only instead she'd foolishly chosen to smash her kitchen window.

Cutting her arm in the process, before passing out on a bed of shattered glass that spread its way out across her kitchen floor.

She'd blamed herself this morning when she'd woken up, cursed herself, thinking that her drunken behaviour last night had all been her own doing.

That this was all on her.

But now she knows that it wasn't. Not entirely anyway.

Women's drinks got spiked all the time in the bars and clubs in London. All across the country. Men drugging women simply for the thrill of it, because they believed they were untouchable, that they'd never be caught.

To them it was all just part of their sick, twisted game.

Preying on disorientated and incapacitated women they'd intentionally rendered powerless.

Powerless. That's exactly what she'd been.

Had she known?

Liam had said he'd seen her fall outside of the bar, that she'd been alone.

If she'd fallen, that meant that she'd been unsteady on her feet, that she'd been feeling the effects of whatever she'd been spiked with.

Perhaps she had been semi-aware of what was happening to her, and she'd been trying to get away. Her memory is so vague and fuzzy, she isn't sure what to think.

She thinks of him. The man in the bar who had bought her that last drink.

Shit.

Stupid, stupid girl.

She'd been so naive, so cocksure that nothing would happen to her, that she was prepared, that somehow, she would be different.

Smarter, more observant, immune from hurt.

Only she could add herself to the ever-growing list now, couldn't she?

She should have known better, Christ! She'd written an article on it, detailing the terrifying spate of attacks that were being made against local women. Women who had been drugged and sexually assaulted. Some even raped.

Drink-spiking was now on the rise, currently at epidemic levels across London. There had been eleven reports of this kind of attack happening in local bars and clubs in the last six weeks alone. Bars just like the one that she had been in last night.

The police had confirmed that the numbers of incidents had more than doubled in the past couple of years. These men didn't just drug women to sexually assault or rape them. They did it to steal from them too.

She thinks of her missing bag now. Her missing front door keys.

Shit!

She could do without this.

She feels the sting of bile threaten again in the back of her throat before leaning over the toilet once more, for the second time this morning, and gagging until her stomach aches with an empty hollowness.

She should leave.

Instead of going back into the newsroom and facing Liam and Kirsten, she could head for the building's main doors, towards the queue of waiting taxis that's lined up on the main road, all vying for their next fare. She could get home and call a locksmith. Call a glazier to replace the window. She'd have to pay extra for the premium of a same-day service. Astronomical prices but worth it if it means that she is safe.

She needs sleep. She wants to crawl into her bed and pull the covers up around her. Cocooning herself inside of her duvet and making the whole world disappear.

But she knows she can't just go, not yet.

Not when that innocent baby's story should be shared with the entire world; and it should be Jenna who shares it.

She owes Holly that much.

'Jenna? You in here? Are you okay?'

She flinches at the sudden shrill sound of Kirsten's voice as her knuckles rap against the cubicle's door.

'Just a minute!' Jenna calls out, flushing the loo in a bid to keep Kirsten from seeing that she's been sick. To keep her from being suspicious that she hadn't been holed up in the cubicle having a rare meltdown.

'I just wanted to check that you are okay,' Kirsten says, her back against the sink, waiting patiently when Jenna finally emerges from the cubicle. 'What Liam said in there... about the baby.' She shakes her head. 'You know what he's like. He speaks before his brain has engaged half the time. He was just being his usual insensitive self. Thinking about ways to spin the article to gain maximum impact for the readers. You know it's always about how to sensationalise a piece so that we hit our numbers. If he knew about your past...' Kirsten pauses, knowing how upsetting Jenna finds the subject of her earliest years. 'He would never have said any of those things.'

Jenna hears the caution in her words.

'It's fine, really. It's not Liam,' she replies, unable to bring herself to look at her friend as she speaks for fear of falling apart. She stares straight ahead at the basin, glad to have the welcome distraction of the water and washes her hands.

'Well, if it's not Liam, what is it? Because I can tell something's going on... Oh my god, Jenna!' Kirsten starts, but her words tail off as her gaze rests on where Jenna holds her hands beneath the fast-flowing water. 'What happened to your arm?'

Her sleeve has ridden up, she realises, along with the makeshift bandage. The lack of material revealing the newly moulded fold of skin botching its way back together to form a scar. Her permanent reminder of another fucked-up night.

'I cut myself on some broken glass last night. It's fine, it's nothing!' Shaking the droplets of water from her fingertips, Jenna drags her sleeve back down, too late, in a poor attempt to hide her newly inflicted injury.

'It doesn't look like nothing! You don't seem yourself, Jenna. And if I'm honest, you didn't seem yourself last night either. What's going on? Because I don't mean to sound horrible, but you look like shit. I thought you said you weren't going to drink last night.'

'I wasn't. I didn't,' Jenna starts, glancing at her reflection in the mirror, and recognising what Kirsten must see too.

The wreck of a woman reflecting right back at her.

Her dark, circled, bloodshot, teary eyes staring out from a ghostly looking face. She recalls the disapproving look on Kirsten's face when she had drunk a shot of tequila the night before as she sinks her wet hands down into the dryer, glad of the few extra seconds she has to compose herself while the loud, noisy blast of air sounds between them.

'I did something *really* stupid last night,' she says, closing her eyes and sighing.

'Okay, when you say stupid, how stupid are we talking?' Kirsten replies, hearing the seriousness of her tone and bracing herself for the worst. 'Oh my god, you didn't go home with Liam, did you?'

'What? Jesus, Kirsten, no! Why would you even think that?'

'Because you looked like you were on a mission to get drunk last night, and you said earlier that you've been home and slept, but you're still wearing the same outfit you wore last night. And you and Liam were both here at the office before me...' Kirsten tails off.

'No! I didn't sleep with Liam,' Jenna replies, shaking her head, incredulous that would be her friend's first thought but, in a way, wishing that's all it was.

'It's something much worse than that.'

'What's worse than sleeping with Liam?' Kirsten laughs lightly, which doesn't disguise the sarcasm there, knowing her own history with Liam and how she's been burned by her boss's advances once too.

Jenna stalls before answering, and Kirsten takes heed of her warning, her concerned expression mirroring that she realises that this is more serious than that.

Jenna takes a deep breath before she hesitantly answers Kirsten's question.

'I arranged for one of the guys from that incel site I've been investigating to meet me at the bar last night. I think he slipped something into my drink,' Jenna admits, finally.

'I think that he drugged me.'

10

JENNA

NIGHT AT THE BAR

He's walking her from the bar and she's not quite sure how she's allowed this to happen.

Earlier, she'd hooked her fingers tightly around her glass, purposely guarding it. Not letting her drink out of her sight. Not even for so much as a second.

Soda water and lime.

Not tequila and soda water like she'd told him. Which was exactly what he had just placed down in front of her when he'd bought her a drink. A fresh glass, filled to the brim with cubes of overcrowded ice that danced in time with the slosh of clear, potent liquid as he placed it down on the table.

She'd eyed it warily.

A huge double measure it seemed. *How generous!*

Jenna had made it her business to watch as the barman had poured it, but when he paid for the drink, he'd kept his back to her. The broadness of his frame blocking her view of the glass as it had sat on the bar.

Deliberately? She wasn't sure. But she thinks it might have

been. She knew better than to touch it, leaving it to sit redundant on the table like a pawn between them, Jenna silently vowing not to drink it.

She wouldn't even bring it to her lips and pretend, she had thought. Call her paranoid or overcautious and maybe that's exactly what she was, but Jenna would rather be paranoid than delusional.

She'd rather be cynical and suspicious of everything and everyone.

The job had done that to her. Always questioning if what she was being told was the truth or just their practised version of it. Being a journalist had taught her over the years that appearances were exactly that. The outward expression of how someone wanted you to see them, how they wanted to be portrayed, which was often seldom what they actually were.

Everyone seemed to have form or motive or secrets, and Jenna liked to be prepared for all situations and every eventuality and, at that moment, her gut had screamed at her not to trust him.

Not to drink the glass that he'd placed down in front of her.

Not when so much was at stake here. She could feel the heat of him, the waves of warmth that radiated from his body as he took the seat closest to her. Too close.

Jenna smiled, unperturbed, as she slid her mobile phone out from the side pocket of her handbag, making out that she was checking a new message that pinged on her phone, all the while secretly thumbing the touch screen display until Kirsten's name glowed back up at her.

She didn't put the phone back in her bag when she was done; instead, she casually sank the phone down so that it was nestled between the warm material of her skirt that dipped down between her thighs.

Her best friend ready on speed dial should anything happen to her.

She hadn't expected him to approach her. To single her out. To talk to her.

But Jenna had been ready. Because this was how they did it, wasn't it? The men in the group. All those men, hiding behind false identities and fake profile pictures in an attempt to conceal the darkness inside of them from the real world.

Normal men. Brothers. Sons. Uncles. Fathers.

Men just like him.

Yet he is the worst of them all.

She'd seen him boasting about it in the forum. How he'd picked out his next unwilling, easy target. A semi-intoxicated woman who would be easier to ply with more alcohol.

It was 'child's-play', apparently. 'Cockteasers, happy to have you buy them drinks all night when they're already half cut. Too self-absorbed and out of it to notice you slipping anything in their glass.'

The very same glass that he had placed down in front of her.

He watched her. Eagle-eyed, like a hunter ready to pounce on his prey. His eyes willing her to take it. To drink from the glass.

Her own glass sat empty, and she knew that she couldn't put it off any longer, not if she didn't want to draw attention to herself. Not if she didn't want him to know that she was on to him. That she was suspicious.

Using her initiative, Jenna slammed her glass into the fresh drink and watched it slide from the table. A loud smash on the floor.

'Oops! Shit, sorry!'

Pretending to be apologetic about that, so that he didn't realise that she'd done that on purpose. That she'd tipped it over so that she wouldn't have to drink it. Because she didn't trust it. She didn't trust him.

'I'm feeling a little light-headed.' She laughed lightly, as if hoping to hide her embarrassment at not being able to hold her drink.

Playing her role too.

Both of them acting.

Only, somehow, she really had started to feel light-headed, and she wasn't sure how that happened because she'd been careful tonight.

Careful enough.

Not expecting him to approach her, she'd thought she'd been safe having just a couple of tequila and sodas. Three or four at the most. Which she had cautiously sipped at. Not enough to make her feel this intoxicated, she didn't think.

Only maybe they were more than enough.

A few years ago, those drinks wouldn't have touched the sides; they would have been the warm-up routine. Pre-drinks before the real alcohol started flowing. Back then, Jenna would have only just been getting started. Knocking back umpteen shots of tequila before she even began to feel the mildest of affects as the alcohol rushed through her.

She'd been reckless back then, desperate for the rush of alcohol to flood her veins and enable her to let her guard down so that she could be herself.

Her real self, she used to naively think.

Tonight, she slipped. She knows that.

She shouldn't have drunk at all.

Only she'd felt the pull of it. The chance to switch off after an awful week having submerged herself in the misogynistic world of the incel group online. After all the videos she'd forced herself to watch that the MP had posted of his PA and other female colleagues. After the numerous reports of all the local sexual assaults.

It was getting to her.

How could it not?

Tonight had been a few hours of much-needed release,

that's all. So that she didn't have to constantly replay all the things she'd read in those forums this past week or so, over and over again in her head. All those warped, unhinged opinions and horrific confessions of crimes men were planning or had already committed had taken a toll on her mental health.

Constant exposure to other people's trauma caused trauma too. Continuously reporting stories about death and violence and corruption was bound to leave an imprint on someone.

It was bound to leave a dent.

She'd let her guard down, she knows now.

'Here, let me help you get some air.'

Now, as he leads her from the bar, she wants to shout at him, to scream at him to get off her, to call out for help. Only she can't trust herself to speak, as she is certain that if she opens her mouth no words will come out.

The noise in the room gets louder, as if someone has just turned the volume up a few notches. The bar is packed, hordes of people all sucking the air from the room and replacing it instead with their constant chatter and laughter that fills her head. Making the bar feel suddenly claustrophobic. As if the walls are closing in around her.

She just needs to get out of this bar, out of this room, away from all of this noise. Away from these people.

Away from him.

And if it means that she'll be able to breathe again, that the cold night air might stop the urge to be sick she can feel building inside of her, she'll allow him to guide her for now.

Until she feels better.

He is guiding her in a straight line, holding her upright but her movement feels slow and clumsy. As if her limbs have become unattached from her body.

One foot in front of the other, Jenna! Come on now, concentrate.

She repeats this mantra inside her own head, or perhaps she is saying it out loud; she isn't too sure of anything right now.

Her head feels strange, her thoughts fuzzy.

Her eyes roll in the back of her head as if they are fighting now to stay open.

Darkness. Then bright, bold light. Darkness. Then light again.

Stay awake she tells herself. *Stay alert!*

Did she just say that out loud? She thinks she might have. Because he is looking at her now. And others are too.

'Too many tequilas,' she hears him quip, his voice projected loudly as they pass a group of onlookers so that there's no confusion at the fact she's had too much to drink.

This is all on her.

He is simply helping her.

The good Samaritan. The local hero.

She tries to keep her focus on him, but his features all blur into one and she can't make out the details of his face. It's just a palette of paint splodges, smudges of beiges, browns and creams all muted into one. Big black holes for eyes.

A demon. A monster.

She feels the bile shoot up her throat as she tries to keep up with it and luckily, this time, she manages to swallow it back down, though she isn't so confident she'll catch it a second time round.

Woosh! A rush of cold air hits her.

Though still not free from the noise, from this godforsaken banging. The thud of the music so loud now that she feels like the speaker is sitting inside of her head.

They keep walking. Further along the pavement.

One foot in front of the other.

Then the slam of the cold, hard pavement.

Then nothing at all.

11

HIM

For someone who seemed to think they were so smart, Jenna Stone wasn't. Women need to be more careful, more vigilant, he thinks.

Hadn't she been watching the news? Didn't she know about all the local women being spiked in the area. The growing number of assaults and attacks made on them. How women round here had been raped.

Of course, she did, she was a journalist after all.

Jenna and her colleagues had written numerous articles on it. Documenting intimate detailed accounts of the attacks from some of the victims, printing their ordeals in black and white for the entertainment of her readers.

Jenna wouldn't call it entertainment, he figured.

She thought that she brought her readers the cold, hard facts, that she warned them of the dangers of the world and all that was going on around them.

The irony that she herself hadn't been aware of what was going on around her. Acting as if she was invincible. As if the awful crimes she had printed on the pages of the Islington Gazette, the harrowing accounts that had aired on the nightly episodes of the ten o'clock news, somehow wouldn't apply to her.

Because she was a journalist, she'd assumed that she'd be safe.

Happily accepting drinks from random strangers and knocking them back without hesitation. Treating it all like a game.

She'd been ripe for the taking.

She'd made it too easy for herself to become the next oblivious, naive victim.

Cocooned by the false illusion of safety a packed bar full of people brings as she had sunk back shot after shot, not thinking about how she'd drunkenly stumble alone to the nearest bathroom later. Or outside for some air when she felt as if she couldn't breathe.

She thought that she knew it all, but she was blind to the predators all around her. Watching patiently, waiting to pounce like vultures, swooping in for the kill.

What did these men look like?

They looked just like him.

Normal looking, average, somewhat nondescript.

The ones who sat and smiled at you, making polite conversation, all the while silently willing you to sip the poison laced in the drink they'd bought you.

Perfectly camouflaged amongst desperate but mostly harmless chancers that only ever approached women at the end of the night, when they were drunk. Believing that they'd stand a fair chance then.

No, these men are worse than that.

They don't ask at all. They just take.

Whatever they want, without permission, on their terms only.

We are the ones that register the look of doubt on your face with thinly veiled amusement, as the drugs start to kick in.

That master that wide neutral smile on your face when you start to feel queasy after that last drink. When the realisation hits you that something might be wrong.

An innocent look then, a few comforting words to gaslight you into believing that you are safe.

You're special, remember. Bad things happen to other women, not to you.

When your chest gets tight, and you find it hard to breathe. When the sweat begins to pool at the nape of your neck and gather under your breasts.

When you feel as if you are going to be sick, going to pass out. That's when we know we've got you.

You're easier to manipulate then, more susceptible to believe the lies.

Instead of fighting us off, you lean into it, wanting so desperately to believe the friendly wide smile on our face, the strength of our hold as we wrap our arms around you and make promises of helping you outside for fresh air.

Easier to guide you away from the throngs of people and the loud, noisy public space.

Easy to get you all alone to do whatever the hell we want to you.

And oh, he'd got so close.

So damn close.

She'd thought she was drunk at first. They all think that.

When they start to feel disorientated and dizzy.

He'd seen it in her eyes then too, the confusion there as she'd tried to tally up what she'd drunk to make her feel so suddenly sick.

The realisation of what was really going on dawning on her, a few minutes too late.

She hadn't consumed enough of the drug to render her completely out of it, but it was enough to make her incoherent, paranoid and untrusting.

Enough to make her vulnerable.

12

JENNA

'You were drugged? Jenna! Are you okay? What guy? Did he hurt you? Did he do anything to you?'

'No. I'm fine. I managed to get away as soon as I started to feel funny,' Jenna tells Kirsten, twisting the truth, thinking of how she'd clawed at Liam's face when he'd tried to help her. How she'd slammed her fist through a pane of glass when she'd arrived home.

How she'd lost her handbag.

'Wait a minute. You arranged to meet up with this guy? Intentionally? Oh my god, you're still in that group, aren't you?' Jenna can see Kirsten's mind going into overdrive as she tries to piece what she just confessed to her actions last night.

'I thought Liam pulled you off the investigation. Wasn't plastering that MP's face all over the front pages of the newspaper enough for you? You gathered enough evidence on what he did to those women for him to serve a lengthy prison term. He'll be brought to justice. You got your guy, Jenna, so why are you still part of that group?' The brief flash of concern that had spread across Kirsten's face is quickly replaced with thunderous anger as she registers the full extent of the danger that her friend knowingly placed herself in last night.

'Because putting away one man isn't enough,' Jenna says finally. 'Not when there's a whole army of men out there, all actively encouraging one another to carry out these awful attacks on women. There are 17,000 incels in that one forum alone. That's 17,000 men, Kirsten, who walk around amongst us, concealing who they really are until they sit behind the comfort and safety of their laptop screens. And don't even get me started on the ones that make no pretence at all. The ones that boast about the shit that they get up to. Egging each other on to slip date-rape drugs such as Rohypnol or GHB into the drinks of unsuspecting women like it's all just some kind of sick twisted game. They keep score, Kirsten, those fuckers tally up points. Did you know that?'

Kirsten shakes her head as if Jenna's answer had just proved her point.

'So why the hell are you arranging meetups in bars while you're on your own and off your face on drink, if they are that dangerous? Are you completely bloody mad?'

'I wasn't drunk last night,' Jenna admits. 'I only had a couple of drinks and those two at the bar, to make it look like I was drunk, so that I wouldn't stand out. The rest of the time I was drinking soda water and lime. Pretending that it was tequila.'

'Pretending to drink tequila? Why on Earth would you do that? Why did you pretend to be drunk, I don't understand?' Kirsten looks quizzical, not convinced that she is being straight with her.

'I know that it sounds a bit crazy, okay, a lot crazy. But I needed to look authentic in case he was watching. In case he got suspicious that I had been the one to invite him there. I only had a couple drinks, four at the most. I thought that I could handle it, that I could stop; only before I knew it, the alcohol had kicked in and I'd started to feel a bit tipsy. I'm not used to drinking any more. When I woke up this morning, I assumed that it had happened again. That I'd gone back there...'

She doesn't finish the sentence: they both know what she means.

Back there again to the Jenna she used to be.

Black-out drunk.

'You used yourself as bait!' Kirsten raises a brow, shocked to hear that last night's little performance had been completely fabricated, all for the attention of one man. 'Deliberately letting me, Duncan, Liam and the rest of the team believe that you were wasted last night.' She purses her mouth, realising as she says it out loud that is exactly what Jenna had done as she recalls the stern words she'd had before she'd left, how Duncan had offered to take her home, but she had loudly refused. 'We were all part of the act too, weren't we? All part of the illusion to make you look *authentically drunk*. I was genuinely worried about you. Did that even cross your mind?'

Kirsten shakes her head. She looks annoyed with herself for not seeing through Jenna's act. For not knowing that there was more to it.

But how could she have known? Jenna had shut her out, and she feels bad about that, because she knows that Kirsten only cares about her.

'I'm sorry, I should have told you, but I thought that you'd disapprove and well, I was right about that, wasn't I? Look, Kirsten, I know how crazy this all sounds and I know that I can't take them all on. There's too many of them. But that guy last night, he's one of the main instigators of the group. He is the one always bragging about how to "ramp up your attacks". You know what the newest sinister phenomenon he pushes is? Injecting women. That sick fuck is on that site boasting about the times that he's got away with stabbing his unsuspecting victims with a drug-laced needle when he's in nightclubs. You want me to just turn my back on that and pretend that I didn't know it was happening? Let some other poor woman deal with the fallout?'

'Can you even hear yourself, Jenna?!' Kirsten is furious now. 'You met him willingly, after you'd had a few drinks. Knowing, KNOWING that he injects his victims with a needle. KNOWING that you could have been his next victim! That's not just crazy, that's insane.'

'No.' Jenna shakes her head. 'It wasn't like that; I had no intention of ever actually meeting him. I just wanted to get him there, to the bar. So that I could see him for myself. Try and work out who he really is when he's not hiding behind a fake username. He thought he was meeting one of the other members. What I didn't anticipate though, was that after he'd figured he'd been stood up, he would approach me at the bar. Mike. He said his name was Mike.' She shakes her head. 'Him buying me a drink had never been part of the plan. But you know how this goes, Kirsten. We take the opportunities that are slung our way and we run with them. That's what we do. That's how we get the job done. Serendipity, fate. Whatever you want to call it.' Jenna tries to explain. To justify her actions last night, but she knows that she is skating on thin ground now. 'I was careful. I promise. I kept my hand on my drink at all times, and I purposely knocked the drink that he bought for me over, not wanting to take any chances. And I had your number ready on speed dial.'

Kirsten lets out a short noise that sounds like a strangled laugh at that.

'Well, fat chance I would have had at rescuing you, seeing as I had no idea what was actually going on last night. Because you kept me in the dark.'

'I sat far enough away from him so that he couldn't physically touch me,' Jenna continues, no longer aiming her words at Kirsten. She is saying them out loud to herself, as if she is still trying to work out how he did it. How he had got to her, because she had been careful. Despite what Kirsten thought.

As careful as she could have been.

Only somehow, he'd managed to outsmart her.

'Does Liam know? Is that what you were talking about when I got here earlier? I mean, I know he can be pretty unethical if it means he'll get his next headline, but surely even he wouldn't condone you putting yourself in danger like that?'

'No and you can't tell him, Kirsten. He wanted me off that site. Said we were lucky that we managed to publish the piece under a pseudonym and not use my real name, this time. He thinks it's too much of a risk to stay on there, digging around. He's worried that someone might work out who I really am. They might try and find me. He said it was too dangerous.'

'Well, he got that right, at least! Jesus, Jenna, if he asked you to stop digging, why haven't you done what he asked?'

'Because, Kirsten, I've somehow managed to find my way in. To infiltrate myself in the group without any of them having the faintest idea that I'm there, hiding among them all.'

'Oh, please! You don't really believe that, do you?' Kirsten says, shaking her head incredulously at Jenna's naivety. 'You lured that monster to the bar under false pretences and yet, somehow ended up getting drugged by him? Sounds like too much of a coincidence, don't you think!'

'He had no idea who I am. All he saw was a tipsy woman, alone in a bar. An easy target. I'm almost certain of it.'

'Well, almost certain isn't good enough! You need to go to the police, Jenna. There might be traces of whatever he drugged you with still in your system; they can do a toxicology report. The bar will have CCTV. If we tell Liam what happened, maybe he can get one of the IT guys to trace this guy's profile from the site. We might be able to catch him.'

Jenna shakes her head.

'Come on, Kirsten. We both know how this works. Chances

are the drugs won't be in my system by now. It was hours ago, and I've been sick twice since then. I can't have ingested it all either, because I was still coherent enough to manage to get away. And even if they found anything, accusing one guy in a room packed full of people of dropping a pill in my drink, won't stand up. I don't have any solid proof. It's just my word against his. If we really want to nail this bastard, then we need solid evidence. Without it, he'll get a tap on the wrist and end up getting off scot-free and, in the meantime, I would have blown my cover. He'll be able to find out who I really am.' Jenna closes her eyes, not even wanting to think about all the things he might do to her. All the things *they* would all be able to do to her.

Because she had seen it: how women were stalked and harassed online. How their home addresses and phone numbers were shared out among other members. How they'd all ganged up together, making women's lives hell. Hacking their social media sites and posting graphic images for all their "friends" to see. Constantly calling up their work and making a nuisance of themselves.

Infiltrating every aspect of that woman's life, so that it would feel as if she was living in Hell.

Some had even been physically stalked. Worse, attacked again. It was a never-ending vicious chain of power and abuse, especially for the women who actually spoke out against them. Women were petrified for their lives – and so they should be.

That's exactly what would happen to her if this group found out who she really was.

'If Liam finds out about any of this, he'll go mad. He'll throw me off the case completely; he might even suspend me for going against him. I can't let him do that. Not now. No. As far as Liam is concerned, last night was a one off. I drank too much and now I've got the mother of all hangovers. That's all he needs to know.' Wanting Kirsten to know that she means it, there's no room for persuasion.

Jenna pauses as if she's not sure she should divulge the rest. But seeing the stern look on Kirsten's face, she knows that she must. If she wants Kirsten to understand why she is doing all of this, why she can't quit just yet, she needs to make her understand what is going on here.

'I think I'm on the verge of breaking another big story. The guy last night, he's been sharing posts and newspaper articles about local attacks that have been happening to women. The rapes and sexual assaults that have happened in the area. And it feels like he does it for something more than just his own amusement. It's like he's obsessed or something. Like they're his own personal trophies.'

'You think he had something to do with them? That they are not all random attacks, that they are all linked?' Kirsten falters, and Jenna knows that she has her.

As much as Kirsten is worried about her, she has worked on these stories over the past year too. She has sat down with some of the victims, with the police sexual assault team, interviewing them. Putting out e-fits of the suspected attacker. Like Jenna, she'd seen first-hand the utter destruction and turmoil the attacker had inflicted on his victims.

The police weren't anywhere near close to catching him. So far, they had nothing to go on. No arrests had been made, and they had no leads.

'I know it's a big ask, but I just need a little more time. I can get something solid on him. I know I can.'

'I can't just stand back and watch you do this. It's too dangerous. You've got too much to lose if it all goes wrong.' Kirsten pauses, and Jenna's heart sinks as she sees her friend shake her head.

She is about to protest, about to beg, when Kirsten silences her by raising her hands to show submission.

'I won't say anything. I'll give you more time. But there's a condition attached to that. You are not doing this all on your own. I want you to keep me updated with everything that happens from here on in. And next time you have a stupid idea to meet another one of those fuckers again for a candle-lit dinner for two, you make sure you bloody tell me, okay? So that you have backup there. Someone on your side.' Kirsten grins at last before adding. 'He'll be hard pushed to take us both on!'

'Deal,' Jenna says finally, feeling the relief of no longer carrying the weight of this alone. Part of her wishing that she hadn't been so secretive and had confided in Kirsten sooner.

'Come on, let's go and get baby Holly's story out there, before Liam's hyperventilating that someone else is going to get the scoop, while we're both in the loos doing something really important like "touching our lipstick up".'

13

JENNA

'Meet Holly!' Placing her mobile phone down in front of Liam, Jenna pointedly taps at the screen as she plays her trump card. Hoping that the image on her phone is enough, that Liam will forgive her for attacking him last night and, going by the huge grin that spreads across his face, her latest offering seems to do the trick.

'You've got to be kidding me! You actually managed to get a photo of the baby! Jenna, you bloody diamond, you!' He grins, staring down at the image of the burly looking firefighter with the tiny baby nestled safely in his arms, as if he's just struck gold.

'How? No! Don't tell me, I don't want to know.' His grin widens, and Jenna knows immediately what he's thinking, because she was thinking it too.

This photo of the tiny infant was the money shot.

The perfect image of 'baby Holly' that they could splash all over the front pages of their newspaper to really get this story out there.

The fact that they had an exclusive on it too.

'We'll have to crop the firefighter out. He can't be seen to have been complicit with me taking the photo. I made him a promise and I'm going to keep it. If anyone asks, the tip off about the baby being abandoned was anonymous. No one knows the mother or her circumstances so that can't be proven otherwise. As far as anyone is aware, I gained access to the child at the fire station by pretending to be a social worker. I'm happy to hold my hands up and say that if it means that there'll be no repercussions back to my source,' Jenna says confidently. Hoping to take the heat off her colleagues and her informant by offering up herself if someone has to take the blame.

Whatever it took to run the story and get this photograph of Holly printed on the front page of their newspapers and all over their numerous social media channels.

Jenna wasn't thinking about the sales figures, or the readership numbers or the money that they'll no doubt generate from this news piece, she thinks only how this story along with Holly's photo could be the catalyst that gets the baby out there. Back into the arms of her mother.

'Holly is the one who is going to sell this story to our readers, so I think we should run with her photo whatever the fallout. It will be worth it,' she continues, knowing exactly how to reel her boss in.

Already she can see the cogs turning inside Liam's head. As Chief Editor of the *Islington Gazette*, he will only be doing what he does best. Working out the numbers while expertly directing the narrative to whatever benefits the newspaper the most. He would be already thinking ahead of the game to whatever would generate the most views and clicks and ultimately more readers and more sales.

She can tell by the look on his face that he knows she's right. The image of Holly will grab readers' attention. Printing this photo is what it will take to break this story.

Kirsten, however, still isn't convinced.

'Worth it for who? For Holly? It might not be worth it for

us, and the fallout might be far greater than you think,' she says, evenly weighing up their options. 'As much as I'd like to publicly launch an appeal to find this woman, and make sure that she isn't in danger, I also don't want to be sued. And neither should you two. Because that's what might happen if we splash all the details we have about her, as well as the baby's photo, across the front page of the newspaper. It won't just be our legals we'll have to watch out for. I've read the terms on the charity's site too, and the scheme grants the missing mother anonymity as part of the service, as long as the baby is under thirty days old, which Holly clearly is. I think we need to respect that.'

'Respect a scheme that is only in the trial process. A scheme that actively encourages women to give up their babies. Just because the scheme protects the mother, doesn't mean we have an obligation to do it too! Not when it's so glaringly obvious that giving up Holly isn't her choice. She's clearly been forced into it.' Jenna shakes her head; having listened to Chris's concerns at the fire station, she too remains unconvinced.

'We don't actually know that though. We don't actually know anything for certain.' Kirsten tries to reason, but Jenna cuts her short.

'I'm the investigating journalist and I'm the one who has done all the leg work so far on this story, so as far as I'm concerned, this story belongs to me.' She pauses for effect, firmly holding Liam's gaze so that there's no question of her backing down, before she taps at the tiny baby's image on her phone screen and holds it out to him.

'Look at Holly's face!' She nods down to the photograph one last time. 'This photo is going to be what draws the readers in. People are going to be invested in this story the second they clap eyes on Holly, how could they not? This baby's photo is what's going to grab the attention of our readers. It's going to grab the attention of the entire country. It's too big an opportunity to pass up.'

Jenna digs her heels in. Knowing full well that Liam will run with this story whatever way he chooses, no matter what she says. Ultimately he calls the shots.

If there was ever a time to sway him, it is now.

This is her one and only chance.

Liam pauses, lost in thought for a few minutes, as if he's taking everything in that Jenna has just said, before finally he speaks again.

'I think Kirsten's right! We can't put out an appeal to find Holly's mum. And we can't publish the note that the mother wrote either. Legal would do their nut and I expect the charity will come after us too,' he concludes, shaking his head.

Jenna feels her heart sink at his words. She'd been hoping that printing the photo of Holly would mean that there was still a chance of the mother seeing her baby and coming forward on her own terms. That the missing mother and child could still be reunited. About to argue her point once more, Liam holds his hand up and continues with what he'd started.

'*But...* maybe we just need to come at this from a slightly different angle. So that we ensure we cover our arses. So that if we do run the story and end up in a ruck with Legal, it would have at least been worth it.'

Bingo! She's got him.

'You said this firefighter wasn't keen on the scheme, right? That he has his reservations. That's why he called you and tipped you off, right?'

'Yeah, but I promised him that this wouldn't come back on him, that I'd keep his name out of it.'

Liam nods in agreement before raising his brow and throwing Jenna a smug grin.

'That's our angle on this then. That's how we get this story out there. We need to focus on the scheme. Baby Holly is the first baby in the whole of the UK to have been placed into one of the boxes,' he says, his voice buzzing with excitement again now that he's worked out how they can do this with minimal fallout.

'How long have the "box things" been installed for?'

'According to the website, only three weeks,' Kirsten confirms, still scrolling through her phone while simultaneously making notes.

'Wow, three weeks isn't long, is it? So, what do you reckon then? Your firefighter source is right, Jenna? That this scheme actively encourages women to abandon their babies? That these boxes offer women an easier way out?' Liam is oblivious to the disapproving look Kirsten is throwing him.

'I don't think it's the easier way out. Women carry their babies inside of them for nine months, Liam, they give birth to them, clothe them, feed them. I imagine that nothing about giving up your own child would be easy...' she says, and Jenna recognises the look of disbelief on her friend's face, which says she hoped their boss would handle the situation with the sensitivity it deserved.

Kirsten's reasoning is wasted on Liam though, because he isn't even listening now. Already off on his own tangent, he fires up his laptop.

'The charity won't be able to take legal action against us for reporting the facts. It would be a matter of public interest, wouldn't it? We'll still be exposing the mother, but this way we'll be covering our own arses. Doing things the smart way, with little comeback on us.'

'And you'll run Holly's photo alongside the piece?' Jenna asks, hopeful.

'We have to. Legal might not be too happy about us plastering Holly's face all over the front pages, but I think we can afford to take the hit for that. Worst case we can issue an apology further down the line. Pay the fine. Whatever, by then, everyone would have seen it anyway. Like you said, it's her face that's going to push this story out there; she is the reason our readers will be invested.'

'What about the letter?' Jenna asks.

'I think we leave that for now. See what response we get. We don't want to push our luck, publishing documents that, at some point down the line, might need to be handed in to the police,' he declares. 'We've missed this morning's print deadline, but we can get the article up online on the website and across all of our social media channels. Do you want to draft the feature from that angle then, Jenna, and ping it over to me, along with the photo? I want to go live with it ASAP.'

'Cool. Well, you both seem to have everything here under control, so I take it you won't need me to stick around and give you a hand. You okay if I head off?' Kirsten asks tightly, clearly not agreeing on what her two colleagues were about to do, but knowing that there was nothing more she could do about it.

'Yeah, you get off,' Jenna answers, distracted, as she fires up her own laptop's screen.

Aware that she has to get this article written up and sent over to Liam to print as soon as possible. The quicker they get it sent to print, the quicker she can get home and crawl into her bed, because she needs sleep.

The sickly feeling is back with a vengeance, but this time the waves of nausea no longer feel like the after-effects of whatever she'd been spiked with last night. This feeling is different, unsettling. More of a bubbling feeling deep in the pit of her stomach – her conscience getting the better of her, realising that when this story goes to print, it would be her name in bold black letters beneath it.

Putting Holly's story out there is the right thing to do, she tells herself as a vague memory from her childhood fills her head...

Nine-year-old Jenna sitting across the table from a social

worker who'd about as much warmth to her as the cold, sterile room they sat in, when she'd informed Jenna that she couldn't make contact with her own birth mother because the authorities didn't know who she was.

Jenna can still recall the raw pain she'd felt burning inside of her all these years later, on learning that she'd been just a few hours old when she'd been discovered.

A tiny crying baby in a tatty cardboard box, dumped inside the communal hallway of a block of flats. She'd spent so many of her younger years feeling insecure and wondering why she hadn't been enough to make her mother keep her, or at least come back for her.

Feeling as if the world wasn't a safe place, that people couldn't really be trusted, because if they could her own mother wouldn't have just left her like that. Wouldn't have cast her aside like rubbish. As if she wasn't good enough.

Wasn't this scheme setting up the same scenarios now, thirty years on?

Wouldn't they too be giving children a lifetime of questions with no answers? A lifetime of feeling like you might be finally getting somewhere, only to come to a dead-end because these mothers were protected, no questions asked.

Kirsten is right, women don't just easily give their children away. Jenna might never know the reason why her own mother abandoned her, but she needed to believe that it was for her own good. For her own protection. That her mother had cared about her. That she had meant something.

This missing mother might really be struggling, and seeing this photo of Holly might just be enough to entice her to come forward and claim her baby back.

Liam was right, screw Legal.

A child's future was at stake.

That made it worth the shot, for Holly's sake if nothing else.

14

EVIE

'They can't do this. They can't fucking do this.' My voice shakes as violently as my hands that hover redundantly above my keyboard.

All I can do is stare. My eyes fixed on the image of the tiny, helpless baby staring back at me.

My baby.

The sight of her takes my breath away. Causing something visceral to ripple ferociously inside of me as I take in every detail of that perfect little face. Her eyes are wide open now, round and dark just like mine. She has a halo of wispy brown hair and two chubby, dimpled cheeks.

I feel a heady rush of love and panic and grief all at once, with such intensity that it floors me. She looks just like me.

I hadn't expected that. Hadn't noticed it before.

I'd expected her to look like him. To *be* just like him.

Rotten and bad and broken.

Him.

I wince as the intrusive memory of him manages to slither its way inside my mind.

I slam my eyes shut and shake my head. Desperate to

dislodge the memory of what he did to me from my mind. Refusing to give him so much as an inch of space inside my head. So much as an inch of time.

I focus on the baby. *My* baby.

'Holly.'

The firefighter who found her has named her Holly, the newspaper article says. It doesn't suit her, that isn't her name. She isn't a Holly. Holly is pointed, and prickly with spines sharp as thorns.

She is a Sophia. Softer, warmer, kinder, after my late nan.

Stop it! I silently scold myself. *She is not yours. You gave her up. You don't get any say now.*

Gave her up. No. I didn't. Giving her up sounds like I don't care. Giving her up sounds like I didn't agonise over my decision for hours. That I haven't been wracked with guilt and pain every second since.

I didn't give her up.

It says it right here in black and white on the screen.

SAFELY SURRENDERED

That's what the headline reads. My eyes don't move from those words, my glare burning into them with such intensity as I will myself to believe them. That she truly will be safe now, safer there with strangers than here in this world with me. I almost don't recognise the low, manic laugh that escapes my lips. For it sounds more like a desperate screech.

Is this where I'm at now? Lying to myself.

Trying to convince myself of my own bullshit narrative that I gave her up to keep her safe. As if I had any choice in the matter. As if I actually had any say at all.

This was his choice. His doing.

I knew what would happen if I didn't do what he said. That they weren't empty threats he had made.

My heart thuds loudly inside my chest.

Distraction. That's what I need. I read the rest of the article. Taking it all in, how 'Holly' was discovered, how the scheme works. What will happen to her now. And when I reach the end of the article and I've run out of words, I scroll down further.

To the place on the screen that I know from bitter, past experience I should never venture to.

Because I know what will be there waiting for me.

'The mother should have been sterilised at birth!'

'She's probably one of the local crack heads. The kid's probably better off.'

Keyboard warriors and trolls.

Cowards hiding behind anonymous profiles, with random made-up names and blank spaces in place of where their photograph should be.

Déjà vu.

I've been here before. Nine months ago. Recounting the entire, terrifying ordeal of what had happened to me in great detail for a journalist in my local newspaper, after the police officer handling my case persuaded me that launching a public appeal might help identify and catch my attacker. That it might warn others of his presence out there. So I'd put it all out there for the whole world to read, laid myself bare.

Only they hadn't found him and, somehow, the vitriol from some of the readers ended being slung back at me.

Nasty, vile words, calling me names.

Taunting me.

ME.

Not *him*. Never him.

'Probably asked for it!'

'Claims she was raped. Just another attention seeking LIAR! Women are all the same.'

Attention seeking.

I think of the numerous invasive swabs that a nurse had

scraped from my body in the examination following my attack. More hands touching me. More pain. More humiliation. More trauma. How the police had taken my clothes that I'd been wearing too. The brand-new trainers that I'd saved for weeks to afford and treated myself to just the day before.

I hadn't wanted them back. I'd told the police to keep them, to throw them in the bin. All of them reminders of him.

These people here in the comments don't know about any of that, or if they did, they don't seem to care.

How I am now the shell of the person that I used to be.

How my life has been completely ruined by his one violent, hateful act.

Now these people are coming for me again.

The spiteful, hate-filled comments beneath the article jab at me as if three dimensional and made from sharp steel, cutting at me with their bluntness as intended no doubt.

'*Some people shouldn't be allowed to have kids.*'

'*Selfish Bitch!*'

I start to cry. My whole body is shaking but this time it is not through fear.

I am done with fear.

I'm angry now.

The newspapers weren't supposed to do this, were they? They weren't supposed to print this story.

The scheme assures the women who use it that we will be protected. That the details about the babies left in Safe Place Baby Boxes are supposed to stay anonymous.

Yet, within just a few hours, here I am. My baby's eyes staring back at me, accusingly, from an online article on the news website.

She is not safe now either.

Tomorrow 'Holly's' face will be splashed all over the front pages of their newspapers for everyone to see.

15

JENNA

NIGHT AT THE BAR

She blacked out. Or did she? Because it only feels like a few seconds, not much longer, that she sees and thinks nothing at all, sees nothing but black.

She is on the ground, she realises, pressing her hands out across the cold, hard concrete beneath her. A torn, jagged ladder making its way up her thigh, gone again. Replaced with a blurred, muted dark image. She feels it, an agonising pain radiating from one of her knees that took the brunt of her fall.

'Shit! Are you okay? Let me help you up!'

Disorientated, she tries to look around her, to work out where the voice is coming from, only her head is spinning. All she can see is swirls of colours, light and dark.

She can't see their face because she is having trouble focusing; all she can make out is the shadowy outline of their figure. The deep, husky tone of their voice.

'I'll take you home.' It's his voice. 'Mike': the man from the bar.

He is helping her.

Which is just as well, as Jenna is no longer capable of helping herself. She feels so tired, so sleepy, and it is all that she can do to not give in to the sudden exhaustion she feels and sink down to the ground again. To close her eyes. To sleep.

That would be nice, wouldn't it?

To give in to the nothingness.

No! Stay awake! You're not safe.

'Ouch,' she murmurs as he grips her too tightly. His fingers pressing hard into the flesh of her arm. Pinching, prodding, squeezing. She'll have bruises there tomorrow, she thinks.

Why is he grabbing her like that?

She twists her body wildly, shaking him off.

Floating in air for a few seconds before her body slams down onto the pavement. An explosion inside her skull.

He is standing over her now and she is suddenly aware of the closeness of his proximity to her.

Acutely aware that he is too close.

He is not going to leave her alone. This is what he wants.

'I'm fine,' Jenna manages, waving him away, though she knows that she is anything but fine. He knows this too.

In fact, she thinks, he's probably counting on it. Her being in this anaesthetised state.

She tries to concentrate, stay focused, homing in on the familiar noise that continues to play out all around her. A loud burst of laughter, excited high-pitched chatter. Someone whistling. Another voice calling out someone else's name.

She is outside the bar in the busy street. There are people all around her.

She imagines them all standing in clusters, drinking from pint glasses, lighting up cigarettes. Pointing over at her. Talking about the state that she's in.

The girl who can't handle her drink.

But while they are looking, while they can see her, she is safe she thinks.

Safe.

Only she doesn't feel safe right now. Because this is how it happens, isn't it? Jenna had heard all the stories, and she'd reported on a few incidents herself, recounting the pure horrors from the victims' stories as they'd described their violent attacks and rapes.

Jenna had once, herself, naively believed that crimes like that happened to mostly women who hadn't been vigilant, who hadn't been careful. Women who took chances, walking home alone late at night. Women who chose a short cut down an unlit alleyway or accepted a lift from a random stranger or someone they only vaguely know.

She knows better than that now.

How one in five women know their attacker.

How more often than not, this is actually how it happens.

Right here, right now, like this. In plain sight of a whole street full of spectators. Jenna on the floor, just another dumb girl who can't handle her drink. While he stands over her, acting like the concerned, protective boyfriend. Mortified at the state his girlfriend has got herself in, as he scoops her up off the floor and whisks her back home to the illusion of safety.

'What's your address?' he asks.

Jenna shakes her head. Refusing to give him an answer, because she knows that this man isn't trying to help her at all.

He is taking advantage of the intoxicated state she is in. Trying to make sure that her abduction looks nothing untoward so that there will be no witnesses. No one to stop him from playing out his sick, depraved fantasies on her once he's got her all alone, locked in her flat.

'Maybe you've got something in here that will give me a clue,' he says as he rummages through her handbag, acting like a kind, concerned person who just wants to get her home safely.

It's all an act, she tells herself. *Reminds* herself.

He is trying to find something that will tell him her address.

She feels sick. The potent, acrid stench of alcohol and cigarettes from his breath as he speaks makes her stomach churn. She doubles over, retching until she's emptied the entire contents of her stomach all over the pavement.

Warm, lumpy, vile smelling vomit all over his trainers.

She is glad. Glad that being sick is enough of a deterrent to make him back off.

Glad that she is managing to get all of the poison that she has drunk tonight out of her system. The couple of drinks she'd allowed herself had been her downfall. She knows that now.

She is thinking about all the local women who had been attacked lately. How prevalent the attacks were happening, more and more often, becoming more violent.

How these women were then subjected to more humiliation afterwards, as details of the attacks were passed around incel sites like trophies. How the sick bastards got off on all the depraved, twisted details. How they seemed to thrive on learning about the victim's fear. Picking apart every tiny detail of the woman's ordeal, before chiming in and adding their own versions of what they would have liked to have done. How they'd made jokes about her as if she simply didn't matter. How they all agreed that she probably deserved it, that she probably asked for it. That what happened to her was all her fault.

Jenna wouldn't be another one of their victims.

She wouldn't become those twisted sicko's entertainment.

'I'm fine. Leave me alone,' she mouths, and there is so much anger in her voice that her words tremble as they leave her mouth.

He grips her harder. Too hard, too firm. Desperate now as he tries to guide her up and away from all the people. Away from the vibrant chaos and bright London lights.

Away, where no one will be able to hear her screams.

Get off me, she mouths, only her words don't leave her mouth.

They are trapped there, lodged like an invisible ball in the back of her throat.

A familiar face in the distance staring back at her from across the road. Amidst the crowds of onlookers.

Duncan?

She is filled with relief that he has come back for her, to make sure she got home safely?

Only when she looks again, he's gone and she wonders if perhaps she imagined him.

'I'll take it from here, mate!' Another voice. Male. It sounds vaguely familiar too. Or perhaps that is just wishful thinking.

The alcohol in her system making her see and hear things that are not really there.

'No, it's fine...' Mike protests, but he doesn't sound so confident now. He doesn't sound so certain.

'I've got her...' the second voice says again, and this time there's a tilt to it.

A veiled threat, some kind of warning.

Yes, please fuck off and leave me, Jenna thinks. Glad of the interruption. Glad that someone is intervening. That someone else is helping her.

Are they?

A hand hooks itself around her arm now. Firmer, with bony fingers that dig into her flesh. Too hard, too rough, as he tries to hoist her back up to her feet.

Jenna just wants to be left alone.

She wants everyone to stop grabbing at her, stop pulling at her. Trying her hardest to shake her body free of his grip and wriggle out from his hold. He is stronger than her, though.

The noise of the street behind them is getting quieter as they get further away. Soon they'll be away from the noise and the chaos and the lights and the people, and who knows what will happen to her then.

Swinging her body around wildly, Jenna lunges at the man holding her.

She has to. What other choice does she have but to fight?

Unsteady, unbalanced as she moves, somehow the tips of her fingers connect with his skin, and she drags her sharp nails down his face.

It works. He shouts out in pain and anger and, seconds later, he is off her, releasing his grip.

She turns to look at him and sees him clearly, staring back at her through bloodshot, alert eyes.

A deep gouge of red across the skin of his face, where she'd tried to claw his eyes out.

To get him off her.

To break free of him.

Only it isn't Mike.

'Fuck, Jenna! It's me. It's Liam. You're safe now. You're safe.'

16

JENNA

Disorientated, Jenna sits bolt upright, and stares over towards the bedroom doorway. Eyeing the empty bed, it takes her a few seconds to work out where she is.

She's home now, safe now.

It was just a dream, she tells herself recalling the two sleeping pills she'd swallowed the minute she'd got home from the office earlier. They must have knocked her out instantly, as she hadn't even made it up from the sofa. She knows that she hasn't just woken from a nightmare she'd become trapped inside: she'd been having flashbacks of the night before. Her subconscious making sense of the fragments of memories from the previous night that had filled her head.

Her being led unsteadily from the bar.

That image of Liam's scratched, bleeding face.

The sight of Duncan, watching from across the road.

Had it been him?

Had he come back for her, to ensure she got home safely?

Or had he been just part of her bad dream? She stares at the clock, registering that it's two thirty in the afternoon, and she has somehow managed to lose almost half the day. She had underestimated how strong the pills that she took had been. The effects of them mixed with whatever else must have still been lingering in her blood stream. Her head feels foggy, her thoughts dense as they settle inside her head.

If anything, she feels worse now, not better.

More confused.

Sleeping pills have always had this effect on her, leaving her groggy and exhausted for hours after she wakes. Which was why she rarely takes them. Why they'd sat discarded in her bedside drawer for months. Maybe even a year.

They were her plan B. Only to be taken in extreme circumstances. In absolute desperation.

She had felt desperate, hadn't she?

She feels now as if she's forgotten something. What?

Something important that was happening today.

The article about baby Holly!

Liam would have gone live with it by now. The story would be up online. Searching for her phone, she finds it wedged down between the sofa's cushions. Jenna taps at the glass, until she lands on the newspaper's website. The familiar photograph that she took of baby Holly filling her entire screen.

The news piece is well articulated and only presents the facts, but it's the photograph of Holly that Jenna is concentrating on. That alone is enough to evoke real emotional reactions from readers, that alone would draw them in and keep them invested.

Some emotions are stronger than others, she figures as she scrolls down further and reads the comments beneath the article, where some readers have already come to their own conclusion about the baby's missing mother. Her eyes naturally seeking out the tirade of abuse that she knows articles like this would bring for the baby's mother.

Sure enough they have.

'*Selfish whore.*'

'Some women shouldn't be allowed to have kids.'

Jenna closes her eyes in despair. The insults are not even directed at her, yet still she feels them. She picks nervously at the skin around her cuticles, relishing the hot sting of pain as her nail digs in harder than she intended and she scrapes a thick bit of skin away and keeps reading.

Ouch!

Blood flows out as the nasty words sink in. *Is it true? Some women shouldn't be allowed to have kids?*

Because she'd thought that of her own mother once too, hadn't she? How she shouldn't have had her if she was only going to dump her in a cardboard box, as if she was nothing more than a bit of rubbish.

If she hadn't really wanted her.

As Jenna had got older, she had realised that life wasn't quite as simple as that. It was so much more complex and complicated: nothing was ever purely black and white.

She had to believe that, that life was a healthy dose of grey, the darkness softened by glimmers of light. That not everything had to be bad.

This mother had cared enough to leave a note.

'She's in danger. Please keep her safe.' Maybe her own mother had wanted that too. To keep Jenna safe? To give her a better life.

Or maybe she'd chosen herself over her own child. Put her own happiness first.

Jenna doesn't have the head space for any of this right now.

Her head is throbbing. She doesn't want to sit with them. All the dark, depressing thoughts that have managed to claw their way inside of her head, despite trying her hardest to stop them from getting in. Painful memories of growing up in care and being passed between the endless foster families and children's homes. Never feeling as if she fitted in or belonged.

Even now. Needing to escape her own company, Jenna

floats aimlessly from one claustrophobic room of her flat to another. Without a cause, without purpose. Too wired and jittery for her usual dependency of coffee. She closes her eyes and tries to shut the negative thoughts out. If she gives in to them now, they will not only overpower her, but they will also consume her completely.

She needs some air.

Pulling the back door open, Jenna steps out onto the damp red quarry tiles, ignoring the wet that seeps into the bare skin of her feet. Part of her welcomes the coolness.

She needs it, that icy blast of cold air that sweeps over her, jolting her from the rapidly darkening mood.

Her phone beeps. The screen lighting up to show a whole list of missed calls and text messages from Liam.

She clicks on his first text message.

Story has gone live. All good, but I need you back at the office. Pronto! Legal are kicking off.

Jenna rolls her eyes before sucking in big, greedy mouthfuls of air into her lungs, as if her life depends on it, as she looks up at the vast sky above her. Grey clouds, thick with a darkness and anger that mirrors her own, dance territorially around each other as if goading each other for a fight.

She casts her gaze across the garden. Her efforts last summer of filling the space with the pretty sight of potted plants and shrubs, in all kinds of bright and beautiful colours, wasted. Pots of stagnant compost housing only decaying twigs and crisped detached leaves now.

How it looks as if everything has turned to rot.

She had felt that too once. Spending so much of her childhood and early adult years pushing down feelings of being contaminated. Tainted. Feeling like nothing more than unwanted rubbish because she just didn't seem to fit anywhere or belong to anyone.

Becoming a journalist had changed all of that. Jenna was good at it, a natural, in fact.

She'd learned from a very young age to observe and question everything and to always be persistent. To never give up, and she didn't. Once she got the bite of a story, she didn't let go until she had everything she needed, to not only uncover injustices but to expose the truth.

To give her readers the answers that they needed too.

That's why she'd arranged to meet the guy from the incel site last night. Except she'd been too cocky following the takedown of the recent MP. So desperate to push for a result that she'd ended up putting herself in real danger.

Stupid girl.

Tearing her gaze away from the depressing sight of pots, away from the overgrowth of long grass that had grown so wildly that it had swallowed the cobbled footpath that runs the length of the garden in its wake.

Another text.

Jenna bites her lip as she reads the message from one of her contacts she'd reached out to, just before she'd taken those sleeping pills.

Telling her that he has something she might be interested in seeing.

Jenna smiles to herself, glad that her hunch has paid off, and then she texts Liam.

I'm on my way. Just gotta make a slight detour first though. I've got something for you on the missing mother. Give me an hour.

Hearing a noise from inside the house Jenna turns towards it.

A knock at her front door.

It's 3 p.m. She remembers she'd arranged for a glazier to come to fix the broken window. Or perhaps it is the locksmith to change her locks and give her a new set of keys. Same-day emergency repairs that had cost almost double in order for her to feel safe again in her own flat.

You've got forty-five minutes and then I'm out of here.

Liam's reply is short and sweet.

Knowing that she won't be able to stay here while the glazier fits the new glass, or her locks are being changed, that she'll have to leave them to it, she takes a final deep breath as she steps back inside and locks the backdoor behind her, before she wipes her eyes.

Tears are a sign of weakness; they make you look fragile and vulnerable and Jenna prides herself on being neither of those things.

17

JENNA

'Did you manage to get some sleep? You do look a bit better,' Kirsten says, getting out of the car and giving Jenna a onceover as she walks towards her, having both arrived at the office at the same time.

'A bit better? Woah! Steady on there, Kirsten, a girl can only take so many compliments before it goes to her head, you know!' Jenna smiles as the two women stroll through the main doors of the office together, making their way up the stairs towards the newsroom.

Though Jenna is secretly glad that she had made the effort to quickly jump in the shower and put on some clean clothes before leaving the glazier to it.

If she looked better, then she could at least pretend that she felt better too.

'You know what I mean. How are you? Do you feel okay, after...' Kirsten pauses, clearly unsure how to put into words exactly what Jenna had just gone through.

'After being drugged? You can say it you know.' Jenna stops directly outside the newsroom door and lowers her voice so that she won't be overheard. 'My ego's a bit battered, and I feel beyond stupid for allowing myself to get into a situation like that in the first place. But other than that, I'm fine. I don't think I ingested enough of whatever he tried to spike me with for it to completely incapacitate me, and it's probably helped that I've been sick a few times now too.'

Jenna falters then, recalling the bad dream she'd woken up from earlier, still trying to make sense of the broken fragments inside her head.

'Duncan didn't go back out, did he? After you got home last night?'

'Duncan? No. He was in his office working,' Kirsten says narrowing her eyes with concern at Jenna's question. 'What makes you think that he went back out?'

'Oh nothing. Ignore me. I thought I saw him outside the bar, but I was probably well on my way to hallucinating by then. Forget I asked. To be honest I really just want to forget all about it now.'

Kirsten nods, before doing just as her friend asks and deliberately changing the subject.

'Whatever this is about, it had better be good, because it's the second time today that his Lordship has dragged me in here. I've just left Janet, in her absolute element, taking over my kitchen. She's insisting that she's going to treat us all to a "proper home cooked meal" when I get back.' Kirsten uses her fingers to draw inverted commas in the air. 'Who knew, eh? Apparently the Marks and Spencer pasta traybake that I shove in the oven at the end of a long busy day just doesn't cut it.'

'Janet is a card, bless her. But you and I both know you'd be lost without her!' Jenna quips, giving a small laugh.

Kirsten's mother-in-law drove her around the bend half the time, always interfering and giving her opinion on the way that Kirsten runs her house and raises her kids and, of course, the way she treats her husband, Janet's one and only golden-boy, Duncan. But they both know that the woman only means well.

Still, Jenna has always found the dynamics between the two women with their dramatic showdowns and constant disagreements highly amusing.

'You love her really!'

'Hmm! Well, I like to keep that quiet. I'm not sure I could handle her ego if she thought I actually secretly liked her. To be honest with you, I'm actually a bit worried about her. She's been having some funny episodes lately. Headaches and dizzy spells. I've told her to go to the doctors but she keeps finding excuses to put it off.' Hearing a ping from her phone, Kirsten reaches into her pocket and eyes the screen before flashing the photo of Holly to Jenna and shaking her head incredulously.

'Oh, wow! This story has gone crazy, Jenna. It's already been picked up by just about every other media outlet and it's all over social media. I bet Liam is in his element right now. Do you think that's why he's asked us back in? His text was pretty vague. Did he say anything to you?'

'Actually, it wasn't just Liam that wanted you in; it was me too. I initiated this meeting.'

'Oh, right! You should have said. Is it about Holly?' Kirsten sounded stung that she'd been left out of the loop by Jenna yet again.

'Yeah, I've got something. I've just come from a shop in the high street literally not even twenty minutes ago, and I wanted to show you and Liam, together. In person.' Jenna doesn't give anything away just yet as she pushes open the door to Liam's office.

'Two seconds, ladies!' He mouths as he holds up a finger, as if to silence the two women, while clutching his mobile phone to his ear.

'I don't give a flying fuck what the charity are implying, we didn't need their permission to publish the photo or break the story. It's a matter of public interest. And judging by the fact that the story has been picked up internationally now, I'd say

that the public are most definitely interested, wouldn't you?'
Liam smarts, spittle leaving his lips as he raises his voice. 'No,
you listen. I've done my job, now you lot need to do yours and
sort this shit out!'

He shouts, ending the phone call and shaking his head
before bringing his attention back to Jenna and Kirsten.

'That was Legal. Surprise, surprise! They were just kindly
informing us of the protocol going forward, now that there's
been a backlash from the charity about publishing that photograph of Holly without permission.'

'So, the Safe Place Baby Box Scheme is threatening legal
action?' Kirsten asks, raising her eyes to Jenna because this is
exactly what she'd warned them about.

'Whatever, it's a small price to pay in the grand scheme of
things. Our lot are kicking off about formalities and permissions,
yadda-yadda!'

Kirsten rolls her eyes at Jenna, and Jenna knows what she is
thinking. This was so typical of Liam. Ignoring and playing
down any negatives and only focusing on what he wanted to
hear.

'Fuck it, that's their job, they'll sort it.' Seeing the unconvinced look on Kirsten's face, Liam waves his hand in the air
dismissively. 'All publicity is good publicity, you know that.
Great publicity in fact. We've never had so many online views
in such a short space of time. People are lapping this story up.'

'Well, that's good to hear because I've just managed to get
my hands on something that may be of interest to you,' Jenna
says cryptically, going to the main computer and inserting the
memory stick into the USB portal on the side of the Mac
monitor.

'You both need to take a look at this,' she says, pressing *play*
and angling the large monitor towards Kirsten and Liam before
standing back, out of the way.

'What exactly are we looking at here?' Kirsten asks, eyeing

with intensity the black and white grainy footage of an empty street as it plays out on the screen before them.

A glare of bright headlights somewhere in the distance throwing a beam of light across the otherwise dark footage. Other than that, there's no movement.

'That's Islington High Street,' Liam says, recognising the dark, empty street immediately. 'It's just down the road from the fire station, isn't it?'

'It is. Do you remember the jewellers just a few shops down from the fire station? The owner was robbed a few months ago. A nasty smash and grab by a group of men in balaclavas, all wielding sledgehammers,' Jenna says, waiting for their faces to register the violent attack they'd covered in the newspaper. 'I was the investigating journalist covering the story at the time. Anyway, the poor guy had been terrified after that and rightly so. He'd been convinced that they'd come back and try their luck again sometime after he'd restocked the place. Swore that if they did, he would be ready for them. He was adamant that he wouldn't allow them to destroy his business for a second time. Well, I gave him a call this morning.' Jenna grinned widely. Pleased with the hunch she'd followed up on, when she'd got home from the office earlier that morning. 'He was true to his word. He's had the place done up like Fort Knox. CCTV cameras installed everywhere. They even cover that strip of pavement just outside. Keep watching...'

The room is completely silent as three pairs of eyes continue to stare at the screen, waiting patiently for a figure to emerge from the shadows. A flicker of movement. Something. Anything.

Jenna holds her breath, her heart pounding inside her chest as much now as when she'd watched this footage the first time round, in the jeweller shop's office. This time without the built-up anticipation, because she already knows what's coming.

Finally, movement, a silhouette of a person, walking hastily across the screen as they make their way along Islington High Street.

'Oh my god, is that her? Is that the missing mother?' Kirsten is leaning forward in the chair to get a better look.

Narrowing his eyes Liam notes the bulges around the woman's middle. 'It can't be her? She's still pregnant?' He points to the oversize coat that the woman is wearing, that fits snuggly around the mound of the woman's chest and stomach.

'She's not pregnant. She's concealing the baby under her coat,' Jenna says. 'It's her. Look!'

They all continue to watch intently as the figure turns and repeatedly scans the street behind her.

'She looks like she's checking to make sure that she hasn't been followed. That no one is watching before she pulls open the top of her coat and peers down inside of it. Which makes sense given the note that she left, warning us that Holly might be in danger. That she needs to keep her safe,' Jenna explains in real time as they all keep their eyes fixed to the screen.

Then, as quickly as the missing mother comes into view, she is gone again. Leaving the street dark and desolate once more. Just the image of lights dancing in the reflection of puddles that adorn the middle of the empty road.

Jenna stops the recording and rewinds it, pausing it just as the blurry image of the woman fills the screen, before she zooms in on the woman's face.

'The image isn't the best; it's very blurred and grainy. It's a low-lens camera and the rain doesn't help. Neither does the fact that it's so dark,' she makes apologetic excuses as she zooms in; the footage she's managed to get isn't as clear as she'd hoped.

The more she zooms in, the worse the image looks. The woman's face becomes distorted and even more pixilated than before. Just a blur of colours and splurges, no real detail there. 'I know that it's not the best quality, but it's something, isn't it? The first and only official sighting of the missing mother that we have so far. Still much more than any of the other papers will have!'

Jenna looks from Liam to Kirsten as she tries to read their expressions. She is met with two blank faces. Neither of them is giving anything away. Jenna isn't sure what she'd expected but no reaction at all hadn't been something she'd factored on.

'Well?' she says finally.

'She's wearing a nice coat!' Kirsten says, giving a small, weak shrug in the form of an apology: she doesn't find this recording of any use to the newspaper.

'It's not a fucking fashion show!' Liam says not quite as polite. 'That's it? That's what you called this urgent meeting for? A two second, barely visible clip of some woman doing a catwalk down Islington High Street, modelling a fucking coat that Kirsten has her eye on?'

'It's not some woman though, is it? It's her. The missing mother,' Jenna protests, but Liam shakes his head.

'Says who? The image isn't clear enough, Jenna. In all honestly this could be anyone. It proves nothing.'

'Come on. It's her, it has to be.' Jenna is growing frustrated. 'I've checked out the timings, this footage was taken just minutes before Holly was left in that baby box. It's definitely her, and it's the one and only sighting that anyone has of the mother.' Jenna tries again. Hearing the desperation in her own voice and hating herself for it. Only she has to at least try and get Kirsten and Liam to listen to her. Whoever the mother is, she might see this image too. Along with the photo of Holly they've already published, it might be enough to make her think that she will be discovered. Enough to make her come out of hiding and step forward and claim her child. To ask for the help that she so obviously needs.

'A woman walking down the street, with a huge bulge under her coat, at exactly the same time a baby was abandoned...'

'Safely surrendered,' Kirsten corrects her.

'Safely surrendered,' Jenna repeats, biting her top lip. Irritated now. Because judging from both her colleagues' reactions, or lack of, the CCTV footage she managed to find of the missing mother isn't as ground-breaking as she had hoped. It's close to useless it seems.

'We can't print this,' Kirsten says, as if reading her thoughts while she gathers up her bag and jacket, ready to make a sharp exit now that they are done. 'If you think that we're in the shit with Legal now, you wait until the charity's lawyers take you to the cleaners for putting this out there. The scheme states clearly that the mother's identity will stay anonymous.'

'Look at these figures, look at the clicks and the views we've had. They're playing it on the news overseas. People are going nuts over it. Little Holly has won their hearts, and people are very vocal about the scheme too. We don't have to cast aspersions or voice our opinions; we just put some images out there and state the facts. What if we can actually do some good from all this?'

'Good? How? Oh, you mean try and make the mother come forward. Guilt her into doing the "right thing". Is that what you're hoping will happen here by trying to identify the woman? Or are you trying to punish her?' Kirsten says now, treading carefully. Knowing how close this subject is to Jenna's heart. How personally she is taking Holly's abandonment. How fixated she seems to be on trying to get this baby a different outcome than the few days of a life she'd already been dealt.

'How do we know that the mother coming forward to claim her child is the right thing? The mother made her choice, and she has every right to do that. We all read the note that she left with Holly. We don't know what mental state she's in right now, and calling her out in the newspaper, trying to identify her, might just tip her over the edge. It might turn into a hate campaign, a witch hunt for the baby's mother, which we all agreed that we didn't want. All you've got if you go with this, is clickbait. You're not going to be giving our readers anything substantial, are you? You're just overpromising and underdelivering by chucking out another sensationalised headline that you've found the missing mother, when all you've found is some shockingly awful quality footage of a woman that we think might be her,' Kirsten says, trying to be the voice of reason.

'Kirsten's right,' Liam says, for once, surprisingly, in agreement with Kirsten. 'I'm all for a bit of clickbait, you know that. For throwing the readers meagre-sized morsels in the hope that it whets their appetite to keep scurrying back for more. But you can barely even call this a sighting.'

'But it is a sighting, and if we don't run with it, one of the other news outlets will,' Jenna presses, knowing how competitive her boss is, in a last desperate attempt to get Liam to change his mind. 'I know it's not the clearest of images, but maybe if we post the video up online too, then someone might just recognise her. Maybe it will jog someone's memory of having walked past her in the street this morning, or I don't know, maybe they'll recognise the coat that she's wearing.'

'I mean, it is a nice coat,' Kirsten adds evenly, as if not wanting to be mean and completely shut Jenna down.

'Or yeah, maybe the missing mother might see it,' Jenna says, finally admitting some of her intention. 'She might think that we are close to identifying her. Which means that she might come forward quicker. If there's even the smallest of chances of the mother being found, of her being reunited with Holly, of keeping her from danger, then yeah, I think we should put it out there.'

'We're not plugging an episode of *Long-Lost Fucking Families* here for prime-time TV, Jenna. And we're not social workers either. It's not our job to go around trying to reunite mothers with their babies. We deliver the news. That's it. The cold hard facts and we're supposed to stay neutral and keep our personal feelings out of it,' Liam says, raising his eyes to let

Jenna know of his suspicions, that somehow this story has got to
Jenna. 'But, maybe it wouldn't hurt to throw it out there. It's
something else to give our readers, isn't it? Another part of the
puzzle. As pixilated as it is. And to be fair, the video quality is
so crap that the mother would still have her anonymity even if
we did put it out,' he adds, 'there's no way anyone will be able to
identify her from this.'

'So you'll do it?' Jenna says full of hope that finally Liam is
listening to her.

It's a long shot putting it out there. But this could be the
only real chance they have at actually finding Holly's mother,
and if there's a tiny, minuscule chance of that happening then
they have to at least try.

18

EVIE

I can't sleep.

Every time I lie down and close my eyes I feel as if I am drowning in a sea of darkness. I'm terrified that if I drift off, the treacherous tide of blackness will consume me completely.

I am beyond exhausted, but I know that even if I slept there would be no real rest for me, because I can't switch my brain off. It's in overdrive now. My head full of terrifying images of him. A flash of that distorted, shadowy face, my mind not allowing me to process the detail of his features.

Or worse. So much worse.

It's full of beautiful images of her.

Holly. No. No! Sophia.

Doll-eyed and chubby cheeked.

SCRUB. SCRUB. SCRUB.

Desperate to keep busy, to shut them both out, I am up now, wide awake. Scrubbing at the bathtub. Dragging an abrasive sponge that is saturated in Cif across the white porcelain, in a bid to remove all traces of her from the place where she was born. Eradicating all signs of her from my flat.

Only my god, she is persistent.

The ghost of her remains here with me, haunting me.

Other reminders too, ones that I can't remove. The permanent marks that have been physically etched on my body. My skin ruined now; thick, red claw-mark slivers that have been dragged down my newly deflated belly. My breasts heavy and tender as they constantly leak milk into the scrunched balls of tissue that I have stuffed inside my bra.

I feel like an empty shell of a person, as if a piece of me is missing. A part of me forever gone.

I did this.

I chose this.

This constant torment and suffering are my punishment.

SCRUB. SCRUB. SCRUB.

I drag the sponge backwards and forwards over the grimy marks on the bath until it gleams white and shiny, like new. I hold the shower head out then and watched transfixed as the hot stream of running water washes away all signs of her ever being there.

Gone. Sucked down the plughole.

The flat is clean. She is gone, and everything feels so empty and pointless now.

I've run out of things to do to keep me busy so instead I move.

Pacing the floor of my flat. Aimlessly, manically, walking around and round in circles. Is she safe now? I am unable to get his words out of my head.

'Get rid of it. Or else.'

'It'. The baby. Her.

That had been the first of many messages he'd sent me. His way of telling me that he'd found me. That somehow, he knew I was pregnant, that he knew that the baby was his.

'Get rid of it, or I will pay you a visit and do it for you.'

Blindsided by fear and terror, too scared to tell the police that he knew where I lived, because hadn't I already done that? Hadn't I already confided that I was pregnant to the dedicated police officer who'd been assigned to my case?

That information hadn't been made public. Yet somehow, he knew, and he'd found me.

I have no idea if he found me through her or not, but I was unable to trust anyone after that. Shutting myself away from the world while constantly living in fear of his next message pinging up on my computer. Terrified that he'd turn up here, at my flat. That he'd try to harm me if I didn't do what he asked.

It's hard to believe that my home felt like a sanctuary once. A place that once offered me solace from the cruel world outside. That I had felt safe here once. Before.

Now, this flat feels more like a prison. I haven't just locked myself away, I've shut the whole world out. I've cut myself off. It feels claustrophobic now. As if the bars of the gilded cage are closing in on me. Hiding away in here, for the past nine months. Enduring the same monotonous daily routine.

Work. Eat. Sleep. Repeat.

Keeping my head down at work, doing only what I had to do to earn enough money to pay my rent and bills and buy my food.

Not daring to start any kind of real conversation with anyone else in case they ask me if I'm okay. Or inquired what I was hiding beneath my oversized jumper.

Petrified I'd come undone, and all my darkest secrets would pour from me.

Her, she was my secret.

'Get rid of it.'

I hadn't gone through with his orders because I wasn't sure I could live with myself if I did. Ending the life of an innocent baby because of what he had done. I wasn't prepared to let him take that away from me too.

That decision. That choice. They were mine to make, not his.

So, instead of doing anything I simply went into denial. Pretending that the pregnancy wasn't happening. That the swollen bulge of my stomach that had started to resemble a watermelon could be hidden away from the world forever. Secretly hoping that by the time I gave birth he would believe that I'd gone through with it, and he would have grown bored of taunting me, of threatening me. That he would leave me alone.

Only he hadn't.

The messages had kept coming. Letting me know that he was still watching.

And now it feels as if she's taunting me too, I think as I eye the soft cotton blanket from where it lies discarded in a heap on the floor. The same blanket that I'd first lain her in just moments after she'd been born. Streaked with sticky residue that had coated her skin.

I pick it up and bring it to my nose, breathing her in. That sweet, heady newborn baby smell of hers that I know will be ingrained in me as long as I live.

I had thought about keeping her.

In that first moment she was born, when I'd felt that tiny unapologetic thud of her heartbeat tapping so defiantly against my skin as if it had been challenging me not to love her. Daring me not to keep her all to myself.

Could I? Because I had made it this far, hadn't I?

Concealing the pregnancy underneath my clothing. Not attending a single antenatal appointment, I'd had no medical advice from a doctor or a midwife. I'd never had a scan or heard my baby's heartbeat.

Anything I'd wanted to know about what my body was going through I had to find out on Google, even down to how to cut the umbilical cord and check that Holly was healthy after I'd given birth completely and utterly alone.

If I was capable of doing all of that, maybe I was capable of keeping her.

Maybe I could hide her away here in this flat with me. Just the two of us.

Kidding myself that he might never have to know.

When somehow, he seemed to know everything.

A new message pinging on my computer just hours after I'd given birth telling me that I could not keep her.

That he would come for me. That he would kill us both.

He wasn't bluffing. The photograph he'd attached to his message of my front door confirmed that it wasn't an empty threat.

I wonder where she is right now? Whose arms she is nestled in, whose warmth is comforting her right now.

If she knows that I'm not there.

If she knows I even exist.

'I did it for her. I did it for her. To keep her safe.'

The words spin around in my head so desperately, like a quiet, constant plea as if part of me is trying to convince myself that it is the truth. That I did do this for her, because suddenly I'm not so sure. Because didn't part of me do this for me too? Having spent so long trying to convince myself that I couldn't possibly love a child born from him. Born from that awful, horrific night. That all I would feel once *it* was here, was hate and disgust. Or indifference at the very least.

Only the swell of love that I feel for her inside of me is overwhelming.

I am lost without her. Incomplete.

He did that.

That thought hits me like a freight train, derailing me.

Despite the way she was conceived, she is still mine, isn't she? She grew inside of my body. She is made up of parts of me.

Flight or fight or freeze, and I am frozen to the spot.

By giving up my child, *my child*, not his, I have allowed him to hurt me a thousand times worse than he did that night.

I've allowed him to win.

Again.

I've made a mistake. I've played right into his hands.

What have I done!

Oh my god, what have I done!?

19

JENNA

'Do you want a lift? Or better still, do you want to come over and join us for dinner tonight? I can offer you a culinary feast cooked by the fairest, most capable of hands of my mother-in-law, which will no doubt be served to us in my finest wedding crockery,' Kirsten jokes as the two women take the stairs.

Jenna smiles. Recognising Kirsten's attempt to dispel her obvious fractious mood with Liam going against her advice of pulling the plug on this next story pitch.

It happened all the time in this job, editors rejecting or insisting on certain stories. The Chief-Ed's word was final whether they liked it or not. It was one of the most difficult parts of the job, especially when a journalist was so vocal and passionate about getting their views across.

'You can help keep me in check when I get the urge to lob the fine china salad bowl at her.'

'It's a good job that I know you love Janet, really Kirsten! Could you imagine if, God forbid, anything ever happened to that poor woman? You'd be the number one suspect! And thanks for the offer, but that's totally out of your way, so I'm going to grab a cab and then I'm going to crawl into my bed and sleep for hours and hours and hours!' Jenna declares. 'I'm exhausted!'

Kirsten nods in understanding, before adding lightly. 'Ooh, sleep? What's that again? I can't quite remember.' She winks at her friend. 'I think I used to do that back in the olden days, before I had two kids under the age of five, and a not-so-house-trained dog. And actually, a not-so-house-trained husband.' She laughs but Jenna hears the sharp edge to Kirsten's voice at the mention of Duncan.

'Is everything okay with you guys?' She knows how stressful life could be at times for Kirsten and Duncan. The two of them working full-time while raising two small children. It was inevitable that they would have problems from time to time.

But this felt different.

She'd felt it at the bar last night too.

How there was tension brewing between the couple. Duncan had been quiet and distracted for the short while he'd been at the bar, constantly tapping away on his phone at every opportunity he'd got and eager to leave to get home so he could get back to his work.

It hadn't gone unnoticed by Kirsten either.

Janet seemed to be a permanent fixture at the house in the form of everyday help lately too.

'I thought I picked up on a bit of a strange vibe between you both last night.'

'Oh, we're fine. Just busy with work and the kids and the million other things that life likes to throw at us. Duncan had to finish up a project he was working on, that's why he was driving and not drinking. Why he left early. He wanted to get back to it. He's just a bit stressed out right now.'

'And that's it? You looked like you were arguing at one point.'

'We had words, yes.' Kirsten rolls her eyes and purses her mouth before admitting. 'I didn't want to put a dampener on the night. He's just constantly distracted. Either his head glued to his computer in the office or he's on his phone. Half the time I feel as if it's like he doesn't even see me anymore.'

'Sorry to interrupt, ladies,' Kelly-Ann's voice calls out from behind the reception desk as she does exactly that, bringing Jenna and Kirsten's private conversation to an abrupt end as they make their way towards the main doors. 'But have you lost something, Jenna?'

Kelly-Ann raises her brow questioningly but doesn't wait, instantly holding up Jenna's handbag and dangling it in the space between them.

'Oh, my bag! Thanks! Where did I leave it?' Jenna asks coolly. Trying her hardest to play down the relief that floods through her that maybe she hadn't lost her handbag when she'd been out last night after all.

She didn't have it with her. She'd left it here at the office somewhere.

Though that relief was short lived.

'Ohh, I don't know. Someone just left it here. Plonked on the desk earlier when Simone was on her break. I was just on my way to come upstairs and give it to you; you've saved me the job now.'

'Did you see who they were?' Jenna ignores Kirsten's burning glare as she takes the bag and briefly peers inside, quickly scanning the contents.

It's all here, she thinks. Untouched, untampered with.

'No, sorry. I've only just come on shift, and like I said, Simone was on the desk last night, but she'd nipped to the toilet. She had a quick nose through it to find out who it belonged to when she got back. Found your press pass in there and your ID. That's probably how whoever found it knew where to find you too. I'm forever leaving my stuff all over the place. Lost my Zara cardigan last week in a café up the road. I keep nipping in there and asking if it's been

handed in but no luck. Still, it might turn up eventually,'
Kelly-Ann continues.

'My mum lost her purse once, only the bastards maxed out
her credit card and treated themselves to a brand-new 52-inch
plasma. Just goes to show that there must still be some good
people out there, huh! You must have got lucky, eh, Jenna!'
Kelly-Ann smiles, and she tries her hardest to return it.

'Yeah, I guess I must have. Thanks for that, Kelly-Ann. See
you later!'

'You lost your bag last night?' Kirsten keeps her voice low as
the two women make their way out the main doors and across
the newsroom's carpark. Her words spoken tightly, in short
angry bursts as if they are being pushed through gritted teeth.
They both know how much an oversight like losing her bag
could have cost Jenna.

'You didn't think you should have mentioned that? Christ,
Jenna. It could have been him! The bloke who drugged you.'
Away from the news building and anyone listening, Kirsten
finally allows herself to raise her voice slightly.

She's angry but Jenna hears the concern there too. How her
words are high-pitched, laced with real panic.

'What if he made copies of your keys, Jenna? Maybe that's
exactly what he was planning all along? Maybe he wanted to
gain access to your flat. Gain access to you after you'd passed
out from whatever he'd spiked your drink with! He would have
had the perfect opportunity then, wouldn't he? He could have
done anything to you.' Kirsten pauses as if something else has
only just occurred to her. 'What if he comes back, later, when
you're alone in the flat? I still think we should call the police.'
She decides, reaching for her phone from her bag.

'Hey, chill out. As it happens, I'm having the locks changed
right now, as we speak. Purely as a precaution,' Jenna says,
hoping that if she acts not the least bit concerned about her bag
being returned to her, then hopefully Kirsten will follow suit

and do the same. Though she knows that acting not bothered isn't going to cut it this time.

She needs more conviction than that if she wants Kirsten to drop this.

'I didn't lose my bag when we were out last night. I didn't even have it with me,' she says, the lie rolling so effortlessly from Jenna's tongue, though she's not sure it sounds convincing, going by the doubtful expression on her friend's face. Jenna could almost see the cogs whirling wildly inside Kirsten's head as she tries to rack her brain to remember if she'd seen Jenna's handbag at the bar last night. 'You heard what Kelly-Ann said, Simone didn't see who left it. It was probably one of the cleaners who found it. I probably left it in the loos before I left last night. I was in a hurry; you know what I'm like.'

She feels guilty for lying to her friend but what other choice does she have?

She also knows that if she calls the police now, and they investigate Jenna's allegations, it would all be over for her. All those weeks of work that she'd put in, investigating the incel group, would have all been for nothing.

'Besides, even if I did report it to the police, they'd have absolutely nothing to go on. I told you earlier there would probably be no solid proof that I'd been drugged by now. Without that, they'd have no evidence to catch this man. What are they going to arrest him for, being a good, honest citizen and bringing my bag back after I got drunk and made a spectacle out of myself outside the bar last night? Because that's all I've got. That and a false name and a fake profile for a member of a forum that the police wouldn't be able to access without alerting the group that I have managed to infiltrate them. And then I'll really be in danger.'

Jenna also has her job to think about.

Liam would go mental if he found out that she had stupidly set up a meet with one of the members of the incel group. That she'd put herself in a position where she'd been alone with one of them, that she'd actually been drugged. He'd warned her already, hadn't he? How digging around in the dark, shadowy corners of the internet in forums like that were too dangerous.

Especially for a woman.

They'd got their man and their story. The MP that Jenna had exposed would be brought to justice.

If he knew, Liam would make sure that she was off the case for good, that she didn't go near the forum again.

And Jenna couldn't risk that, not when she'd got this far. Because it would mean that she'd lose all hope of finding out Mike's real identity. She just needs a bit more time.

'Look, I made a stupid mistake last night. I should never have spoken with that guy in the bar, especially as I was on my own and I'd had a few drinks. Not when I knew who he really was, what he is a part of. It was completely unprofessional and, to be honest with you, I feel more embarrassed now than anything else. I know better than to take risks like that. So please, can we just drop it now? I'd really like to just draw a line under last night and pretend it didn't happen. Lesson learned the hard way; I won't let it happen again. Trust me.'

'Okay, okay!' Kirsten sighs finally, just as she reaches her car, as if part of her recognises the conviction in Jenna's voice and so desperately wants to believe it. 'I'll drop it, but if anything else happens, no matter how small or insignificant you think it is, you need to tell me. Okay?'

'Okay. Deal.'

'Okay,' Kirsten says; she will know from experience that's the best she's going to get right now. 'I'll see you tomorrow. Shit!' she adds then, closing her eyes. 'I forgot about dinner tomorrow night!'

'I'm babysitting, aren't I?' Jenna raises her brow questioningly so that Kirsten can elaborate further, unsure what the problem with tomorrow is. She is due to sit for the kids so that

Kirsten and Duncan can go out and celebrate their wedding anniversary.

'I can't ask you to do that, not after everything that's happened...' Kirsten falters once again. Not wanting to break her promise after she'd agreed never to mention it again. 'Janet's busy, but maybe we can do it another night. To be honest, the way things are going lately it's really not a big deal.'

'No! You absolutely won't change your plans. I said I'd babysit the kids and that's what I'm going to do. You know how much I love spending time with them. Honestly, it's fine. Please don't change your plans. Besides, it will do me good to get out of the flat for a bit.' Jenna knows that Kirsten won't argue with her about that.

'Are you sure?'

'I'm absolutely positive! I promise. You know how I love seeing the kids.'

'Okay, only if you're sure?! Have fun tonight, with all that "sleeping" malarky.' Kirsten wrinkles her nose as if it's the last thing she'd ever be caught doing, given half the chance, before giving Jenna a kiss on the cheek and getting into her car.

Jenna stands, watching her pull out of the carpark, clutching her handbag tightly to her.

BREATHE.

Willing her trembling legs to hold her, she makes her way over to the nearby bench.

She needs to sit down, before she collapses.

20

HIM

He is wired. Still restless and full of adrenaline from the events that had unfolded the previous night.

Tipping the contents of the handbag out across the floor, he spreads the items out before carefully inspecting each one in turn.

A well-worn lipstick, a bunch of scrunched- up used tissues, a half-eaten protein bar that is open and has left crumbs everywhere.

The contents of the bag just as messy and chaotic as she was.

There's no phone here though. She must have kept that on her.

He picks up the work ID card. A lanyard with a press pass attached to the back of it.

Her name is printed in gold swirled handwriting across the front of it.

Jenna Stone:

Investigative Journalist of The Islington Gazette.

He knows who she is.

A notebook.

He thumbs the tatty, biro-scrawled pages and reads all her notes.

Notes about him.

He thinks of the damage that she could do if she succeeded in her plan to take him down. Thinks about the shit storm she'd create by poking her nose in.

She thinks she's so smart, doesn't she? Untouchable.

Lurking in the darkest corners of the internet, trying to dissect the minds of the thousands of men that had more than earned their place there inside the forum, whilst miserably trying and failing to pick apart the women-hating ideology that members spewed from their keyboards about women just like her.

That was irony right there.

That even after trawling through hundreds and hundreds of comments and posts that she'd still remained oblivious to the fact that it was because of women like her that they now lived in such a sinister, toxic world.

Her tiny mind isn't capable of deciphering the violent threats that are tossed around so casually. Can't even comprehend the levels of hate and vitriol that festers there.

That her, being there in the group, uninvited, unwelcome proved their very point. That nothing was sacred any more, because this is what they all did, wasn't it?

Women.

So entitled, so superior to men.

Greedily taking what isn't theirs to take, with no thought of the repercussions or consequences.

And there will be consequences, of course there will.

Skulking around on the online forum that she'd infiltrated herself in under a false name. Scrolling through thousands of their private posts and discussions.

Believing that she would remain unseen.

Only he'd seen her.

Luring him to a public space purposely under the false pretence of being the same as him. 'One of them.'

She'd wanted to play with him, and lucky for her, he liked a game.

Though personally, he preferred a smarter opponent, someone who posed more of a challenge.

He preferred games where if you wanted to defeat your rival, you needed to think strategically. To be several moves ahead of them at all times.

Like chess – the moment of checkmate means that the game is already lost.

He is filled with a morbid fascination then, at how midway through her sentence she would have faltered, her words slurring as they left her mouth, and she lost her train of thought.

The raw, terrifying panic that would have set in as she realised what was happening to her.

That feeling of sudden powerlessness.

Oh, how he loves those moments. Lives for them in fact.

He'd almost had her. He'd been so close.

Only she'd proved a more worthy opponent than he'd given her credit for.

She'd managed to get away this time.

But not unscathed. Not without a warning.

She still hasn't learned her lesson though. But she will.

She'll soon think twice about poking around in groups where she doesn't belong in the future

To him, that's still classed as a win.

Checkmate.

21

JENNA

Finally, alone, Jenna tips out the contents of her handbag onto the wooden slats of the bench and begins sifting through them. Urgently scanning her belongings and checking properly that everything is all still there. That it's all intact.

House keys. Work ID. Press pass. Check.

It is all there. All of it.

Spread out amongst the pile of random items are her make-up bag, and an open packet of chewing gum, and half a dozen screwed-up dirty tissues that have been spewed from the jumbled, disorganised heap they'd been in at the very bottom.

Closing her eyes Jenna fights the urge to cry again.

This was all her fault.

Kirsten had every right to be concerned, of course she did. Because whoever took her bag knew where she worked now, and they would know where she lived too.

Nowhere would be safe now.

Cursing herself for stupidly thinking that she had been so careful last night, when the reality was she had been anything but: spending all that time trying to conceal her real identity from him, not giving anything of any significance away while they spoke.

She'd been on guard, keeping her wits about her.

Only she hadn't done any of that.

She'd fucked up, big time.

Mike had outsmarted her last night, hadn't he?

He'd somehow managed to slip something into her drink when she hadn't been looking.

How had he done that?

And then to take her handbag and simply disappear into the night like a ghost. Gone without a trace, almost leaving her wondering if it was all in her head.

If *he* was all in her head.

Her memory so fragmented and blurred and full of flash-backs and images that she doesn't know quite what is real and what is not any more. Recalling how she'd punched through her kitchen window before passing out on a pile of broken shards of glass.

He was real, Jenna. He was real.

But surely if he'd gone to all that effort to drug her and take her handbag, then why had he taken it upon himself to bring it back to her?

Unless this was all part of his plan, so that he could catch her off guard.

Maybe this is exactly what he wanted her to think. That he wouldn't bring her bag back to her if he'd wanted to harm her, would he? That would have been pointless.

He wouldn't need to make a copy of the keys when he could have just used the set that he took? Unless he was playing the long game and letting her bask in the false sense of security that he'd orchestrated for her.

And Kirsten was right about that too: that he might come back, in the middle of the night while she was alone and sleeping. That he might really hurt her.

She shivers thinking about the type of men hiding out in that online forum. Men capable of doing awful, despicable things to her. Men who thrived on making the lives of women like her a living hell.

Shit! She is just being paranoid now. Overthinking things. Kirsten had done that. Sewn seeds of doubt in her mind. Because it might not have even been him who had taken her bag in the first place. Someone else might have found it and handed it in.

She holds on to that thought. She has to.

Googling the number of the bar she was at last night, she dials it and waits patiently on hold, the monotonous sound of classical music that plays at the other end doing nothing to soothe her.

'I just wondered if a handbag was found there last night, hanging on one of the barstools at the far end of the bar?' she asks, full of hope when someone finally answers.

There's a muffled sound as the barman places his hand loosely over the phone's receiver before calling out to several people around him, each of them answering that nothing had been found last night.

Jenna thanks him and hangs up. But she's not willing to let that dishearten her. Anyone could have found her bag and handed it in. Maybe she'd dropped it outside on the street and a passer-by found it, or she'd left it in the Uber last night and the driver had dropped it off for her.

No. She knows that doesn't make sense. He would have dropped it to her flat not to her place of work. She could have lost it anywhere.

Even so, she needs to stay calm. She's already had her locks changed. The locksmith was there right now. Just to be cautious, just to be on the safe side. She'd had to, even before her bag had showed up, or she'd never sleep again.

Taking out her lip balm, Jenna slathers the pink gel into a

smooth layer over her dry lips before popping gum into her mouth, which feels dry. Her hands are still shaking.

But the main thing is that she is safe and that she has her bag back. This doesn't have to be the beginnings of a sharp spiralling downward descent of paranoia.

She'd got cocky and complacent, and she'd made a whole series of costly mistakes. But she wouldn't be doing that again. She'd be more careful than that going forward.

She had to be.

This had been the wake-up call she'd needed. The reminder that she wasn't invincible. These people weren't messing about, they were reckless and unpredictable, and she needed to remember that. She needed to remember to keep her wits about her at all times.

Tucking her lip-gloss back down into the side pocket of the bag, she notices the flash of white paper that she doesn't immediately recognise.

Her notebook is missing, she realises.

This neatly folded piece of paper tucked down into the inside pocket of her bag has been torn from it.

Her heart sinks as she pulls it out to take a closer look, only to see the thick black smudge of letters that have been scrawled across the page with what looks like her eyeliner pencil.

I know who you are '4EvAlone'
And I know where you live.
Stop digging or you'll be sorry.

Dropping the piece of paper as if it's just scorched her skin, Jenna stares out across the carpark. Suddenly feeling very scared and vulnerable that she isn't alone. Fearful that someone might be lurking in the shadows, watching her.

Kirsten was right about that too it seems.

It had been too much of a coincidence that Mike made a

beeline for her, when he thought whoever it was he'd been meeting hadn't shown up.

She thought she was so clever, sitting the other side of the bar as she silently observed him. A false sense of security that at that distance he wouldn't be able to harm her.

Smug in the knowledge that she'd secretly set him up, when he'd been on to her from the very start all along.

Whoever this Mike really was, he knew who she was now. He knew where she worked, and where she lived.

He knew everything he needed to know in order to get to her.

Him and a whole army of men just like him.

Oh, she got the message this time loud and clear.

Spiking her drink last night had been his first and final warning.

22

JENNA

'Well, don't you look stunning!' Jenna whistles approvingly as Kirsten pulls open the front door and does an exaggerated twirl to show off the new fitted black dress that she's wearing for her date tonight.

'Why thank you! At least *someone* has noticed the effort I've put in!' Kirsten says with a small smile, stepping aside to let her in.

'God! Be careful in those heels, you'll do yourself some serious damage if you fall over in them.' Jenna nods down to the ridiculously high heels on Kirsten's feet as she slips off her frumpy-looking trainers and hangs her coat on the hook behind the front door.

'I feel wobbly just looking at them. How do you walk in them?'

'Duh! They're not meant for walking! They're meant to look sexy.'

'Oh, I definitely got that memo.'

'Well, let's just hope Duncan does too, then!' Kirsten twists her arm around the banister before leaning her weight against it and bellowing up the stairs.

'Duncan! Jenna's here and the cab's outside.'

She waits for a second before they both hear the muffled sound of a grunt, which Jenna assumes is Duncan's answer.

'Still working, is he?' she asks, seeing the look of irritation that flashes across Kirsten's face despite how she's so clearly trying to hide it.

'Apparently so. Can't seem to drag him away from his computer these days,' Kirsten adds, leading her friend into the lounge. 'I think it had gone 2 a.m. this morning when he finally finished whatever it was he was doing on his laptop and crawled into bed.'

'I take it things are no better then?' Jenna asks, picking up on the tension in the house and not wanting to pry. The last thing she wanted to do was start Kirsten off on a tangent about all the things that were pissing her off right now, but it was clear to see that one of them was quite blatantly Duncan.

Jenna sees the fake smile fixed to her friend's face, not wanting to let on that she was still angry with him.

'Yeah, we're fine,' Kirsten says, though the word *fine* could have meant a thousand things and Jenna got the impression that in this case, whatever fine was, had become the norm for them both.

'Oh, ignore me!' Kirsten sighs as if catching herself and realising how unreasonable she must sound, for being angry at Duncan for simply being busy with work.

'It's probably just me being silly and overthinking things.'

'You don't think he's working?' Jenna says carefully, secretly wondering if there was more to all of this.

'I think we're both just busy and tired and stressed.' The words are spoken with such conviction that Jenna isn't sure who Kirsten is trying to convince here more, her or herself.

'Duncan's been really busy working on this new project for work; he practically lives in his office lately. Can't seem to drag him away. And obviously we're busy with the newspaper and then of course there's the kids, as much as Janet helps. When she's not making things worse by fussing over her golden child; it's never-ending around here. We just never seem to have any real time for each other. I just wanted tonight to be different, you know.' Kirsten lifts her arms as if to display the effort she'd gone to tonight. A new dress. Her hair and make-up done to perfection.

She was trying.

'Well, you look gorgeous and I'm sure Duncan will be blown away when he sees you,' Jenna says with a smile, just as a chorus of noise floods the room, cutting short their conversation.

'Auntie Jenna!!' Amelia and Christian screech excitedly, bursting into the room and making a beeline straight for her, their cartoon character themed slippers padding across the wooden floors as they run towards her. Flinging their arms around her and hugging her tightly as if they can't quite believe their luck that she is here.

Auntie Jenna.

God, how she loves that. How she loves feeling a part of this family. Part of something so much bigger than just herself.

Jenna doesn't take the responsibility of being Auntie Jenna lightly either.

She always shows up. Christmas, birthdays, babysitting duties. She always makes time for the kids, and for Kirsten and Duncan too. Helping out in any way she can. She often finds herself here on a Sunday, peeling potatoes in the kitchen with Duncan, ready for their Sunday roast dinner. Or placing strawberries and huge dollops of whipped cream 'messily', as per Kirsten's instructions, on top of a ready-made cheesecake so that Janet wouldn't know Kirsten had cheated again with a shop-bought one.

Kirsten and Duncan's house was the polar opposite of Jenna's flat.

It was full of noise and mess and chaos and laughter and so

much love. When Jenna is here, she soaks it all up like a thirsty, dehydrated sponge.

Even the bits that seem to drive Kirsten and Duncan nuts. How the TV is always blaring with garish cartoons, and there always seem to be a million tiny discarded toys spread out all across the carpet.

'Auntie Jenna, can you read us a story? Auntie Jenna, do you want to come and see the hamster's new house in my bedroom?'

'Hey! Give Auntie Jenna a break, she's only just got here. Let her sit down for five minutes,' Kirsten says, prising her children away from her friend before rolling her eyes apologetically with a small grin, clearly delighted at her children's reaction to her surprise. 'I didn't tell them you were coming over! They would only have driven me nuts all day long asking what time you're getting here. Go, on, kids. Back upstairs you go. Jenna will come up and see you shortly.'

Jenna watches as the children leave the room, just as Duncan walks in, running his fingers though his dishevelled hair, a frown fixed to his face as if he's still deep in thought.

'Hey, Jenna!' he says, immediately snapping out of his trance as he sees her. Duncan walks towards her and gives her a kiss on the cheek, and Jenna is glad when he tactfully doesn't mention anything about the other night at the bar.

Did he know? Jenna was certain that he did. Certain that Kirsten would have told him because she would have been so worried for Jenna that she would have needed to confide in someone. And Duncan, being a good husband, was now making a point of keeping his wife's secrets for her.

'Sorry, I was in the middle of something,' he continues, before turning to his wife and almost doing a double take.

'Oh, wow! I didn't realise that we were going all out.' He takes in the effort that Kirsten has made, before looking down at his own crumpled shirt and the trousers that he'd worn all day, working, as if it only just occurred to him that he should have probably showered and got changed.

'Well, it is our fifth wedding anniversary. Worth making an effort for, no?' Kirsten mouths tightly, a rigid smile fixed to her face.

'I'm so sorry, babe. I was caught up with work stuff. I can go and change. It will take me five minutes to iron a clean shirt.' Realising his error, Duncan at least had the good grace to look flustered.

'No. The cab's already outside. You look fine,' Kirsten decides, grabbing her bag from the side and trying and failing to hide the look of irritation on her face as she turns her attention back to Jenna.

'We won't be late,' she says, as if making a prediction, and Jenna is sure she can almost hear the hurt in her friend's voice.

Kirsten had mentioned a few times lately how she and Duncan were like ships passing in the night, how they were both so busy and stressed all the time. How they rarely saw each other, let alone spent much quality time together.

They both very much needed tonight, and Jenna felt bad for them both that their evening had already got off to a shaky start.

'Have fun!' she says weakly as she stands at the door, waving them both off.

23

JENNA

Setting the storybook down on the bedside table, Jenna does a double take as she eyes the alarm clock and notices the time. She hadn't realised that it had got so late.

Glancing back over to where the two sleeping children lie tucked up in their beds, she shakes her head and lets a small smile escape her lips, realising that these two cheeky little monkeys had been purposely keeping her occupied reading them stories tonight, so that they could stall their bedtime and spend more time with her.

'Just one more, Auntie Jenna. Please. Pretty please.'

She was a soft touch, the children knew that and they had her wrapped around their tiny fingers. One more story had turned into three, all of which the children had animatedly chatted and giggled their way through, which of course, had been another ploy to guarantee they got to keep her up here with them for even longer.

She can't help but give a small chuckle at that, because the truth is there is no other place that she would rather be. She'd probably enjoyed the evening just as much, if not more than the pair of them put together.

Pulling their duvets up around them and tucking them in, Jenna switches off the bedside lamp and carefully tiptoes from the room, closing the bedroom door quietly behind her. She treads lightly across the hallway, making sure to avoid the creaky floorboard just outside the children's bedroom. The movement is subconscious; this house is as familiar to her as her own.

Except there's no comparison between this old, beautiful house with its high ceilings and original stunning features and Jenna's cold, boxy rented one-bed flat.

Jenna craves this house like a drug sometimes.

She's never told Kirsten that because she knows just how mad it would sound. How Kirsten probably wouldn't get it.

But it was true.

There were times when Jenna physically yearned for the warmth of this place, for the pull of it. For all the noise and the chaos and the laughter and, mainly, for the sense of belonging. Because this is exactly the kind of home and family that she had gone to sleep dreaming about as a small child. It saddens her to think that Kirsten and Duncan have so much and yet sometimes it's as if neither of them sees any of it at all.

She sees it, how lucky they are.

She eyes the gallery of framed family photos that Kirsten and Duncan creatively placed at the top of the stairwell, as if to remind themselves to soak it all in. A lifetime of memories captured in colour and displayed proudly on the wall. Her gaze rests on the earlier ones, the ones of just the two of them, when Kirsten and Duncan had first met. Both of them smiling at the camera, locked in each other's arms. A crowded bar. A sandy beach. Young and happy. Before the kids had come along.

Jenna looks at the other photos; her favourite is the photo of Amelia minutes after she was born, lying in the arms of her flushed-cheeked, adoring mummy. Her proud daddy gazing down at her with a look of disbelief on his face that she is finally here. That she actually belongs to them.

Another photo of Christian, placed in Amelia's arms as a newborn baby, a couple of years later. A wide-eyed moment of complete awe on the little girl's face at finally meeting her new baby brother, captured so perfectly.

A lifetime of their memories that make her feel warm and fuzzy and loved, yet the irony is that none of these are hers. None of these memories belong to her.

She's been thinking about that a lot lately. She is almost thirty now, and yet she is still no closer to getting any of this for herself.

The big, beautiful house. The cute, giggling children. The loving husband. A family all of her own.

How would she? Her landlord keeps putting the rent up every couple of months and blaming it on the cost-of-living crisis and, more so, she hasn't had any kind of serious relationship for years.

The only example of a real loving happy family that she has ever had in her life, is this one and it pains her to think of her two friends struggling like they are.

Kirsten had tried her best to hide it, to play down the hurt on her face at Duncan's lack of effort and attention lately, but Jenna had seen it. And her heart had broken for her friend when Kirsten had admitted that she'd been overthinking things. Because she knew exactly what Kirsten had been thinking.

The same thing that she was secretly starting to feel suspicious of too.

That maybe, Duncan wasn't distracted with work at all. Maybe he was preoccupied with something, *or* someone else.

Because he'd done that before, hadn't he?

The second that thought enters her head, Jenna feels bad for even thinking it. For even allowing herself to entertain the idea. It had only happened the once, she reminds herself, and

Duncan had been so plagued with guilt for what he'd done, that he'd immediately confessed all to Kirsten. Swearing to her that it had been a huge mistake. That he had been drunk and had felt flattered at the forward advances from a new PA at his office work night out.

A young, attractive PA.

He'd said that it had been nothing more than a snog. One stupid drunken kiss that had meant nothing to him. Meant nothing at all.

Only it had meant so much more than that to Kirsten.

That had been years ago, not long after Amelia had been born and she was four now. They'd worked through it somehow.

But Jenna often wondered if it lingered. The betrayal, faintly wafting around them in the air, like a bad smell, that no matter how they tried to cover up or block it out, it was always there.

Simmering just beneath the surface.

Surely Duncan wouldn't be so stupid as to do something like that again.

Not now, when he had so much more to lose.

She stops outside Duncan's office, noting how the door sits slightly ajar.

Almost like an invitation to step inside.

The journalist in her is justifying what would be the harm in it, if she did happen to casually wander in there and take a look around, because that's what Jenna did, wasn't it? She searched for clues, did her own research before jumping to any conclusions.

Gathered the cold, hard facts.

Liam had always commented how she seemed to have a good nose for a journalist, and she liked to think that was true.

Because it was definitely twitching now.

Duncan would never have to know.

Before she has time to talk herself out of it, she slips inside through the door and makes a beeline towards Duncan's desk.

The obvious place for her to start.

Opening the notebook that has been left discarded next to the keyboard, Jenna scans the first few pages of scribbled notes, trying to make sense of Duncan's scrawl that sweeps across its pages. Before thumbing her way through a pile of paperwork stacked high on his desk, only to find more of the same.

Jenna can't make head nor tail of any of this stuff. It is like trying to read in another language.

Duncan had told her once that the difference between a data analyst and his job, a data translator, was that instead of gathering information and processing data, Duncan translated the numbers into plain English for others to understand.

Only written down like this, means his notes read like a different language.

Jenna picks up a folder and flinches as a page falls out, floating to the floor.

A photograph. She picks it up and smiles.

She is in this one.

They all are. It was taken here in this house, standing in front of the Christmas tree in the lounge.

Jenna's mouth is wide open, her face twisted with laughter. Janet stands beside her, doubled over in hysterics.

Jenna can't recall exactly what it had been that Duncan had said, just before the camera's timer had gone off, but she knew that it was something silly by the way that Kirsten is laughing too. Her face contorted into fits of giggles, tears streaming down her face. They all look so happy. So, picture perfect.

One big happy family.

Unable to help herself, she takes her phone out and snaps a photo of it.

Catching herself as she slips the photo back inside the folder and questions what the hell she is doing in here.

Snooping around in Duncan's things as if she's some amateur wanna-be Miss Marple, accidently stumbling into murder scenes, ready to solve them. When the truth is that she doesn't even know what she's looking for.

Duncan would never risk cheating on Kirsten again. She is sure of it.

She shouldn't be in here.

She should go downstairs, make herself a hot drink and curl up on the sofa underneath one of Kirsten's faux fur throws, and watch one of *The Real Housewives'* programmes on catch-up, exactly as she'd intended on doing tonight once her friends had gone to dinner and the kids were asleep.

That's exactly what she should do, she thinks, and she is about to, only as she glances at Duncan's computer screen she falters slightly. It's the one place she hasn't checked. The most obvious place and it's right in front of her. Staring her straight in the face. If Duncan was hiding anything at all, this would be where she would find it.

Pressing the keyboard hesitantly, Jenna resigns herself to the fact that if the screen stays black when she presses the keys, then it's not meant to be.

But as soon as her finger hits the first key, the screen flashes a bright blue hue into the room as the monitor springs to life. In Duncan's haste to leave tonight, he'd left it on power saving mode and was still logged in.

Sitting down on Duncan's chair, Jenna eyes the screen before clicking the mouse onto Duncan's browser's search history.

It's completely blank, as if it's been recently cleared.

As if Duncan has purposely deleted whatever it was that he'd been looking up.

All of it.

Jenna sits back in the chair and wonders why Duncan would have done that.

Why would he have taken the trouble to delete everything that he'd been looking at, in his own private office, on in his own personal computer.

A computer that no one else has access to but him.

What is Duncan hiding?

24

JENNA

Control Panel > Desktop > Show Hidden Files.

One of the tech guys in the newsroom had taught Jenna about invisible files when she'd gone undercover as a legal assistant in the courthouse, investigating allegations of a corrupt judge and his involvement in a blackmail scandal. The files she had found hidden on his computer had revealed vital documents of evidence that would have sent notorious, local gang members to prison for a very long time. Only the judge had chosen to make that evidence disappear and, ultimately, the gang to walk free. Jenna had found out why in the end: the gang had been blackmailing him. He'd chosen to save himself and his own sordid secrets about the affair he'd been having with the young male office intern behind his wife and children's backs.

It turned out that the files she had found had been enough to incriminate both the judge and the gang in the end.

She almost hadn't done it tonight.

She'd almost clicked off and let the computer go back to sleep mode, because her search had been so futile. Scrolling through all Duncan's social media posts and private messages, she found nothing. No hints of flirtation, or anything else that seemed inappropriate.

The perfect husband.

Yet he'd taken the time and the effort to delete his search history, so he must have something to hide?

She had only searched for hidden files out of habit, running those words through the system as a very last resort on every computer she searched before she gave up.

BINGO.

There it is.

Jenna looks at the small blue folder that appears on the screen, only becoming visible when she hovers her mouse across it. She pauses, daring herself to be brave and look. Bracing herself for what she might find when she does.

Is this where Duncan is hiding the intimate details of his dirty little secret, evidence of his cliche, flirtatious messages to another woman, perhaps a couple of nude photos he'd been sent or sent to her?

She opens the file.

The first page is a list of women's names, which are all dated. She falters, wondering if it's not one affair she's stumbled upon here, but a whole conquest of indiscretions that he's logged down like some kind of trophy list. Women he'd met on a dating app perhaps and had one-night stands with. Only as Jenna makes her way down the list of names, she stops when she reaches one that is familiar to her.

Lizzy Day.

She bristles, thinking that it can't be the same Lizzy Day that she knows. Because that Lizzy has only just turned eighteen, and she only knows her because she interviewed her once, shortly after she had been out at a club celebrating her eighteenth birthday, when she'd been spiked.

Lizzy had made it to the toilets before she'd passed out and, luckily, it had been her friends who had found her and managed to call an ambulance and get her straight to hospital.

They'd acted so quickly that the doctors were able to do a toxicology report and confirm that she'd been spiked with GHB.

She'd been lucky, that's how Lizzy Day had described the aftermath of her ordeal. She'd been lucky that her friends had got her to hospital in time and away from any harm.

Lucky.

That word has stuck, lodged itself somewhere deep in Jenna's brain, because it was *not* a word she would use to describe being drugged and almost raped on the night of your eighteenth birthday.

Lizzy's eighteenth birthday.

Jenna googles the details of the article she'd written at the time and, sure enough, it's the same date that Duncan has typed next to Lizzy's name.

It's the date that Lizzy was attacked.

Jenna scans the rest of the list, googling the other women's names and their coinciding dates.

Lizzy Day. Sharon Hargreaves. Evie Monroe.

Most of the information online is vague, and she realises that there's only some information for some of the woman on this list. Nothing for others.

A few of them only actually came forward and reported what had been done to them. That was why. What if the others were victims too, only they hadn't reported their attacks to the police?

But then, that didn't make sense, did it?

That Duncan would have this level of detailed information when it wasn't available publicly to others. When no one else would have known about the attacks.

Other than the victims.

And the attacker.

Jenna Stone.

Blood whooshes wildly inside of her ears, before a faint ringing starts there and she feels suddenly light-headed at the sight of her name right there at the very bottom. The most recent addition to the list. Staring at the computer screen trying to make sense of it all. Trying to think of a better reason that would justify why Duncan would have this. Why he had created a database of local women being attacked and stored them all on a secret hidden file like this.

A fleeting memory invades her mind as she tries to gather herself. The stern words from one of the many foster carers she'd lived with as a child, that had been imprinted in her brain one time that Jenna had asked when she would be able to try and make contact with her birthmother.

What's unsought will go undetected.

The foster carer's vague answer: Jenna had been too young to know what that meant.

'It means, Jenna,' the foster carer dragged her words out slowly as if she was explaining to a simpleton not a curious child, 'if you go looking for trouble, you'll be sure to find it. And sometimes the answers you are looking for are not the ones you'd hope they would be. Sometimes the people you seek out, are not the people you hope them to be either.'

Jenna had believed for years after that the woman had been blunt, almost to the point of being cruel, and it wasn't until years later that Jenna had realised that the woman had only been speaking the truth.

People only showed you what they wanted you to see. The rest was all just a facade. Played out on a stage in which they were all acting out their parts.

And people often let you down.

Jenna knew that from experience.

As a journalist she had often had a front row seat to some of the darkest, most disturbing news and acts. Sifting through the debris and chaos of other people's stories in order to get to the truth, she'd uncovered things that would make most normal people want to curl up into the foetal position and block the world out completely.

It turned out that her foster carer had been right. Truth was often a bitter pill for people to swallow.

But Jenna needed the truth, no matter what it cost her.

Clicking through the file, opening the numerous other folders, she studied the screenshots of photographs taken from the same women's social media accounts.

Sharon Hargreaves.

They were profile pictures mainly, but some were other photos that had been taken from their publicly available accounts.

There was an address too.

He must have done some extensive research to find out who these women were and where they lived. Had Duncan been stalking these women?

Jenna could feel the hot, burning liquid threatening to expel from the back of her throat at the thought of her friend being capable of such despicable, heinous acts.

Duncan had drugged her; he had drugged all these other women too. With the intention of attacking and raping them.

It was all here in black and white in front of her, and yet, somehow it was as if she couldn't make any sense of it. Part of her didn't want to believe what she was seeing. Part of her wished she'd never looked.

How would she tell Kirsten about this? Where would she even start because this would devastate Kirsten. Her entire family would be completely destroyed; she would be destroyed.

She clicks on the other links that have been added further down the page.

Newspaper extracts. Interviews from some of the victims too. Appeals for witnesses to come forward. A police report.

She has seen some of these screen grabs before, she is sure

of it. They'd been shared on the incel group as if used to bait all the other members to jump online and antagonise the victim further. Publicly humiliating and attacking these women in every comment section of the newspaper's articles, and all over the paper's social media.

They did it on purpose, while the women were at their weakest, at their lowest, begging for help.

Shaking, Jenna types in the web address into the search bar of the incel forum she'd been secretly investigating, and is almost sick when the page pops up on the screen with Duncan's sign-in details already saved to the log-in screen.

Duncan is part of that group.

He is one of them.

25

JENNA

NIGHT AT THE BAR

'Why did you get another round in? We're leaving, aren't we?' Kirsten says, her tone curt enough to make Duncan realise, as he placed the drinks down on the table in front of Jenna, that this wasn't a question and that by getting this round of drinks in, he'd somehow managed to royally mess up.

'Leaving already? But we only got here an hour ago. Come on, let's just have one more drink,' Jenna says, hoping to change Kirsten's mind as she takes the drink from Duncan and sips it gratefully.

'I'm exhausted and we need to get back. Janet texted saying that she's not feeling too great, She's having another one of these migraines she keeps getting, so I need to get back for the kids and surprise, surprise, Duncan's working again tonight,' Kirsten says tightly. 'Do you want us to drop you on our way?'

'Oh no, I hope Janet's okay? No. You both go. I'm going to stay here for a little while longer.' Then seeing Kirsten eye her full glass she adds, 'Don't worry I'll make this my last one.'

Jenna had a sneaky suspicion that staying here longer wasn't the only thing that had annoyed Kirsten tonight.

She'd seen it.

Her two friends having 'quiet words' up at the bar.

To an outsider, they probably looked like a normal couple engrossed in a private conversation, but Jenna knew them both so well.

How Kirsten had the same familiar tight smile plastered to her face after making pleasantries and polite conversation, that she usually reserved especially for occasions like this.

Occasions that she didn't want to be at.

How she seemed irritated by Duncan, because unlike Kirsten he wasn't willing to put on an act and pretend that things were fine between them both, when clearly they were not.

He had seemed moody tonight, distracted. His steely gaze fixed permanently to the screen of his phone.

Jenna had watched them as they had both stood at the bar. How Kirsten had leaned in and said something quietly into Duncan's ear. Causing a flicker of irritation to flash across his face before he replied, rolling his eyes as if Kirsten is overreacting. As if she's picking up on something that isn't even there.

Jenna figured they could probably do with some time alone. Away from all the noise and chaos of the packed bar. Because something is clearly going on here, the arguments were happening so often lately.

Kirsten tried her best to hide it, but tonight isn't the first time that she has felt the tension pour out from her two friends.

'Oh don't tell me you're both leaving?' Liam says animatedly, without any real conviction, throwing his arms up in the air as if he's suddenly overwhelmed with despair at the thought of Kirsten and Duncan leaving.

As if they are all such good friends. Though no one is falling for it.

'Jenna, are you coming with us?' Duncan says, ignoring Liam's comment completely and purposely turning his back on him.

Duncan doesn't want to be here tonight either, Jenna can sense it and she doesn't really blame him.

Stuck here, in a room full of Kirsten's work colleagues while Liam lords it over him, working the room, plying everyone with drinks to get them in the mood for a real celebration.

Duncan tolerates Liam at best, for Kirsten's sake. At worst, like tonight, he blatantly ignores the man. Irritated by how loud he is, how brash he sounds, how excitable he's become.

Though Liam, of course, is completely oblivious to Duncan's permanent sour scowl and his dismissive body language every time Liam looks as if he's going to approach him.

Or at least if he notices, he doesn't let on.

Which only riles Duncan up even more, Jenna suspects. That he can never seem to evoke the same reaction in the man that Liam stirs in him.

She feels bad.

Her friends have only come here tonight for her.

She knows that. To raise a glass to her and celebrate the successful week she's had. To congratulate her on her growing success.

Yet they both look as if they'd rather be anywhere else in the world but here. 'The offer's there, if you want it,' Kirsten says, clearly in a hurry to leave before things escalate, now that Liam is standing so close to Duncan, in one of his windup moods. Tugging her coat on in a hurry, ready to brave the elements of the cold, icy night outside as they make their way to the carpark behind the high street, where Duncan has parked.

'No, you go. I'm going to stay a while longer.'

'Too bloody right she is!' Liam beams, placing his arm around her shoulder and giving her a light squeeze.

'This is Jenna's night. She's the reason we're here celebrating. You can't whisk her away this early. The night's barely started.'

'Are you sure you don't want a lift, Jenna?' Duncan tries again.

'No, really. You guys go. I'll call you tomorrow,' Jenna replies. She picks up her glass and takes a big gulp.

'I can come back for you. I'm only going to be in my office, working. I'm going to be up for hours.'

'God, no! I couldn't let you do that. Dragging you back out, that would be insanity. I'll get a cab, there's loads out on the high street, or failing that I'll call an Uber.'

'Honestly, it's no trouble,' Duncan says again, and Jenna feels it. How Duncan's mood has shifted. There's an undercurrent of something that she can't quite read or understand as he stares at her intently. His body in such close proximity to hers that it makes her shift uncomfortably back in her seat. Away from him.

Jenna looks over to Kirsten to see if her friend is seeing this too. If it isn't just her. How there is something unsettling about him. How he's being too insistent, almost to the point that it is inappropriate.

Jenna catches it then.

That secret conspiratorial look that married couples sometimes share. No words spoken out loud but in a blink of an eye a whole coded conversation has just passed between them.

About her.

Full of guilt, Kirsten looks down at the floor.

She's told him, Jenna realises.

Even though she'd told her not to, as she didn't want to make it a big deal, didn't want anyone to worry. Kirsten went ahead regardless and told Duncan about the phone calls she'd been receiving.

That's why he is behaving so overprotective towards her now. As if she is fragile and made of glass suddenly.

It was only heavy breathing. No voice. No conversation. No other sound at the end until the ring tone sounded and the caller finally hung up.

Kirsten is worried that the harassment is linked to the MP that Jenna managed to expose in the newspapers. That there will be a reprisal for taking down a man in such power. That she needs to be careful. To keep her wits about her. Which is another reason she's angry at her for having a couple of drinks tonight.

'It's no trouble, Jenna. Let me drop you?'

'Seriously you two need to stop being a couple of killjoys, and let Jenna have some fun for once. She's bloody earned it after the week she's had.'

And Jenna had felt that.

How she had earned it, hadn't she? A couple of drinks, to take the edge off. To help her unwind.

She's taken it too far though. Knows deep down that she should stand up for her friends. She should tell Liam that Kirsten and Duncan are only looking out for her. Only doing as Jenna had asked of her earlier in the night.

Keeping an eye on her and making sure that she stayed out of trouble.

Only, instead Jenna stays silent.

Glad that someone is not only allowing her to let her hair down for once, but that they were actively giving her permission to do so.

Maybe Liam is right. Maybe Kirsten and Duncan did need to let Jenna have some fun for once.

'I'm a big girl, Duncan. Don't worry about me. You go! The night's still young.'

Young, and dumb and stupid and naive, Jenna!

26

JENNA

Jenna shakes her head, as if her brain is not computing what her eyes are seeing and needs a physical jolt to kickstart it. Duncan is one of *them*.

Her friend. Her best friend's husband.

He is one of the vile men on that disgusting forum.

Jenna thinks of all the times that he stayed up late into the night while she and Kirsten had discussed the newspaper and the cases they were covering while they'd both put the world to rights. All the times he'd sat there and listened to them talking about the victims that they wrote their articles about. About the local women who had been attacked.

How he sat there and said nothing, but really, he was soaking it all up like a starved sponge, taking in all the intimate details, all of their pain, to share with the forum later on.

All the times she'd sat across from him at his dining table on a Sunday, devouring one of his legendary roast dinners. All the while thinking what a wonderful man he was, as he chatted and played attentively with his two small children. Before lovingly squeezing the hand of his wife and topping up her wine.

There must be some kind of a mistake.

Duncan isn't like that. He isn't like them.

She thinks about how Kirsten told her that Duncan has been distracted lately.

She thinks again of what Kirsten said about how Duncan is constantly hiding away in his office until the early hours of the morning, claiming that he's busy with a work project.

How Kirsten had told her that he'd crawled into bed at 2 a.m. this morning.

And if he is part of the disgusting group, chances are that he knows Mike, because it is too much of a coincidence, isn't it? That they are both part of this group and they were both there at the bar last night. They'd both spoken to her. Both bought her drinks. There's only one way to find out.

Jenna clicks the sign-in button, logging in as Duncan before scrolling down his activity log to see if he had posted anything incriminating here in the early hours of this morning.

Click. Click.

Jenna feels sick. She feels as if she is floating. As if she is outside of her body. Blinking a few times, trying to give herself time to make sense of what she is reading.

Duncan commenting on posts about other women.

'Stupid slut!' 'Prick tease!'

His vile words.

His scornful comments.

Another demonised woman, Jenna thinks. If you wanted almost guaranteed hate, write about a female victim of crime in a newspaper article or on social media and watch all the misogynistic women-haters crawl out of the rotten woodwork where they fester.

Blaming women for the abuse that was committed against them. Justifying the crimes by making cheap, nasty jibes and cruel scathing personal comments about their appearance or their morals.

As if the pain and ordeal of the attacks these women had suffered wasn't enough already.

As if what had happened to them was all their own fault and their punishment wasn't nearly enough for any of them.

The rise in toxic abuse online lately. The vitriol towards women was growing, flooding the newspaper comments sections and social media once the newspaper's stories had gone live.

'*Stupid fucking bitch!*'

Jenna closes her eyes. Wishing she could push what she's seeing from her mind, forcing it out.

She'd often wondered who the vile, poisonous people were who shoved their misogynistic, hate-filled opinions down people's throats in the cesspool that was the comment sections. Not normal, decent people, she'd always assumed, because normal, decent people wouldn't behave like that.

Only Duncan is a normal, decent person. Or so she had thought. Happily married, a loving father.

He has a tiny four-year-old little daughter for Christ's sake, yet here he is, sharing articles about some of the recent attacks. Purposely driving members' attention to the posts, as if to goad them into piling on and prolonging the victim's suffering even more.

Which they all do so willingly.

Like the vile, misogynistic monsters that they are.

Wading in the muck that they all created as they torment real victims. Publicly crucifying women who are at their lowest. Who are reaching out and asking for help.

They are gutless.

Hiding behind their fake profile photos and a pathetic username.

Anonymous on here as if that makes it any better. As if that makes them any less of a troll in real life.

Yet Jenna knows that was all part and parcel of publishing.

That the comments sections of every article posted online was one of the known downsides of the internet. Every opinionated arsehole out there felt entitled to state their point of view on situations and circumstances that they knew nothing about, and worse, they had access to mobile phones which enabled them to spout their vitriol to anyone who cared to listen at the press of a button.

But she also knows that the comment sections also mean that these types of stories gained traction. Traction means attention and attention, good or bad, means that the articles have more chance of going viral.

More chance of being seen.

She scrolls down to Mike's fake profile name and sees that Duncan has liked some of his posts. Leaving his own comments of agreement and encouragement beneath them as if to spur Mike on.

They *do* know each other.

Jenna tries to recall if she'd seen Duncan having any conversations at the bar with anyone outside of their group, if he'd spoken to Mike then, only she hadn't taken much notice of Duncan until much later, when she'd observed the weird dynamics and tension that was simmering between her two friends.

Kirsten and Duncan seemed as if they'd had a row or disagreement about something and Kirsten had wanted to leave. Is Mike the reason why Duncan had reluctantly left Jenna there in the end, finally accepting her refusal of a lift home from him?

He knew that Mike would take over from where he'd left off.

Were they both in this together?

Mike had been the one to approach her.

He had been the one to initiate their first conversation.

Up until now she'd been so certain that Mike had drugged

her, but thinking about it, she'd been so careful to protect her own drink around him, hadn't she?

What if she'd already been spiked by someone else?

Duncan.

She trusted Duncan, didn't she? She hadn't had her guard up around him, and he had been the last person to buy her a drink before he left.

What if the poison was already swirling inside her as she'd kept it covered and away from Mike? What if the drugs were already taking hold in her system when she'd 'accidently' knocked the drink over that Mike had bought her?

There is a creak of floorboards on the landing.

Not taking any chances, Jenna logs out of the forum just as a voice comes from behind her.

'Jenna? What are you doing?' Momentarily startled, she jumps in her seat. Turning to the figure standing in the doorway.

'Shit, Kirsten! You scared the life out of me,' she says, desperate to regain her composure. To stifle the flash of heat that creeps up her face as she taps the mouse, simultaneously coming out of that screen.

'My phone died, and I just wanted to check my emails. Make sure that nothing new had come in from Legal about Holly's photo. See if there had been any updates. I hope you don't mind?' Jenna knows that she is saying too much, speaking too fast, she's giving herself away.

Calm the fuck down, Jenna!

'Is Duncan not with you?' she asks, staring past Kirsten at the door, half expecting him to be out there, standing in the dark void of the hallway behind her.

'No. We had a disagreement about something. I got a taxi home.'

'Without him?' Jenna turns back to the computer and closes all the open applications as quickly as she can.

Leaving Duncan's computer exactly as she'd found it.

Tell her. Tell her what you found.

She should, she thinks, and she is about to. About to blurt out how she'd found a secret database of female victims that Duncan had compiled on his computer.

That there were more women on there than they knew about. Women that hadn't yet come forward, yet Duncan knew all about them.

She could show her the disgusting comments that he'd shared with the other members. With Mike.

Only as she goes to speak, she realises she can't. Her voice won't come out. It feels trapped, as if her throat is closing over.

'I'm sorry, there's something I need,' Jenna coughs, and it's only then that she realises that Kirsten has been crying. How her eyes are puffy and lined red.

'Kirsten. What's happened? Are you okay?' Jenna gets up, going to her friend.

'It was a stupid fight,' Kirsten says, shaking her head and stepping back, and Jenna gets it as she notes the tremble of her friend's words, how she's so close to losing it again. How Kirsten is too upset to be comforted right now.

One kind word or gentle hug could tip the woman over.

But she needs to tell her. She must.

'There's something that I...' Jenna starts only to be stopped mid-sentence by the sound of Amelia's teary voice, calling out as if on cue from her bedroom.

'Mummy?'

'Coming darling!' Kirsten calls out before bringing her focus back to Jenna. 'Look, do you mind if we talk about it some other time? I just can't right now.'

'Mummy!'

'No of course. Of course,' Jenna mumbles gathering her things as Amelia's cries grow louder. Part of her relieved that she doesn't have to do this right here, right now.

Not only was this a conversation they'd both need to have without either of the children present, but she needs to process what she's just seen. To make sense of it first in her own head before she shares it with Kirsten.

The fact that Kirsten ended their date early and came home without Duncan spoke volumes.

Things were already really bad between the couple.

If Jenna was going to be the one to break this news to her friend, then she needed more proof. She needed solid evidence to back up her suspicions. To learn this about the man she was married to would completely devastate Kirsten. It would destroy their marriage completely.

'I best get off before he gets back,' she says, making her way down the stairs and grabbing her coat and shoes before turning to face Kirsten who is stood at the top of the stairs. 'I'll leave you both to it.'

Kirsten nods in understanding, which is ironic, because she couldn't possibly have a clue that the real reason Jenna is so eager to get away from this house before Duncan returns is because she's not sure she can bring herself to even look at him.

She's not sure she's capable of being anywhere near him.

Because he isn't who they think he is.

He isn't anything like the man he pretends to be.

He's one of them.

27

EVIE

The phone rings for a second time, maybe even a third and I ignore it.

I zone back out from the sounds in the room and concentrate on the image on the screen.

The dark, wet street in the background sets the scene.

A faint silhouette of a woman with a huge bulge in her coat, the footage is too grainy to make out any real detail. The images are too blurred to make out the features of my face or anything distinguishing enough to identify me. Even the coat I wore, which is a vibrant baby pink, is muted in these photos into various shades of black, white and grey.

To any other person looking this could be anyone.

I should be happy about that, relieved. But I am not.

Because the fact that they've released this footage online, that they've printed the stills of it on the front pages of their paper, means that they are getting closer to figuring out who I am.

What I've done.

They are a step nearer to finding out the truth that I've fought so hard to conceal.

I close my eyes and cradle my pounding head in my hands as if trying to keep my wild angry thoughts from exploding out through the top of my skull.

Why? Why are they doing this to me?

The charity said that I would be given full anonymity. I heard it again, on the news yesterday. How a spokesman for the charity confirmed on national TV that they are not looking for me.

That I haven't done anything wrong. That they are not searching for the Missing Mother, as the newspapers have so aptly named me.

So why are the media so set on finding me? Hounding me.

It's her.

I stare at the reporter's name that is printed in bold directly beneath the article, and my heart lurches inside my chest with recognition.

Jenna Stone.

The same journalist who posted a photo of my daughter in the newspaper and started this entire witch hunt against me.

'Bad mother. Doesn't deserve children. What sort of woman gives away her baby like that.'

And now, as I look down at the image of me walking along Islington High Street that night, with Holly tucked away inside my coat, I have no doubt that Jenna Stone is coming for me.

Why is she doing this to me? She hasn't worked it out yet.

Hasn't worked it out that I was the woman her newspaper launched an appeal about, following my attack.

Only to find out weeks later that my attacker had inflicted more on me than just the violent act of rape.

He'd impregnated me with his spawn. Left me with one final, permanent reminder of what he'd done to me.

I had pretended that it wasn't happening at first. When my periods didn't come, and every slight smell made me run to the toilet and violently wretch.

When my clothes and skin became so tight and stretched, and the bulge protruding as if I had a rapidly growing tumour inside of me, I pretended that I'd just put on weight.

Which was impossible seeing as the alien life form that was growing inside of me feasted on all the goodness and nutrients that I put inside my body, sucking me dry. Sucking the life from me.

Leaving me feeling constantly sick, and dizzy and weak.

The blogs and articles I looked up online about pregnancy looked nothing like this.

The morning sickness they spoke of that lasted for just a few hours a day during the first few months of pregnancy came every hour of the day for me. For six whole months.

Only to be replaced once it had stopped with chronic burning heartburn.

And I hid it all. I hid her.

Beneath layers of baggy clothing, despite whatever the temperature was outside. Not registering the pregnancy with a doctor or midwife.

Not going to a single anti-natal appointment.

I couldn't because if I did, he would know.

'Get rid of it, or I will pay you a visit and do it for you.'

Jenna Stone's newspaper had somehow led him to me.

Her newspaper, publishing all the intimate, graphic details of what happened to me all those months ago, in the hope that it would help them appeal for other witnesses to come forward, other women who'd been attacked to speak up. For some clue to find him. Her paper had ultimately led him straight back to me.

First he made the threat about me not being able to keep my child. The messages he sent me, telling me to 'get rid of it', and after that came the comments on my social media. Then came the private messages. Vile and graphic from so many different accounts that I knew it couldn't be just him.

There was a whole army of men like him out there.

I felt as if I was being followed. Got paranoid that random men were turning up, at night, when I was working in the supermarkets. That they were watching me all the time.

So, I couldn't let on that I hadn't gone through with his demands.

I couldn't let him know that I hadn't had an abortion.

Because he would have crucified me if he'd found out that I was still pregnant.

I pushed her out into the world expecting to see a monster, a devil's child, *him*.

She had been tiny and squishy and pink and the most perfect little thing I've ever seen.

And I knew in that moment, that if I wanted to keep her safe,to keep her away from the animal that created her, then I needed to keep her far away from me.

Jenna Stone is going to work it out, isn't she?

She is going to work out that I am the missing mother, and when she shares that with the world, it will all have been for nothing.

Holly's life will be in danger again.

28

JENNA

Jenna stares down at the barely legible scrawl that sweeps across the page of her notepad, from where she'd quickly scribbled down the list on Duncan's computer.

Sharon Hargreaves, 17 Waterside Road. One of the most recent additions to his list. She is convinced that the only way she can get to the bottom of the issue is to come here and ask the woman herself, because Jenna had looked the woman's name up online and googled the date to see if anything had been reported at that time, but she'd found nothing.

This is the right place. She knocks again, louder this time, and sees the small flash of yellow light that peeps out from the gap around the edge of the curtains at the window beside her. How the glow expands as the fabric twitches, as whoever is inside fails miserably at peeping out undetected.

'Sharon?' Jenna calls through the letterbox. 'My name's Jenna Stone. I'm a journalist from the *Islington Gazette*.'

She waits for a short while, hopeful for a reply that deep down she knows she won't get.

She's met with only silence.

'I know you're in, Sharon, I saw you at the window. I just

want to talk to you.' She tries again. 'It's about some incidents that have happened to women in the area, Sharon. I wondered if perhaps you could help me. Two minutes of your time, that's all I want.'

Seeing the faint outline of a silhouette move across the hallway floor inside. She's there, right there on the other side of the door.

Curiosity has got the better of her, Jenna has her attention now.

'Well, I don't want to talk to no journalist.' Sharon's voice is firm and unwavering as she shouts back.

Jenna purses her mouth in annoyance. She had thought about that before she knocked, thought about not telling the woman who she really was or what she really did for a living. Of tricking the woman into thinking that she was here as someone else.

That she was selling something, or that she was conducting a survey in the area. Anything other than a journalist, because she knows how it might put the woman off talking to her. Especially if a crime had been committed and Sharon hadn't reported it, and if she hadn't told a single soul what had happened to her. Which is what Jenna suspected.

Jenna had taken a huge risk and decided not to lie. If she wanted this woman to open up to her, to tell her why she was on Duncan's list then she knew she was going to have to give her some honesty too. Especially if she wanted her to trust her.

She has to be truthful with her from the start.

'I'm not here as a journalist. My visit has nothing to do with the paper. No one knows I'm here. I just want to talk to you. Woman to woman...' Jenna pauses, trying to articulate what she's about to say next, because she knows how difficult this might be if her hunch is right and this woman is indeed a victim of one of the attacks.

'I was spiked, Sharon. A couple of nights ago at a bar in the high street. Someone spiked my drink.' She hopes that Sharon is listening and, more importantly, that she believes her.

That she can hear from her voice how this isn't a ploy.

'I managed to get away, Sharon. But I know that there is a whole list of others who didn't.'

Don't say they weren't the lucky ones. Don't you dare say lucky ones.

'I think you're one of those women too, Sharon. Am I right?'

She is met with silence again, only it doesn't deter her from continuing to try. If anything, the silence only makes her more determined to get through. Because as long as the woman is quiet it means that she is listening.

'I just wondered if you would talk to me. Just for two minutes. That's all I ask, Sharon. Completely off the record, just you and me, you have my word. I promise you I won't be writing about this in the newspaper.' Not yet, Jenna thinks. Not until she has cast iron proof.

The house is silent once more. The shadow on the other side doesn't move.

Jenna wonders what it is she'll have to say to get the woman to consider opening the door to her. Or if this is pointless. A complete waste of her time. If the woman had wanted to come forward and talk about her attack, she would have by now.

'Look, I know this is hard and I know how you must be feeling, trust me I do. Because I feel exactly the same. I thought I was drunk.' She gives a small, stupid sounding laugh. 'I thought that it was my fault. But the man who did it to me, to us, he's going to keep doing it until someone stops him. And I think that I can stop him, Sharon. But I need your help.'

Jenna holds her breath. Hopeful now. Expelling it a few seconds later when she hears the metal chain slide across the inside of the door.

'You can't be round here shouting things out like that,' Sharon says, her face peering out the crack in the front door as she susses Jenna out and makes sure she's alone. 'My neighbours will be having a field day listening to all that. You better come in.'

Sharon leads her into the lounge and nods her head for Jenna to sit on the sofa. She doesn't offer her a drink, and she gets the message.

The woman is giving her the two minutes she asked for – no more and no less.

'He did it to you too, didn't he?' Jenna says gently. Not wasting any of the short amount of time she has. 'He spiked your drink?'

'How do you know? You can't know. You can't possibly know, because I never told anyone,' Sharon says, looking like a deer caught in the headlights, as if she hadn't expected Jenna to go straight in and ask her outright, clearly having no time to compose herself from such a direct question.

'I'm a journalist, I've been investigating a number of spikings and sexual assaults that have happened to women over the past year in this area. I believe that they are linked. I found a list of names and dates, Sharon. I recognised some of the names on there.' Jenna coughs to clear her throat as if she has trouble saying the next bit out loud. 'My name was on there, the date that it happened to me. Your name was on there too.'

Sharon nods as if understanding the enormity of Jenna being here right now. The woman knew the truth and there was no point lying about it.

'Look, my husband will be back with the kids soon, and the truth is, I didn't tell anyone. Not him, or my mates or the police. But yeah, I was drugged. I knew straight away because I hadn't been drinking. I had an eye infection and was on a course of antibiotics. So, when I started to feel drunk, more than drunk really, dizzy and sick and confused and unable to keep my eyes open, I knew straight away what had happened.' Sharon shakes her head as the tears she's trying to hold in stream down her face with relief at finally being able to talk about what had happened to her with someone.

Someone like Jenna who would understand.

'I told my friend I didn't feel well and asked her to put me in a cab, and she did. She got me a taxi and I made it as far as here.' Sharon nods to the sofa that Jenna is sitting on. 'My husband, Mark, he thinks that the copious amount of Prosecco I'd knocked back while I was out with the girls reacted badly with my meds. Thinks I had the worst hangover of my life, as I was laid up for the entire weekend; he often makes jokes about it even now.' Sharon looks at the floor.

Full of guilt that she'd never confided in him.

That it had gone this far, and she still hadn't told him the truth.

'Why didn't you tell him? It wasn't your fault. You did nothing wrong.'

Sharon shrugs. 'I was flirting. God, I know how pathetic that sounds, I mean look at me. I'm hardly a catch.' Sharon nods down to the oversized onesie she is wearing, her hair scraped into a messy bun on the top of her head and not a scrap of make-up. Jenna thinks she looks lovely.

Normal. Nice.

Still Sharon was clearly her own worst critic.

'I'm married, and I don't think someone's flirted with me for what feels like years. I was flattered. So, when the guys offered to get us a round of drinks, I didn't see what harm it would do. Just having the one.' Sharon rolls her eyes. 'What's the saying about hindsight being twenty-twenty? You can always see so much clearer after it's happened, huh!' Sharon tries to make a joke, tries to lighten the mood, but neither woman pretends to laugh.

'Mark is the jealous type; he'd go mental if he knew I was out accepting drinks from men I don't know. Men who were clearly trying to get into our knickers.'

'And you were the only one drugged in your group of mates?"

'Yeah, seems like the bloke talking to me would have preferred it if I was unconscious,' Sharon says bitterly. 'My friends were all drunk by then, and I don't think they were really paying much attention to what had happened. I didn't want a fuss. Like I said, as far as anyone is aware, I wasn't feeling well. My mate put me in a cab and I came home, threw my guts up and passed out there on the sofa.'

Jenna nods. Glad that the woman didn't have a far more horrific encounter to share with her. That was something she supposed.

Still there was something about her demeanour, something about the way she is acting, nervously scratching her arms as she spoke, her eyes constantly darting to the door and the window. She might be nervous about her husband and children walking in on them, but Jenna can't help but feel there is more to it than that.

'Is there something else, Sharon? Something you're not telling me.'

Sharon starts to shake her head, and then thinks better of it.

Maybe because finally she is talking to someone who will actually listen to her, someone who will really understand.

'It started with phone calls at first. Nothing major, just heavy breathing. I thought it was kids at first.'

Jenna shifts uncomfortably in her seat as she thinks about the similar phone calls she'd been getting, only hers had started before she'd been spiked.

'Until finally, he threatened me, he told me not to speak to anyone. Not to go to the police. Told me he'd find out where I live and he'd make my life hell,' Sharon says quietly, her eyes constantly going to the front door, and this time Jenna knows it is her husband that she doesn't want to hear this.

'Then he found me on social media. Sent me some nasty

messages, threats about what he'd do to me. Calling me names, you know. A slut. A tease. I deleted it all in the end. Everything, because other accounts started joining in. And I was worried that they'd make contact with my friends and family that I have on there. That they'd start commenting on other people's photos about me. So, I came off social media completely.'

Sharon closes her eyes, holding them tightly shut for a few seconds before she opens them again and continues.

'A few times I've seen people outside the house. Men. Loitering at the end of the drive, or on the corner of the road. I don't know, maybe I'm just paranoid but sometimes I feel like I'm being watched. Like maybe it's him watching me. Like he's getting off on tormenting me.'

'Did you tell him where you lived? When you spoke to him in the bar. Did you tell him all this information about yourself?'

'No, I only gave him my first name. But afterwards, days afterwards, I realised that my driving licence was missing from my purse. It had been on the table that night. I tried to tell myself that it probably just fell out. That I probably just lost it somewhere.'

'Do you think you'd recognise him again if you saw a photo of him?'

'Maybe.' Sharon shrugs. 'But I didn't speak with him for that long and it was much earlier in the evening, so I don't even know if it was him who did it.'

Taking her phone from her pocket, Jenna shows her a photo from her phone and zooms in. It's the picture of them all that she took from the photograph she'd found in Duncan's office. The most recent one she had of him.

'I'm not sure. I don't know.' Sharon shakes her head flustered. 'He does look familiar, so maybe yes, he might have been there in the bar, but he wasn't the man I had been speaking to.'

'Do you remember anything about the man you spoke to? Do you remember what he looked like?' Jenna asks, thinking about the man from the incel group that she thought had spiked her drink.

They were both part of the same group: Duncan and Mike were in this together.

'He was tall, dark hair. Good looking. I don't know...' she says vaguely, shaking her head.

'Shaz. We're back. Grab the plates, will you?' A man's voice booms from the front door, cutting their conversation short just before the house is filled with the sound of children's chatter and footsteps as they run through the house towards them. 'It's probably freezing already, as we got stuck behind a learner the whole way back here.'

'Oh!' Mark says, eyeing Jenna from the doorway with a curious look on his face. 'I didn't know we had company!'

'I was just introducing myself to your wife.' Jenna smiles. 'I'm the new Avon rep in the area. I live in the next street. I was trying to do the hard sell on signing some more women up as reps, only Sharon isn't sold on the idea.'

'I thought about it,' Sharon says quickly. 'Thought maybe the extra money might come in handy for our next holiday. But I'm not sure. I don't know if I'll be able to fit it all in. Thanks for all the info though, Jenna.'

'No worries,' Jenna says, getting up from where she's been sitting. 'I'll leave my number with you just in case? If you change your mind and you want to chat again, you can always give me a call.' About to get her card out of her purse, Jenna remembers how they are on headed paper, advertising the fact that she's a journalist. Instead, she grabs a pen from the bottom of her bag and scribbles down her number on a scrappy bit of paper.

Before nodding over to Mark and throwing him a grin.

'Right, I best get out of your way and leave you to it. That smells delicious by the way.'

29

HIM

He watches as she picks up her cup and drinks the liquid down.

Such a devoted mother.

She's so busy talking about herself, full of monotonous empty chatter about what she's done since the last time he'd seen her, that she hadn't noticed him slipping anything into her mug of sweet tea.

She never notices, which makes it so much easier for him.

But then isn't that what she had wanted once upon a time? For him to be discreet and quiet and not to make a fuss. Isn't that how she had wanted him to be?

Children should be seen and not heard.

Those had been the words that she had regularly fed to him as she'd hurriedly pulled the bed covers up and tucked him in at night as a small child.

A lie, really. As she didn't want him to be seen either.

She wanted him in his bed, in his room.

Out of the way so that he wouldn't disturb her plans for the night. Again.

Because he'd done that before. Interrupted her when she'd been entertaining one of her 'gentleman callers'.

Though when he'd boldly tiptoed downstairs that one time and stood in the lounge doorway, watching, the man who had been stood in the middle of his lounge with his eyes firmly closed and his trousers tugged down around his ankles, hadn't looked anything like how he'd envisaged a gentleman would look.

He'd thought he was having a fit. As his body convulsed violently with a shudder and he let out an animalistic groan as if he was in agony.

He remembered wondering what his mother was doing down on her knees on the floor. Why she hadn't helped the man whose tongue was stuck out like a panting dog, his eyes white from rolling to the back of his head.

'Is he dying?' he'd asked, accidently voicing his thoughts out loud and realising the immediate error as he registered the sudden look of horror that had quickly flashed across the man's face, as he'd yelped loudly and yanked his trousers back up.

His mother, immediately back up on her feet, shouting at him to go back upstairs. Screaming at him.

Louder and angrier than he'd ever heard her before. He'd been terrified, stood motionless on the spot until he'd felt her grabbing him roughly by the arm as she hoisted him back up the stairs towards his bedroom.

'Why can't you just do as you're told? Stay in your bed. Do you hear me. Do not come out of this room.'

There were no bedtime stories in his house after that. No soft glow of a night-light lighting up the dark corners of the room nor bedroom doors cracked slightly open.

Instead, he was met with a spoonful of medicine forced into his mouth before his mother left the room. Turning off the light and shutting the door, plunging him all alone in to darkness.

He'd felt scared. Lying in that dark room all by himself as his heart began beating wildly, he feared that it would burst right out of his chest.

Unable to get up as his legs felt weighted and heavy. His limbs rendered useless.

Then dizziness. If he tried to move, to get up, to get out of his bed. It forced him back down, made him submit to it. Trying and failing to fight the heaviness of his drooping eyelids.

Giving in to blackness. Nothingness. Until he woke again the next morning feeling groggy and confused.

Children should be seen and not heard.

He'd thought of those words the first time that he'd drugged her.

His mother.

The first time he'd slipped something into her drink when she wasn't looking, watching her expression for the fear to quickly take hold as he knew that it would do.

He'd thought that once would be enough to get the urge out of his system too, to make her pay for what she did to him.

But it hadn't been.

He'd done it so many times to her now, that he was convinced she must secretly believe that she has the onset of dementia setting in.

She's at that age, he figures and what with the regular headaches and blackouts she experiences now. The big chunks of missing time from her memory. The way she seems to be unable to concentrate properly any more. Her sudden unpredictable mood swings. It's a fair assessment.

She's scared and instead of putting her out of her misery, he enjoys it. The fear she feels. The same panic rising up inside her that she'd made him feel as a small, helpless child.

Not realising that it's the side effects of the drugs he's regularly feeding her.

'Children should be seen and not heard. Did you know that there's irony in that proverb, Mother!' he says as she begins to lose the fight of keeping her eyes open. Growing weaker, more frustrated as her body disobeys her orders. 'It dates back to medieval

times; *did you know that? Brought into force because of religious reasons. The saying was directed at women, in fact. How they should be seen and not heard. Women were not permitted to speak in the presence of adults. It was only later that the saying evolved to include children,*' he says as his mother's fight to keep her eyes open fails miserably and her head lolls to one side. Losing all power, losing all control.

'*Well, I found it interesting anyway,*' he smarts, taking the cup from her hand to prevent her spilling it down herself, making a note to rinse it out before he leaves.

To leave no trace of what he'd slipped into her drink. No evidence behind.

A silent assassin, neither seen nor heard, just like she'd always wanted.

30

JENNA

The sound of her own name blaring from the TV pulls Jenna from her trance. She's been distracted, she realises. She's been sitting staring absently at the TV screen for what feels like hours.

She should have gone to bed, but she knew if she did, she wouldn't sleep.

She couldn't, she was too wired.

Staring past the flashing images and colours as if the screen was still and black. Her brain not registering anything else but what she'd seen on Duncan's computer the night before.

Now, she watches the screen, watching as the camera zooms in on Islington High Street, which Jenna recognises immediately, with its diverse mix of trendy bars and boutique shops. Hordes of people walking the pavements either side of the grid-locked rush-hour stream of traffic that runs down its centre.

Even more crowded than usual with clusters of people, chaos pursuing as predominantly female pro-choice and pro-life protesters form outside Islington Fire Station. The large group all holding up a huge display of placards and boards, in a bid to offer support to the scheme.

Turning the volume up, the TV now has Jenna's full, undivided attention.

'*Islington Fire Station, the first official site for the trial location of a Safe Place Baby Box in the UK, has seen its first baby anonymously dropped off. I am here with one of the charity's representatives, Jessica Marks. Jessica, can you give us any more information on how baby Holly was found and how she is doing?*'

'*Thanks to the silent alarms fitted inside the boxes, the firefighter on duty at the fire station was able to tend to the child in less than two minutes after her placement inside the box, and we are very happy to report that "the baby",*' the woman says tartly, clearly not happy about the baby's sex being revealed, '*is healthy and doing well. On behalf of the scheme's founders, I would like to reiterate that they are not searching for the missing mother who "safely surrendered" her infant to a Safe Place Baby Box here at Islington local fire station. I would also like to convey that the baby's mother has the right to total anonymity and that her actions are perfectly legal.*'

The reporter turns to acknowledge the crowd of protesters behind her, all backing up the scheme as if to show the support it received.

'*The scheme has been brought into question by members of the public following a legal case that has now been brought against lead journalist, Jenna Stone, of the Islington Gazette,*' the reporter continues, '*who published an article featuring a photograph of the safely surrendered child, without obtaining the necessary consent or permission. We are aware of numerous groups that have been set up on social media to search for the missing mother, which has come with a lot of public speculation about locating and identifying the mother. However, the police have urged members of the public that no crime has been committed here and that they are not looking for the baby's mother. But not everyone is happy about these trials. Joining us now is Phillipa Rose from the UK Adoption Rights Agency.'* The reporter holds the microphone out towards an older woman, her grey hair dressed tightly with curls and a stern expression on her face, her jaw tense and jutted forward.

'What are your thoughts, Phillipa? Do you agree that the newspaper had a right to bring this information together to the public forum with the photograph of baby Holly, as well as CCTV footage that's just been released, potentially of the infant's mother?'

'I do, yes. I believe that Jenna Stone and the Islington Gazette had every right to share the information, in the interest of the general public. Safe Place Baby Boxes are still in the trial process, and we believe that they are completely unethical and, quite frankly, a slap in the face to every parent who has followed standard relinquishment procedures. Not only that, but how can we know that the mother has made this choice of her own accord? What if this isn't a cry of help from the mother? What if the decision was taken out of her hands by an abusive partner, or a controlling family member? The baby may not be the only victim of circumstance here. Regardless what this scheme claims, we believe that the mother was clearly in a desperate need of help. And because of that, we believe that she needs to be found.'

The woman's words are drowned out by jeers and shouts from the protesters behind her. Shaking their heads and holding their placards higher in disagreement.

Switching the TV off and throwing the remote control down on the sofa, Jenna has heard enough.

Her head is swimming with the mess that this has all become.

In the midst of all the chaos is a tiny baby who had been placed alone in a box in the wall.

A baby who is now without her mother.

A sadness envelops her entire being at what will become of that child now.

What life will she lead? What lies will she be told that she'll forever believe are her truths?

Getting up, Jenna makes her way to her bedroom. Bending down to retrieve the shoebox that she stashed beneath her bed, she wipes away the film of dust that covers the lid, unsure of how long it's been since she'd last looked at the contents inside.

Tonight, she is drawn to it. Lifting the lid, she reaches inside and pulls out the tatty, worn blanket. Neatly folded, she places it down next to her before picking up the pile of tatty old newspaper clippings that sit just beneath it.

A solid mass of something catching in her throat. She swallows down the emotion as she stares down at the image of the baby in the photo.

How tiny she had looked. How helpless.

Just like Holly.

This baby had been left just inside the communal hallway doors of a block of flats in west Sussex.

She'd been found by one of the residents. An old lady on the first floor, who had heard the sound of crying and thought it was an injured kitten or cat. The woman had gone out to the main doors to investigate, only to find a cardboard box just inside the flat's doorway.

The tiny baby wrapped in a blanket, cocooned inside.

Jenna.

She'd only been a few hours old, according to the social worker's reports. She still had her umbilical cord attached and, despite the blanket and the fact that she'd been placed inside a doorway, away from the elements, her skin had been tinged blue with the cold.

Jenna had gone on to spend the earliest years of her childhood not knowing the truth about herself, and after age nine, when she'd finally been told what had happened to her, she'd spent the rest of her childhood and teenage years obsessing over being reunited with her birth mother. Daydreaming about her turning up one day, overwrought with emotion at giving her baby girl away.

Hope had turned to desperation, and her optimism about her birth mother had turned to a feeling of deep sadness and rejection, as she had been left to wonder how different she would be if she'd had that love and stability instead of being passed from one care home and foster family to another.

Her whole life feeling as if she never really belonged to anyone at all.

Jenna can't bear to think of that for Holly too.

Being abandoned as a baby played such a big part of why she does the job that she does. Why she'd chosen to spend her career telling the stories of others, when she couldn't bring herself to tell her own.

How she fought for answers, even if initially people didn't want to hear them.

They deserved that.

To know the truth about themselves, no matter how painful it might feel at its discovery.

And maybe, subconsciously, she'd never stopped searching for answers of her own. Maybe part of her had held on to the fact that, one day, she might actually find her biological mother.

Thirty years, Jenna! It's been thirty years. Who are you still kidding?

Placing the blanket and the newspaper clippings back inside the box, Jenna sees another call from Liam flash up on her phone, having probably just watched the same news report that she had. She sighs.

'Hi, Liam,' she says with fake joviality, because she doesn't have the headspace for any of this right now. For Liam breathing down her neck about how Legal are driving him crazy, for all this stuff that baby Holly has bought up in her own life.

'Have you seen the news? This story has gone nuts. Other

countries are jumping on and questioning the scheme. There are protests taking place all over the country.' Jenna can hear the amusement in his voice, the satisfaction he gets knowing it was his paper that brought this story to the world.

'I've seen it, yes,' Jenna says, flatly, feeling utterly drained from it all.

'Are you all right?' Liam asks; he must be wondering why Jenna isn't as thrilled about all of this as he is.

'I'm fine, I've just got a lot on right now. What did you call me for?' Jenna asks, knowing how blunt she sounds but no longer caring; she just wants Liam to get to the point.

'Do you still have the letter from the missing mother?'

Jenna hesitates.

'I thought we agreed that we weren't going to run with it. That it might be too much of a risk if we published it. It might put the mother and Holly in even more danger?'

'People are looking for her now regardless. Even without the letter, they are concerned and want to find her. Did you hear what the woman from the adoption agency said, questioning if this isn't a cry of help from the mother. Implying that the baby may not be the only victim of circumstance here. We know the answer to that and she's right, isn't she? I think, if we print the letter, it will give us more leverage against Legal too, to justify why we printed the photo and the CCTV footage in the first place. It will make our motive for doing that even stronger, and we need to do something as they are not going to drop it. I say we go ahead and publish it. That way we can keep the story going for as long as we can too.'

Jenna takes a deep breath, letting Liam's words sink in. That's what this is really about for him. Another front page exclusive. All eyes on the newspaper. All eyes on him.

She's exhausted from it all, though she's still holding on to a tiny bit of hope that the more they can push this story out there, the more chance they'll have at finding the missing mother.

The more chance they might have at reuniting her with her baby if she comes forward. Maybe putting the CCTV footage and the letter out there will be what it will take to let the mother know that people actually care.

That she doesn't have to suffer in silence, alone.

Tucking the box with the newspaper clippings and blanket back underneath the bed, she thinks about that for Holly too. How one day, she might only have memories just like this. Newspaper clippings, screen shots from the online paper. Recordings on the news about her being abandoned.

Liam wasn't doing any of it for those reasons, for the *right reasons*. He was only thinking in numbers. How many clicks the online newspaper article would receive. What kind of income they would generate from this.

Despite the risk it might pose to the missing mother, there was a chance that it might help her too; it had to be worth a shot, didn't it?

'Yeah, I have it. You want me to scan it and email it over?'

'No! I'll come over and grab it. This is our exclusive, I want the original copy. I don't want to take any risks of anyone else getting their hands on it, before we have a chance of getting it out there.'

31

JENNA

'You sounded as if you could do with some cheering up, so I brought you this!' Liam says, holding out a bottle of wine towards Jenna as soon as she opens her front door.

'Ahh, thanks!' Smiling, Jenna takes his gift, stepping aside so that he can come in. 'It's a lovely thought but if you don't mind, I think I'll pass on that tonight. I'm not really in the mood for any more alcohol,' she says politely. Drinking with Liam is the very last thing Jenna has on her agenda tonight.

Especially with the mood she is in.

'Oh, come on! Just one glass. You saw the news. This story breaking is all thanks to you,' Liam urges, following Jenna in through the flat to the kitchen, 'You should be celebrating. Join me, please. One teeny-tiny, small glass.'

Placing the wine bottle down on the counter, she doesn't want to seem ungrateful. Besides, maybe a small glass might help to take the edge off the awful couple of days she's had. It might help her to sleep tonight.

'Fine. One small glass. Oh, here let me get you that letter,' she adds, grabbing the envelope from where she'd tucked it down inside her laptop satchel and handing it to Liam.

'I've already written the piece; in case you changed your mind. I've emailed a copy of that over to you too.' She nods to the extra piece of paper that she'd folded up with it, before she begins filling up two wine glasses.

'Impressive!' Liam smiles, but she knows he didn't expect any less. She has worked hard from the minute she got this job to prove herself worthy, to show everyone she worked with that she was the best at what she did. That she never gave up.

'When are you planning on going live with it?'

'As soon as possible. I'm heading back to the office after here. The sooner we get it out there the better,' he says as she hands him his glass and leads him into the lounge.

'You'll have to excuse the mess!' Jenna apologises as she places her glass on the coffee table. Before she starts moving the piles of discarded notebooks and paperwork that were scattered across the seat next to her on the sofa from where she had been going over everything earlier. Mortified at the state she's let the place get into, she makes a mental note to give the flat a thorough clean as soon as Liam leaves.

'You don't hang about, do you?! Are you working on the next breaking headline already?' he asks.

'I'm just looking into a couple of things. Nothing concrete yet, just seeing what I can pull together. You really think publishing the letter,' Jenna says vaguely, changing the subject so she doesn't have to delve any deeper into exactly what it is she is investigating right now, 'will help convince Legal to stop coming for this?'

'Personally, I don't think the missing mother can be identified from the clip we've put out. The image is too blurred and grainy to make out any real detail. But then we knew that.' Liam shrugs. 'So, I don't think we need to worry about the scheme coming for us in that regard. The photo of Holly might be frowned upon, but I believe it was necessary. Our readers are lapping it up. People are going nuts about this story, Jenna.

They are protesting out in the streets. And have you seen how many groups are popping up all over Facebook? The armchair detectives are out in their droves, desperate to be the ones to find the missing mother. That's on them, not us. The letter shifts the focus away from us and back onto the missing mother. We need to throw whatever we have out there while it's still hot and while everyone still gives a shit.'

Jenna nods in agreement at that, as she takes a big mouthful of her wine.

Savouring the familiar wave of warmth that runs right through her as she drinks it down.

Because she knows that Liam is right. This would be old news soon.

Soon there will be no more leads, no more breakthroughs, the protesters will move on to fight a different cause and the readers will stop caring. Once this media circus was over, people would go back to their normal lives and forget about baby Holly completely.

And maybe one day Holly will go to the tatty old shoebox that she too has shoved beneath her bed, full of old newspaper clippings and recordings of her on the news as a baby and wonder what became of the woman who gave birth to her. Wonder why her own mother hadn't kept her or came back for her.

Maybe she too would have a million questions swirling inside of her head.

'Hey, are you all right?' Liam asks, breaking Jenna's train of thought as he notes the tears that she can feel slipping down her cheeks.

So caught up in her thoughts, she didn't even realise she has started to cry.

'Sorry! Yes. I'm still not feeling a hundred per cent, that's all,' she lies, wiping her face, before taking another long glug of wine. Something to do as a distraction.

Something to help numb her pain.

'From the other night? Yeah, that was a bit of a state you managed to get yourself in.'

She's about to agree. To lie.

Only it all suddenly feels like too much for her.

Holding all of this in and keeping it all to herself.

How she'd put herself in so much danger, how she was *still* was in so much danger.

She thinks about her handbag turning up with that note stuffed inside of it.

Stop digging or you'll be sorry.

Then she thinks of Kirsten, how she hasn't even been able to bring herself to answer her friend's calls, when she knows that Kirsten probably needs her now more than ever, but she simply can't. Because what would she say?

What she has seen on Duncan's computer has changed everything.

It's made everything so much more personal, and she isn't sure she can cope with anything else.

'I'm sorry, ignore me, I've just had a lot going on lately,' she starts to explain, but really where does she even start with it all?

Where does she even begin?

'I just, I thought,' spluttering now, unable to get her words out, her whole body shakes violently with each wracking sob. Mortified that she is breaking down like this, in front of her boss of all people. Only she can't stop. It's like the floodgates have opened and everything she's been holding in is pouring out from her.

'Tell me, Jenna. Let me help. What's wrong?' She hears it, how Liam sounds just as shocked as she feels at her sudden out-of-character outburst.

How he can't comprehend what has led her to this state.

'I'm sorry. I'm sorry!' Jenna manages to say between sobs as she feels Liam taking the glass from her hand and moving it on to the table so that she doesn't spill it.

'Don't be sorry. Come on, tell me, maybe it will help,' he says gently, as if feeling her resistance to confide in him as he tries to coax whatever it is from her.

And maybe it will help. Because right now it doesn't feel as if it could make things any worse than they already are.

'I didn't get drunk the other night.'

'Okay!' he says, a strange tilt to his voice that implies he doesn't believe her, because he saw her with his own eyes.

The bewildered look on his face tells her that he isn't sure where she is going with this, yet he is prepared to be patient and listen.

'I didn't get drunk, like I told you. I was drugged, my drink was spiked at the bar we were at. After you all left to go to that club.'

'Are you kidding me?' Liam grips his lower face as if he doesn't want to show the shock that is there, but Jenna already sees it. 'Are you okay? Did something happen?' There is real panic in his voice. Then he falters. 'Wait. You were drugged when I found you? When you fell outside? When I tried to help you and get you a cab? How did I not know? Why didn't I realise? I just thought you were drunk, and you said you wanted to be by yourself. To go home by yourself. You were adamant.'

Jenna can tell that he feels awful at not being more insistent at taking her home and making sure she was all right.

'It's no one's fault. Besides, I don't think I ingested enough of whatever he put in my drink for it to have worked fully. And it was because you were there, that I managed to get away and get home safely.' Jenna nods, convinced that if Liam hadn't come along when he had, Mike might have been more forceful and she might not have got away so easily.

'But you didn't tell me! Did you call the police at least?'

Jenna shakes her head. Wondering how she is going to come clean and confess that there is still so much more.

'It wasn't just some random attack. It was my fault; I should have been more prepared.'

'More prepared?' Liam screws his face up, not understanding her reasoning. 'More prepared for what? What do you mean it wasn't a random attack?'

'The man who spiked my drink, Mike – at least, that's what he called himself. I'd been talking to him at the bar after you left. It wasn't a coincidence him being there, it didn't just happen by chance. I invited him there. I organised him to be there and I knew what he was capable of.'

'You invited him to the bar even though you knew what he was capable of?' Liam shakes his head. 'I'm sorry, you've lost me, I don't understand...'

Jenna pauses, knowing that the worst of her confession is yet to come, and he is not going to be happy to hear what she has been up to for the past few weeks.

'He's a member of the incel group that I infiltrated, the group I was investigating to take down that MP,' she continues, seeing the anger flash across Liam's face as he joins up the dots.

'But you left that group weeks ago...' he starts, stopping as he sees the guilty expression on Jenna's face. 'You're still in there?'

She looks at the floor.

'For fuck's sake, Jenna! Are you mad?! Do you know how dangerous that place could be for you? If they find out who you are, where you work, where you live, who knows what they'll do to you.'

'What they've done to me,' she says, thinking about the couple of tequilas she'd drunk back for Dutch courage, how they'd made her feel more confident than she'd truly felt, how she'd carelessly let her guard down.

How she hadn't been as careful as she'd hoped.

'I think they've found me. He's found me,' she says quietly. Before opening up to Liam about how her handbag had been left at reception at work, and the note she'd found inside.

Grabbing the piece of paper from where she'd kept it on the shelf of her lounge, Jenna lets Liam read it for himself.

'"I know who you are *4EvAlone,* and I know where you live. Stop digging or you'll be sorry."' Liam reads it out loud slowly, as if his brain can't believe what he is seeing.

'He knows who I am.' Jenna drains her glass. Relishing the last dregs as they slip down her throat. 'He hasn't shared it with the rest of them. Yet. But he will I guess.'

'If you keep digging,' Liam repeats quietly, as if the gravity of the situation is only just sinking in.

'There's more,' Jenna says tentatively. 'I don't think he acted alone; I think there are two of them. I've been thinking about this. Thinking about how he could have got to my drink and, honestly, I was so careful, I didn't leave it out of my sight, and I didn't drink the one that he bought for me either.'

'So, you think someone else might have spiked your drink? Someone else who was there from the group?'

'Before Kirsten left, she and Duncan offered me a lift home. And Duncan was pretty insistent. He kept saying that I should leave with them, wouldn't take no for an answer, to the point of being annoying. And, I know this sounds crazy, but he bought me my last drink, and well, he could have slipped something into it. Thinking I was going home with them. I don't know, maybe he planned to drop Kirsten back home first and then...' Jenna stops talking. Stops thinking out loud because even after everything she knows, she still can't believe that Duncan is capable of doing something as horrific as this. And judging by the look of disbelief on Liam's face right now, he isn't sure if he believes it either.

'Duncan? Kirsten's Duncan?' Liam almost laughs at the suggestion.

'I know how it sounds and, trust me, that's the last conclusion I would ever have come to, only I found something on his computer last night.' Jenna goes to her pile of notes that she'd been pawing over earlier in the evening and takes the list of names and dates that she'd managed to scrawl down in her notebook.

Handing it to Liam.

'This is what I've been working on. These are some of the women in the area who have been spiked and sexually assaulted recently. At least one of them was raped. I looked it up. Kirsten launched the public appeal for the paper.'

'So what? It's a list of people who were assaulted. Maybe that's who he's getting his information from then. Maybe he's trying to help Kirsten play detective to gain some brownie points. It must be hard for her, seeing all the success you've had lately.' Liam shrugs clearly not convinced.

Which is exactly what Jenna had expected. She'd expected that from Kirsten too. Complete and utter disbelief.

'Most of these names do not come up when I search them, and most of the dates beside them don't coincide with the dates of anyone reporting being spiked and/or assaulted. Which means not all of these women have come forward and reported these crimes at all. There's no way that Kirsten would know these names. I went to see one of the women earlier today. Sharon Hargreaves. She confirmed it, told me that she hasn't told a soul about what happened to her. That she too had her drink spiked. She hasn't told her husband, her friends, not the police. She's the only one who knew. Other than the man who spiked her drink.'

'Duncan?' Liam shakes his head, incredulous, as it sinks in. 'I mean, whatever I think about the bloke, he's hardly criminal mastermind material, is he? Doesn't he work doing something mundanely boring in IT? You really think he's capable of doing all of this?' Liam waves the list at Jenna. 'That somehow he's managed to keep all these dark sordid secrets hidden from Kirsten. That he's really capable of being this calculating?

'Have you told Kirsten any of this?'

'How can I? Where would I even start?' Jenna shakes her head. 'They are having some problems right now, too,' she confides.

'No shit!'

'She keeps calling me, but I can't bring myself to answer the phone to her. I don't know what to say. I can't tell her any of this until I have more proof, because she won't believe me. She won't want to believe me.'

'And how are you going to get that? Because you can't stay in that group, Jenna. You can't risk your identity being revealed. You can't risk those kinds of blokes finding out who and where you are and coming after you. You know what they are capable of doing.'

'I've started to visit the women on the list. Maybe, just maybe, I'll be able to gather enough information and evidence that we'll be able to uncover his identity. That we'll finally have the proof. One way or another.'

'What you need, Jenna, is to leave this well alone.' Liam shakes his head in disagreement. 'If, and I mean if Duncan is involved, then this is too close to home. Too personal. And this other bloke, Mike? If he's from the incel group too and they are both somehow connected and carrying out these acts together then you're really not safe. That group is dangerous, Jenna. I know what happened to you was awful, but you got away. Thankfully there was no harm done. This isn't down to you to solve. Sometimes you've got to put yourself first. No story is worth your life.'

'I know,' she says, genuinely lost for words. Genuinely lost for a way of getting to the truth without one of them getting seriously hurt.

She starts crying again as she realises the severity of what she is involved in.

But she knows she can't stop now, Liam is right: it is personal.

She also knows, when Liam leans in and wraps his arm around her, how he is completely unaware that he is holding her together right now. All of her broken pieces.

Him being here is the only thing keeping her from falling apart.

She isn't sure if it's the warmth of the wine as it surges through her, or the relief she feels now that she's said it all out loud, or maybe it's the heat of him against her, but when Liam reaches down to kiss her, Jenna does the one thing she had promised herself she would never do, and kisses him back.

3 2

EVIE

I want her back.

As soon as I admit this to myself all the feelings of guilt and regret and sadness that swell inside me suddenly melt away. I need to get her back. I stare at the envelope that I took from the baby box. My pitiful exchange for my child. A list of numbers I can call for support should I need to. An emergency hotline.

Such a pathetic swap, I had thought to myself at the time, when I'd taken it. So convinced that I wouldn't need it, that I would never choose to make the call.

I don't need these people's help or support.

What I do need though, is my baby back. I'll explain everything. I'll tell them how I'd been forced to give Holly up against my will. That it had never been my choice. Not really. That I'd only ever wanted to keep her safe, to keep her far away from him.

Him.

He did this. He took everything from me and left me hollow, with nothing. I did what he demanded I do.

She's gone, and now I am suffering more than ever. The

excruciating pain inside of me worse than anything he physically did to me. I don't feel safe, and how can I know if she is?

How can she be? Out there somewhere in the world, held by the arms of complete strangers that aren't capable of loving her even half as much as I do.

I wonder if she feels it too. The vast echoing void of emptiness and nothingness growing rapidly inside of her. Just as I feel it expand inside of me.

Will she grow up believing that I didn't care or want her? That she wasn't enough.

No. I can't let him do this. His threats and taunts are one thing, but keeping me away from my daughter is something else completely.

I can't do it. This.

I can't just sit here and do nothing. Say nothing.

My hands shake with rage and fury and I tap out my angry words in the message.

You raped me. She is proof of what you did to me. Her DNA is proof of that. If you come anywhere near me and my daughter ever again I will make sure they find you. That they lock you away for good and throw away the key.

It was stupid of me. Foolish even. Thinking that I was finally standing up for myself. Fighting back with my own loaded threats, playing him at his own game for once. Thinking that somehow, I could win. That he was an equal opponent.

What chance do I stand against him?

Biological fathers have rights to see their children too. You'd never be able to keep her from me. That will be nice, won't it? Co-parenting.

The words spin out from the screen of my phone, and I sink down to my knees on the floor, as if I don't I will lose my mind.

There it is. The price I would pay if I went through with trying to get her back.

Biological fathers? Rapists!

He is right about that.

Rapists have rights too. I've looked it up, as I've lain awake at night distraught about it. Already on the brink of turning crazy, this latest threat might just do it.

I start to cry.

That's his trump card. If he gets caught, this is how he'll punish me. That's how he'll still be able to get to me and continue his sick and twisted games. Admitting to what he did would prove he was Holly's father, but he'd make that work for him too by using it against me forever.

He could pretend to be a reformed man, and get visitation rights.

More rights than me, because I have none now.

I gave her up. I gave her away.

He would love that. The power and control that he'd forever hold over me.

The damage he would do to her, just to get to me.

I can never get her back.

33

JENNA

Jenna opens her eyes. Her head is pounding, and she feels slightly groggy as the onset of a mild hangover sweeps over her. Grabbing her phone from the side, she winces at the harsh glare of light, pleased to see that she's woken before her alarm.

It's still early: 6 a.m.

Liam.

Thoughts of him, last night, fill her head.

Him kissing her. His mouth hot and firm against hers, pressing against her with force and wanting, and she had wanted him right back. It had all happened so quickly, so naturally. Before she had time to think about what they were doing, she was almost naked on the lounge floor and Liam was writhing away on top of her.

Remembering the heat of it all, the intensity of his thrusts, how she had thrown her head back and groaned loudly as she had climaxed, she winces now at her vulnerability.

The cliche they'd become.

She'd slept with her boss. She'd slept with Liam.

Feeling her face flush red, she sits up in her bed and stares around the room, looking for traces of him. Glad that the room is empty, and all Liam's things have gone. A wave of relief rippling through her that he has decided to leave early and spare them both from that awkward dance around each other this morning, while both secretly wonder if the other was feeling regret.

And there is so much regret.

Pools of anxiety swell inside of her as she recalls how it only took a few mouthfuls of wine until all of her pent-up secrets had so willingly poured out of her.

She could trust him, couldn't she?

Liam might be a lot of things, but a gossip wasn't one of them. He wouldn't tell anyone. He had sworn to her. Promised her, and Jenna had believed him at the time.

Did she believe him now?

It had been the second glass that had tipped her over the edge.

Perhaps it had been the relief of finally saying everything out loud. Perhaps it was because she didn't drink any more, or the fact that she hadn't eaten all day, or that her body was simply exhausted, or a mixture of all the above. Whatever the reason, the wine had gone to her head.

Making her feel light and untouchable and numb. Making her do things without thinking about the consequences. The repercussions. The people who could get hurt.

Her. Him.

Kirsten.

Kirsten would usually be the first person she called in a situation like this, when she woke all flustered and panicked, knowing that she'd royally fucked up. Her best friend always knew what to say, always gave her the perfect advice. But there was no way that she could call her now.

She'd broken the code. The unspoken rule of not sleeping with your best friend's ex. Especially when said ex had been a notorious shit.

Liam had hurt Kirsten all those years ago, before moving on swiftly to his next conquest as if Kirsten had never existed. Even if that hadn't happened. Her and Liam. Liam and Kirsten. Jenna still couldn't bring herself to call her friend.

She'd purposely ignored so many missed calls, still unable to bear to speak to her, knowing what she did about Duncan.

Where would she start? Where would she even begin?

Getting up and padding her way out to the kitchen she sees the note that Liam has left by the kettle.

Had to leave. I took the letter. Going to post it online. Talk later x

Jenna eyes the kiss and winces. It feels too intimate. As if it's crossing too many boundaries.

Tapping the newspaper's website into her phone, Jenna reads the Missing Mother's letter that's been published on the site. She notes the time. Four hours ago.

Liam mustn't have slept. He must have left after she'd fallen asleep so that he could prioritise breaking the story first thing this morning. In time for the paper to go to print. Already the news had traction. Reshared online by other news outlets and plastered all over social media. Which of course brought a fresh influx of comments and speculation about who this woman could be and why they should be looking for her.

Work.

This is what she needs to stay focused.

This is what would help her stay out of her head.

Jenna licks her lips noting how dry her mouth is, how she needs a strong cup of coffee and to jump in the shower before she is able to face the day.

To face another victim of the attacks.

That's what she is going to do she decides. Despite Liam's

warnings not to, she's going to visit the next woman on Duncan's list.

Because Liam was right about one thing. This had become personal. Which only gave her even more reason to want justice for the victims, as well as herself.

34

EVIE

I don't know what possessed me to open my front door. Usually I call out first, to check who's standing out there on the other side. Other times, when I don't even feel like doing that, I stop dead, no matter where I'm standing in the flat and hold my breath. Pretending I'm not home until whoever it is out there gets bored of waiting for a reply and finally takes the hint to leave.

Only the CCTV footage that was published yesterday, and the letter that was printed this morning have turned my brain to moosh and I'm clearly not thinking straight.

I'm not thinking at all.

Because the last person I expect to see as I pull the door open is her.

Jenna Stone.

'Hi, it's Evie Monroe, isn't it? I'm sorry to just turn up like this unannounced: my name is Jenna Stone. I'm a journalist with the *Islington Gazette*,' she starts before holding up the bouquet of brightly coloured flowers and making some weak attempt to persuade me that she isn't here professionally. She only wants to talk, she says. Nothing we say will go on the record.

At least I think that's what she says, only suddenly my hearing is replaced with the warped sound of loud ringing in my ears. My vision starts to blur to a muted dark grey and thousands of tiny white spots form in front of my eyes, and I start to sway on my feet, about to lose my footing. My body is pricked with waves of panic and terror as I try and work out why she is really here.

Why she is standing at my door, now. So soon after the CCTV image and the letter were released into the world.

She knows. Oh my god, she knows!

She knows about Holly. She knows who I am.

She's finally worked out that I am the missing mother.

She's good I'll give her that. Making out that she's only here under the guise of a friendly chat, when what she really wants is the next instalment of the story so she can share it with the world.

My story. I grip the doorframe just as my legs give way beneath me, and she is next to me then, wrapping her arm around me, holding me up.

'Evie? Are you okay, here, let me help you...'

She guides me back inside, to the kitchen table, and as much as I want to shrug her off, to push her as far away from me as my strength will allow, I'm scared that without her I will collapse to the ground.

Reluctantly, I allow her to lower me carefully onto the chair.

'Let me get you some cold water,' she says, slamming around in my empty cupboards before picking up a dirty glass from the side and rinsing it out.

She places it down in front of me, and I gulp it down greedily as the dense fog in my head starts to gradually settle.

Desperate to compose myself, to bring myself back inside of

my body, I wonder if she can see that every part of me is quivering silently with fear of what she is about to say, as I grip the glass tighter to disguise how the water sloshes against the sides.

Breathe.

'I'm sorry to just turn up, I did try calling a few times first but you didn't answer,' she says weakly. Awkwardly. Guessing there was a reason why I didn't want to take any calls, yet she came here anyway.

Today, I don't want to see or talk to anyone. Especially not her. I don't want anything to do with her.

Turning up like this, unannounced.

Unwelcome.

I want to say all of that to her, but right now I can't find my voice.

So, I bide my time, and drink the rest of my water, letting her talk first while I compose myself some more.

'Are you okay?' she asks finally, now that we have sat for a minute or so, though the tension in the room is so taut that the awkward silence could have spun out for an hour or more.

I nod and watch as her eyes sweep the room, as if she's quickly assessing the dirt and chaos of my kitchen, as if she is assessing me.

She is trying her hardest not to outwardly judge me. Not to show the shock or disgust on her face, but I see it there anyway, how she's looking around at all of the filth and the grime and wondering how I can live like this.

The curtains drawn to block the world out, a sour pungent stench of an overflowing bin filling the air around us. A pile of dirty dishes towering in a sink filled with scud-filmed water.

When she puts her eyes back on me, they soften.

I wonder if she sees it in me too. The disgust I feel for myself. How I deserve to live in this squalor. How I haven't washed or showered for days. I don't have the energy or the inclination, because let's face who cares about me? Not even I care about me now.

She must see it too, as she takes in my greasy ponytail that is tied at the nape of my neck. The baggy, shapeless clothes that I'm wearing, creased from being slept in.

Oversized, elasticated, to hide the deflated, hollow mess of a body beneath them.

I'm festering. In my own sadness. In my own misery.

Locked away from this world inside these four claustrophobic walls.

And now she is here judging me.

I don't bite. I don't dare. Not until I know what her real reasons are for being here.

'Why have you come here?' I ask, my heart pounding in my chest as I brace myself ready to tell more lies. Because just because she says it out loud, accuses me of it, doesn't make it true.

She'd have to prove it, wouldn't she?

She'd have more than just a hunch. More than just a feeling that I look vaguely like the shadowy, blurred figure in the CCTV footage. That's all she has, I tell myself. That's all she's got.

'I wanted to talk to you about what happened.' She clears her throat as if she is searching for the words with less damage attached to them. 'When you were attacked.'

I push my bottom lip over my top lip subconsciously, as if I'm frightened of what will come out of my mouth if I don't physically stop myself from speaking.

'I know that it's been difficult—' she starts and that's enough.

That is all that it takes for the eruption of rage to explode out from me.

'Difficult?' The laugh that leaves my throat is a bitter, aggressive cackle. So raucous that it almost makes me choke.

'Difficult? You know, do you? You know how it feels to be raped? Then to have that rape splashed all over the papers. Have people reading all those horrific things that bastard did to me, for their own entertainment while they're casually sipping coffee and eating their Coco Pops.' I slam my hand down on the table, sloshing water from my glass all over the wood. 'You know what it's like to have comments written all over social media, to have all those disgusting things written about me. Sent to me in private messages. All those threats of what other men would like to do to me.' I can feel the tears gathering in my eyes, but I will not cry. I will not bloody cry. Not again. Not any more. 'I listened when the police said that they would help me, and they lied.'

Jenna hangs her head and looks ashamed, and I am glad.

Glad when she doesn't answer. Glad when she can't find the words. Because there are none. None good enough for me.

'It was your newspaper that led him back to me. I should never have listened to the police. By getting me to go public about my attack and doing that fucking appeal, you all led him straight to me.'

'I know that you think that...' Jenna starts before she shakes her head. 'I know that's how it looks. But you weren't his only victim, Evie. You weren't the only one he did any of this to. I don't think he found you through the police or the paper. I met another woman yesterday that he did this to, too. He didn't rape her but he'd drugged her probably with that intention. She hadn't told a soul. Not her husband, not her friends, not the police. But he'd done it to her too. Stalking her. Trying to make her life miserable. It's all part of it for him. Tormenting his victims. It's part of his game. He gets off on it.' Jenna takes a deep breath. 'There are other women out there, too scared and traumatised to come forward. Other women just like you.'

Jenna pauses, her eyes fixed on mine, and she knows she has my full attention now.

But still I look away. My gaze fixed on the pretty bunch of flowers on the table that I assume she brought to soften me up before she broaches the subject of the baby, only she hasn't mentioned her and she doesn't look as if she intends to.

It's only when we sit there for a few more seconds in silence that it finally clicks.

She really doesn't know, does she? She has no idea.

She's not here about Holly; she's here about *him*.

She's got something to tell me about him.

'I was spiked too, Evie. He did it to me.'

'He did it to you? So, you got him then? You finally caught him?' I ask, eyes full of hope. That this is why she is really here.

Finally, she's got him. Finally, there's news.

She shakes her head. And that's all I need to know. That's all I really need to listen to.

She continues talking regardless, explaining that she's been investigating a group of men on an incel site. There's a list apparently. With all our names.

She thinks there are possibly two men carrying out the attacks, but there are plenty more joining in afterwards and taunting the women. Making their lives hell.

When she's finished, I feel a strange feeling of solace, to know that I'm not suffering alone. That's why she is here.

This is personal for her now too.

'I wanted to show you a photo. I wanted to see if you recognise this man.'

She gets her phone out and holds it up, and I stare at the face on the screen with heightened fear and suspicion, just as I've done with every man I've seen since. Taking in their features, staring at their eyes, inhaling their smell.

Paranoid of every single one of them, because any one of them could be him.

'You know him?' I ask. Because she is there in the photo too. She'd tried to crop herself out but her finger has slipped revealing the entire image. A group of them, a family, friends, laughing, love.

'It doesn't matter, I just want to know if you recognise him.' Jenna shakes her head. Knowing that I would want to know, that I have a right to know. Only Jenna can't tell me. Or rather, she won't tell me.

'It doesn't matter?' I nod as the finality of her words sink in. 'This might be him; this might be the bastard that did *that* to me, and it doesn't matter who he is? Why are you protecting him? Is that why you are really here? So that if you do find out that your friend or whoever the fuck he is to you, did this to me so what? You can make it go away.'

I stand up and go to the door of my flat and open it wide.

'Maybe that's what I should do. Make it all go away. Make him go away. Why not, huh? I've got nothing left to lose. Maybe I should put an end to it all. An end to him. Destroy him like he did to me,' I say. And when she tries to talk to me, tries to explain, to appease me, to talk me round I scream.

'GET OUT! GET OUT! GET OUT!'

I slam the door and sink down to the floor as the sobbing starts.

Time is running out for me; I can feel it.

How the clock is ticking, as the feeling of impending doom hangs over me.

I've felt it from the minute I set eyes on the footage they posted in the newspaper of me earlier. The letter they printed, pleading with them, begging them all to keep my daughter safe.

How it's only a matter of time until they work it out.

Until Jenna works it out, because as much as I despise her, I know that she isn't stupid.

She is getting close.

If she even so much as suspects that I am the missing mother, what's to stop her from printing my secrets all over that rag of a newspaper she writes for?

Another exclusive story to share with the entire watching world of complete strangers invested in the tragedy that has unfolded before them.

My tragedy.

My life.

If Jenna pieces the stories together and works out that they are linked, she could use Holly's DNA to gain the evidence she desperately seeks in order to take the man down who did this to me.

She'd have her proof then, wouldn't she? That the rapist's blood is running through my tiny daughter's veins.

What am I supposed to do now? Just stay here like a petrified deer, caught in the bright, stark headlights of an oncoming vehicle as it comes hurtling towards me, waiting patiently for the inevitable slam of metal into me.

Like I've been doing the past nine months, hiding away, hiding from him.

I saw what Jenna saw today when she was here.

A weak, broken woman.

Forever his victim.

I'm not doing it any more; I'm not spending my life worried about him finding me, finding her. I'm not spending my life hiding away.

There's only one way to stop him coming for me, and that's if I get to him first.

35

HIM

She hasn't deleted her fake profile. She's still there in the group.

Festering like a bad smell.

Worse than that, she's managed to get her hands on that fucking list and she's contacting all the women. Building a case against him so that she can expose him. She's proving to be a royal pain in the arse. Because she won't let this go. She is like a dog with a bone now.

Clearly drugging her and threatening her with notes wasn't enough of a warning, because she isn't going to drop this now, is she?

If anything, it seems to have become more personal. She wants to be the one to catch him and reveal his actions to the world. To bring him to justice.

Take him down in a blaze of glory.

He was going to have to work harder to scare her off.

Jenna Stone is proving to be a bigger problem than he'd anticipated.

A problem that he needs to eliminate.

36

JENNA

Jenna turns again in the dimly lit street, the second time in as many minutes as she scans the road for the noise she had heard behind her.

Footsteps. Close.

But when she looks there is nothing. No one.

The street remains quiet and empty as the streetlamps flicker through the downpour of rain, casting their eerie dancing shadows as the droplets come down heavier now.

She is soaked through; most smart people have taken shelter in the warmth of their houses, she thinks as she jealously eyes the warm yellow hue of lights that eminates from the windows.

Home, inside in the warm. Which is exactly where Jenna wants to be right now.

Snuggled in her cosy warm tracksuit, on the sofa, with a hot mug of coffee.

Instead, she is out here, with wet clumps of hair stuck to her freezing cold face, her coat soaked, stuck to the sodden outfit beneath it.

She shivers, clutching her keys in a tightly balled fist. Not just through fear but from habit.

She is not being followed, she reassures herself as she turns and continues, quickening her pace.

She is just being paranoid. On edge after visiting Evie Monroe.

She knew that it was going to be hard. That Evie wouldn't appreciate the unwelcome intrusion of her unannounced visit, dredging up the painful memories of the brutal attack she'd endured, with open arms, but she hadn't been expecting what she'd found waiting for her.

That shell of a woman, who had seemed so on edge, so terrified.

Living that half-life behind those closed curtains.

After all this time.

Jenna hated herself for thinking that way, for thinking that what Evie went through was something she could simply pick herself up from, brush herself down and move on.

She was raped, Jenna. Violently raped and left for dead. You don't just get over that. You never get over that.

She hears the noise come again behind her.

Definite footsteps that time. The scuff of a boot, the stamp of a puddle.

And as much as she wants to tell herself to stop being stupid, stop feeding into her paranoia, she isn't one to keep her back to danger and hope it goes away.

Jenna turns around ready to face whatever the threat is head on.

Whoever the threat is.

Eyeing the figure of a man further back, who is walking with purpose towards her. His coat pulled up covering half of his face.

She feels her body tense with fear, as she grips her keys tighter.

It's him, Mike, the man from the bar the other night. Even from this distance, in this heavy downpour, without being able to see his face properly, something deep within her alerts her that it is him.

Closer. Closer still.

She fights the urge to turn and run.

No. She will not run. She will not show fear.

She will call his bluff and show him that she is not scared of him. That she is not like the others that he has tormented: she won't be his victim.

She is on to him.

Raising her arm, her fist locked tight around the sharp metal of her keys, ready to strike out if she needs to, and she thinks she might need to, she watches in dismay as he makes a sharp right turn, in through the garden gate just a few feet from where she is standing.

She stares, her eyes fixed on the pool of bright yellow light pouring out onto the wet pavement as the door is pulled open and the excited sound of a child as they run into the man's arms yelling: 'Daddy!'

Catching a glimpse of his face lit up in the doorway, she realises that it isn't him at all.

Shit, Jenna!

She drops her arm and lets out the breath that has been lodged deep down in her chest, watching as the door closes and the street is plunged back into silence once more.

Silence apart from the rhythmic drumming of rain as it hammers down all around her.

Pulling her coat up around her own face, she walks faster, silently cursing herself for being so stupid, so foolish as to let herself freak out at the sight of every man she met.

Reaching her flat Jenna hurries inside, stripping her clothes in the bathroom and chucking the sopping wet pile in the bathtub to deal with later, before she pulls on a comfy tracksuit and pours herself a hot mug of coffee to warm herself up.

Only she can't relax.

She can't stop thinking about Evie and her torment since her attack. How she, just like Sharon Hargreaves, had been subjected to such vile abuse and stalking since. How he allowed these men to have tormented them both, and the other women he'd attacked for so long. Willingly given them all ammunition.

Though compared to the other women it seemed that Jenna was getting off lightly for now.

Grabbing her laptop, she sits cross-legged on the sofa and – even though she knows she shouldn't, she'd promised Liam she wouldn't, that for her own safety she would stay away from the forum, that she wouldn't risk putting herself in any more danger than she'd already exposed herself to – Jenna logs in to the incel site.

Because she wants to see if Duncan has been online again and posted anything. She wants to see if she can find any more links between him and Mike.

Mike hasn't posted anything. So, Jenna skims her way through the vitriol, trying not to focus too hard on the vile, disgusting comments posted there. Trying not to allow her energy to stray, because she's not sure she can stomach much more of this.

She clicks on Duncan's username.

His first post is a blurred photo of the CCTV image of the missing mother taken from the article they'd printed in the paper. Underneath that are two links.

One is the article about Holly. Her tiny innocent face staring out at the camera, not knowing that she is any part of this.

The second article is what makes Jenna sit up straighter, instantly adjusting the angle of her laptop screen as if she's not seeing something right.

Her eyes home in on the article that's been posted beneath the image. Her head spins as she tries to make sense of what she's seeing. As she tries to piece the two things together.

It's the article that Kirsten wrote. The public appeal she'd put out following the interview she had done with Evie Monroe following her attack.

Kirsten had launched the appeal for witnesses to come forward, to urge other women to be brave and reach out. To let the attacker know that they were coming for him.

Why was this posted underneath the photograph of Holly?

She thinks about how Evie Monroe had looked as if she was about to pass out when she'd seen Jenna standing on her doorstep earlier this afternoon.

How on edge she had been.

Hiding away inside that filthy cesspit of a flat.

Jenna had assumed that what she'd told her was true. That she was still being anonymously hounded by her attacker and his army of cronies. That she was still struggling, still trying to pick up the fragmented pieces of her destroyed, shattered life.

How her legs had buckled beneath her, and her skin had drained of all colour at the sight of Jenna, at the reminder of what she represented, all those painful memories: though that hadn't been why at all.

Evie Monroe had almost passed out at the sight of a journalist standing at her front door, just hours after that CCTV footage and her letter had gone live.

Jenna clicks back on Kirsten's article, zooming in on the date that was printed underneath.

The attack Evie had endured had happened nine months ago.

An audible gasp leaves her mouth as she realises that Holly is her baby.

That's why Evie had been acting so on edge earlier this afternoon.

Because of what she has to hide.

Evie Monroe is the missing mother.

37

JENNA

'Jenna? Open the door. I'm not going away until you speak to me. I just want to check you're okay!' Kirsten pounds on Jenna's front door.

'Hi,' Jenna says as she reluctantly opens it, knowing that Kirsten means it. She will stand there all night if she has to. She is stubborn like that.

'Hi? You haven't answered my calls for two days, you almost didn't answer the door to me tonight, but hi! That's it?' Kirsten eyes Jenna with a genuine look of concern on her face that makes Jenna feel bad for avoiding her.

'I was worried about you, Jenna, after the other night and what happened to you...' She pauses knowing how Jenna doesn't want to be continuously reminded of that. 'I just wanted to check you were okay. But you didn't answer my calls and then you didn't even return them. Are you okay? Has something happened?'

Jenna shakes her head, because she knows if she speaks, her lies won't hold any real conviction and Kirsten will see straight through them. See straight through her.

'I'm fine,' she says finally. 'I'm sorry, I've just had a lot on.'

'You wanna talk about it? It's horrible out there, I could do with a cuppa. Janet's at home with the kids.'

'Where's Duncan?'

'I don't know, seeing to this project he's working on probably! Don't ask me, I'm only his wife.' Kirsten tries to make light of the real emotion in her voice as she speaks about the man she is married to.

'I take it you didn't sort things out then, after the row you had the other night?'

It's Kirsten's turn to shake her head.

'No. I've barely seen him and when I have, he seems preoccupied. So, are you going to invite me in then?' Kirsten says after a few seconds of Jenna standing awkwardly in the doorway, making no such attempt.

'Ahh, I'd love to, but I'm just about to call it a night actually. I've had a busy few days.' Jenna lies again, her head still spinning with all the things she's yet to share with Kirsten. Duncan's posts on the incel thread, her being with Liam, Evie Monroe being the missing mother. That they both knew her all along.

'Yeah, I saw that you've been busy.' Kirsten nods, clearly getting the message loud and clear. 'Take it that was your idea getting that letter up online. I thought we agreed that we weren't going to share that. In case it put the missing mother in even more danger. How did you manage to persuade Liam?'

'I didn't,' Jenna says, unable to hide the defensive tone. 'It was his idea, actually. He thought it was worth putting it out there while everything was still so fresh in people's minds.'

'For the clickbait you mean.' Kirsten rolls her sarcastically; like Jenna she'll know that Liam would be loving the drama that's unfolding and the fact that it's his newspaper that is holding centre stage.

'He thinks it might soften things with Legal.'

'And what about you? Do you still think there's a chance

that the missing mother might see it? That she'll come forward?'
Kirsten asks.

'Yeah, I think there's always a chance,' Jenna says vaguely,
hoping that might be true.

She'd seen for herself the way Evie had behaved when she'd
seen her, the way she was living.

Maybe she regretted giving Holly up.

'Look, Jenna. I don't know what's going on right now, with
us, but I feel as if you're shutting me out. Have I done something wrong? You've stopped confiding in me. You're not
answering my calls. And now you and Liam have clearly made
the decision to publish the letter behind my back. Was it
because I told you not to? It wasn't personal. I know how much
Holly's story means to you, Jenna. But you can't change fate;
maybe her destiny is with a different family altogether. We
don't know the mother's reasoning for giving her up. But maybe
she did the right thing. I just don't want you getting too
involved, too consumed by it all.'

'Liam and I didn't make any decisions purposely behind
your back. He asked for the letter, and I gave it to him. And as
for Holly's story, I can't just sit back and do nothing, not when
there's even the tiniest chance that I might be able to make a
difference. And I'm not mad at you, you haven't done anything
wrong. Like I said, I just have a lot going on.'

'Like what? Has something else happened?'

'No.' Jenna shakes her head. 'I just decided that I'm going to
start looking into the victims of the spikings again. The sexual
assaults, Evie Monroe's attack. I feel as if they are all linked to
the man I met in the bar the other night.'

Linked to your husband.

That's what she doesn't say. *Your husband who has played a
role in this too. Only I don't know how much of a sick, twisted
part he is playing in all of this. And I still need more proof.*

'Please tell me that you're not still on that incel site?'

Kirsten immediately knows by the look on Jenna's face that she is. 'It's too dangerous, Jenna. If they know that you, a journalist, a female journalist at that, is digging around, it wouldn't be hard to track you down. And you've seen what some of them are capable of, Jenna. These people are not right in the head.'

'Oh, I know. Trust me, I know, but please, don't worry about me, I'm a big girl. I know what I'm doing.'

'Okay, well, as long as you're okay.' Kirsten nods, a look on her face that tells Jenna that she senses that there is more to it. That Jenna is keeping things from her, important things, but whatever they were, tonight wasn't going to be the night she confides in her. Knowing that something doesn't add up, but she isn't going to get her answers.

Not tonight.

'Look, I'm really tired. I'll speak to you soon okay?' Jenna says, stepping back inside, ready to close the front door.

'Oh, that's Liam's, isn't it?' Kirsten stares past her, her eyes fixed on something behind her.

'Liam? No.' Her words coming out flustered, as she turns to see what it is that has caught Kirsten's eye. She sees Liam's green chequered scarf hanging from the hook on the wall. He must have forgotten to take it with him when he left in the early hours of this morning.

'Is that why? Is he here now?' She looks like she thinks she has finally worked it out. Why Jenna is being so standoffish and hasn't invited her inside.

That she has figured out her secret.

'No,' Jenna starts, caught off guard at the directness of Kirsten's question.

'But he's been here though?'

'Well, yeah. He was. He's gone now. He popped in last night...' She feels the flush of heat spread across the apples of her cheeks giving her away. 'For the letter.'

'Oh my god, you have to be kidding me. Are you serious

right now? We don't talk for what, two days, and suddenly you and Liam... Something happened between you, didn't it? Is that why you've been avoiding me?'

'No. We're not a thing. It isn't like that,' Jenna realises too late that by trying to explain she'd just inadvertently admitted that something had gone on between them. 'And I'm not avoiding you,' she says, hoping to keep Kirsten's attention focused on that part of the conversation.

Only it's out there now and Kirsten has no intention of letting it go.

'It isn't like that?' Kirsten repeats, shaking her head. 'I can't believe that you would do that, go there, with him. After everything.' There is a look on Kirsten's face that Jenna can't read but it looks more like disappointment than anger.

'Christ, Kirsten. It's really not a big deal. It was nothing, besides, you and Liam were what? Five years ago, now?' Jenna exclaims knowing how defensive she sounds, knowing how instead of coming from a place of attack she should have told Kirsten about this before she found out; she should have had more tact.

'And you weren't together for much more than five minutes,' she adds, knowing how her words would sting but it was as if she had no control over that.

'There was a reason for that,' Kirsten says tartly.

'Because you weren't right for each other and he moved on.'

'Rapidly. With just about every girl in the office since. You were the only woman in our office he hadn't slept with; you were probably like the ultimate prize for him. My so-called best mate. I bet he's loving that.'

'It's not all about you, Kirsten,' Jenna says defensively. 'Look. Just because you're unhappy right now, doesn't mean the rest of the world has to be too.'

Kirsten shakes her head, an expression on her face that says she is about to say something. That she was going to stand up for herself and say something equally as cutting, only she decides against it at the last second.

'You know what, I'm sorry that I bothered you! I'll leave you to it.'

Kirsten steps back from the door. Holding her hands up as if calling a truce. A look of hurt on her face, telling Jenna that she's gone too far.

'Shit! I'm sorry, Kirsten, I didn't mean that,' she calls out but it's already too late. Kirsten is already heading out of the flat's main doors.

Jenna walks back to her flat and shuts the door before leaning her back up against it.

She had been cruel, unnecessarily cutting. And deep down she knew that what she had done with Liam had been wrong. She knew that it would hurt Kirsten to find out that they'd been together like that, after the way he'd hurt her.

The problem was that now that she and Liam had become a thing, Jenna felt as if she actually quite liked the idea.

38

EVIE

The rain streaks across the windscreen distorting my view of the street that runs along the front of *Islington Gazette*'s offices.

Tonight, in this downpour, the notoriously busy London road appears eerily quieter than usual.

I pull to the kerb and switch the engine off, instantly killing the bright white head beam that spans mesmerising patterns across the puddled-filled potholes in the tarmac.

I like it out here. Sat in my car, hidden away, under a blanket of darkness. It gives me a sense of security, a sense of isolation. As the rain drums outside and the metal roof of the car cocoons me inside from all the elements.

Shifting my body back in the driver's seat, I get comfortable, prepared to settle in for however long this might take.

Until Jenna comes out. That's if she's even there. Because this might just be the worst idea I've ever had, but where she works is the only address I have for her. The only place that I know there's a sure chance of finding her.

I'm hopeful, hopeful that the CCTV footage and the letter that was published in their paper will mean that they are all in there, being kept busy.

That *she* is in there.

I'd been too reactive earlier when Jenna had turned up at my flat, too emotional. I know that now. I have thought about nothing else since she walked out. I should have stayed composed and not reacted, instead of screaming at her to leave the first time the conversation got too uncomfortable and the burning fire of rage inside me got the better of me. I might have been able to persuade her to give me his name.

My attacker.

I know she knows his name. I know she knows who he is. I saw the expression on her face, how she'd grabbed the phone away as soon as she'd realised her error.

How she was in the photograph too. A group of them, standing smiling around a Christmas tree.

Smiling with *him*.

A family member perhaps? A friend?

She is linked to him.

If I'm going to find him, it's going to be through her.

I feel as if I'm going crazy, still not having any answers. If anything, I have more now. Why is Jenna Stone protecting him? Is this what it is really about? The tirade of bullying and torment I've been receiving online every time she announces intimate events and details about my life in the newspaper.

The attack. Leaving Holly, and now the CCTV footage and the letter.

It's as if nothing is sacred.

Does she know?

Does she have a personal vendetta against me? Can I even trust her?

I must. And she owes me that much at least.

I watch the reflections of rainwater shimmer as they land in the pools of water on the road, the streetlights above them creating a hypnotic play of light. Feeling calmer now, more tranquil, at making my decision. I am angry, I am furious, but I'm not scared any more. I am not prepared to hide away in my flat alone any more. As if I'm the one who's done something wrong.

I'm going to take my power back; I'm going to find the man that did this to me and I'm going to make him pay.

That's the only way to end this for good.

Jenna Stone is going to give me his name.

I'm not sure how long I have sat here, long enough to feel my eyes start to droop, for my breath to slow and the warmth of the car start to lull me to sleep. But I sit up alert at the sudden movement at the front of the building. A smartly dressed man pushing his way out of the office doors.

Not Jenna, I think, about to settle back in my chair, only I see a second man following him.

There is something about the speed he is walking, the exaggerated movement of his arms.

They are arguing about something.

Sitting forward to try and get a better look, I strain to see through the pouring rain. Wiping my hand against the windscreen as my heavy panting breaths start steaming up the glass, blurring my view.

I lower my window so that I can hear what's being said, only the sound of the rain drowns all the noise out and I'm too late anyway.

One of the men is storming off.

I watch the door for anyone else leaving the office. For anyone else following them out the door. Only the street is quiet again.

Eerily quiet.

And that's when I see him. *And I know in that instant that it is HIM.*

The memory of what he did to me is back inside my head after nine months of purposely blocking it out.

I no longer have to try and conjure up an image of him, or imagine what his face looks like.

It's there, even after trying to erase it from my mind.
It's always been there.
And I am immediately back there again.

39

EVIE

THEN

Am I dead?

I think that I might be as a brilliant white screen of light floods my vision.

There's a feeling of numbness, of nothingness. A feeling of being outside of my body.

The glare of light is blinding. Haven't people claimed that they see it when they die? A long tunnel of light that they feel enticed to walk towards.

Only I don't feel the pull of it.

Instead, the harsh brightness causes me to flinch. Making me want only to close my eyes tightly and block it out.

Part of me is relieved that my reflex is to shut it out.

The next time I open my eyes, I know for certain that I am still here.

To me, that resistance is proof that I'm still inside of my body.

Proof that I am still very much alive.

Where am I?

I am lying on my back, I realise. Staring up at the early dawn sky.

Somewhere outside.

It's cold and my body trembles violently, frozen, as I sink down into the wet dewy grass beneath me. Why am I lying on grass? A flash of memory then. Pitch black looming high above me, a blanket of a thousand twinkling stars.

His face. Sharp jutted features and a chiselled jaw.

A flash of intensity in his eyes, unwavering as they stare into mine.

A glint of malice there.

Gone again. Replaced with this brilliant ball of yellow sunshine as it creeps slowly from behind the clouds.

Please? I beg, desperate for some warmth.

'Cooper!'

An unfamiliar female voice startles me.

A name that I don't recognise. The sound so loud and magnified inside my ears is glorious. Breaking the looming silence that came before it. The high-pitched ringing inside my head has finally stopped, and I can hear again. Properly. The noise no longer muted and drowned out. Distorted. The sound is real; I am not alone.

I try to move my head towards it, to lift myself up from where I lie, but every part of me feels so heavy, it's easier to just continue to lie here and gather my bearings.

Someone will come for me now. Someone will help me.

Where am I? Homing in on the noises nearby as I wait for help. The low, continuous hum of moving traffic from a busy road. The usual sound of early morning rush hour in London, still, I am none the wiser.

I could be anywhere. Anywhere in the world, as the birds chorus high above me, soaring across the vivid blue skies. Oblivious to me so broken and numb beneath them.

Unmoving.

Only, there is movement then beside me.

Close.

The flattening of grass, the sound of a grunt or a snort I'm not sure which, and then miraculously, there is skin on mine.

Warm and wet.

A tongue I think, recognising the moist glide of a firm, strong tongue as it licks at my face. Then the warmth of fur roughly nudging into me, snuggling into my neck.

A dog.

A beautiful fluffy dog!

I smile as tears full of both relief and delight start to fall. Running down my cheeks, my chin, my face. I feel it, how somehow this dog just knows how broken I am. He can sense it. How frightened I feel. How scared I am. Though I'm not scared now that he is here. I am grateful.

Praying that he'll stay with me now, and he will if I am quick.

And I *am* quick.

Looping my shaking fingers around the strip of leather, gripping his collar tightly, as if my life depends upon it. Which I think that maybe my life does depend on it.

Don't go, I silently beg. *Don't leave me. Please.*

I hold him there at my side with every last bit of strength that I have inside of me, so that if he is called again, he will have no choice but to stay here and defy his owner. I'll be found then, with this dog at my side.

If I just wait patiently, just a little longer. Relishing the warm pant of his potent breath on my face, while I wait. The wet splatter of drool that trails down from his lips and lands on my chin.

'Cooper! Cooper.' The voice continues, calling out from somewhere off in the distance.

Far away. Still too far away. I grip on to the collar tighter as I feel the pull of him.

HELP! That's what I want to shout, only my words don't come. They are stuck there, shoved down inside my throat.

I turn my head, scanning the view in every direction. But there is nothing: only grass and sky. Green and blue. And that blinding brilliant white sunshine.

'Cooper. Come!'

No, Cooper. Stay.

But the dog is obedient, his ears pricking up at his owner's firm, impatient command. Giving me one more vigorous lick as if offering me a form of apology, before he tugs his collar from my bent, limp fingers. No strength there.

He is leaving me.

'Come back.' My words come in a whisper now, so softly spoken that I'm not even sure that they left my mouth. My hand drops back down to the wet grass.

I am all alone again.

More tears come. Nothing like the tears full of self-pity and sadness, the numbness I'd experienced only seconds ago when I'd first woken. These tears were new, my sadness replaced with almighty pain now that I am suddenly aware of my body.

And it is everywhere all at once. Everywhere. Everywhere.

Head pounding, body tender, limbs sore.

I can't just stay here.

I can't just give up.

Fighting the temptation to close my eyes once more, to sink back down into the ground beneath me. To allow the light to wash over completely for one last time, I use every last bit of strength that I have inside of me, and I roll onto my side.

Slowly then, ever so slowly, I sit up.

'Help!' The sound of my voice breaks from somewhere deep inside of me. Carrying across the vastness of the almost empty park.

To where the dog barks excitedly in the distance.

His owner turning to see who or what has got his attention.

And our eyes lock.

'Help me, please,' I say again, exhausted. Barely managing a whisper, before I allow myself to collapse back down onto the cold, wet ground.

40

EVIE

The engine roars, a loud, deep-throated growl as the car accelerates towards him.

Faster.

The tyres skidding, spinning out of control, desperately trying to grip the road to gain more traction, only the ground is too wet.

The car glides as if in slow motion.

I hold my breath in anticipation of the slam of metal smashing into him.

Watching in fascination as his body, weightless, flying, spins through the air reminding me of the rag doll that my nanna had made me as a child.

Its soft useless cotton limbs hanging flaccidly from its body.

A double-sided face showing two expressions.

A laughing, happy face. A crying, sad face.

As he lands with a thud on the cold, wet road, his face is the crying, sad face.

I watch as blood pools from the freshly inflicted wound on his head.

As the rain keeps coming, washing the flow that is building down the nearest drain, along with his blood.

41

JENNA

'Kirsten, I'm so glad you called, look what I said earlier...' Jenna starts, glad that Kirsten has returned her call so quickly; she'd only left not even an hour ago, but Jenna felt wracked with guilt.

She wanted a chance to explain. Everything.

Because if she didn't all these secrets were going to come between them for good, and Jenna couldn't bear to think of losing her friendship.

Kirsten was like family to her.

Shit, Duncan had been too. But Jenna couldn't keep this from her friend any longer.

'Look, I didn't know how to say this, but Duncan—' she starts, knowing that she needs to stop cutting Kirsten out and treating her like she is too fragile to deal with this. Kirsten deserved to know the truth about who she was married to.

'Duncan! It's Duncan!' There is panic in Kirsten's voice, she is close to hysteria.

'Kirsten?' Jenna wonders if she is too late, if someone has got to Kirsten first, before her. If Kirsten already knows.

'There's been an accident, Jenna. An awful accident. Duncan.' Jenna can just make out the words through Kirsten's frantic sobs. 'He was hit by a car outside the newsroom. A hit and run. The driver didn't stop. They've taken him to Whittington Hospital, Jenna, but the doctors they said that…' She starts to cry then, huge wracking sobs making the rest of her sentence completely inaudible. 'They said that I need to prepare myself. That he might not pull through.'

'Christ! Kirsten!' Jenna can hear the despair in her friend's voice, but is unable to find the right words to comfort her. 'Are you there with him now?'

'Yes, I am here with him. They are just taking him down to surgery now. He has a bleed on the brain. They're going to put him in an induced coma. God, Jenna. What if he doesn't wake up from this? What will I do without him? What will I tell the kids?'

'Kirsten, you need to stop thinking like that. He is going to wake up and when he does, he's going to need you to be strong for him, do you understand? Text me what ward you're in, give me twenty minutes okay. I'm on my way.'

'Thanks, Jenna,' Kirsten says weakly as Jenna hangs up the call, and she stares at her mobile phone that she's holding limply in her hand, processing what she's just been told.

It's too much of a coincidence, isn't it? That today, the same day that Jenna went to Evie Monroe's flat and showed her the photograph of Duncan, he was run down just hours later.

That the driver didn't stop; they'd purposely driven off.

Purposely not wanted to be caught.

Jenna recalled how calm and composed Evie had sounded as she had told Jenna that she'd had enough of suffering at her attacker's mercy, that she wouldn't stand for any more of his constant torment.

That she'd lost enough.

She had nothing left to lose.

That she was going to put an end to it all. *An end to him.*

Those were her words.

Regardless of what Jenna thought about Duncan, despite her suspicions, she hadn't wanted this.

It is all her fault.

42

HIM

He stands on the pavement, looking over at the warm yellow glow that emits from the edges of the closed curtains of the ground floor flat.

Closed intentionally to block the world out.

He wonders if she is in there.

Lighting up his cigarette his eyes don't move from the window above him as he waits patiently as the darkness out here will allow him, hoping for a tiny glimpse of narrative that isn't owed to him, to tell him if she's in there.

If she is home. If she's struggling to get to sleep.

He imagines that she is. That every time she's laid her head down and closed her eyes, since that night her mind has been plagued with graphic nightmares of what might have been, if she hadn't made her lucky escape.

Lucky this time.

He draws a plume of smoke deep into his lungs and breathes it out again, watching as a cloud of white smoke dispels into the blackness of the night air.

The situation has become too messy.

The walls are closing in on him. It won't be long now until it all comes out.

Until his whole life unravels right before him.

It's all her fault.

Jenna.

She thinks she's so smart, so clever.

That she's above everyone else.

She got her hands on that fucking list and she's contacting all the women. Building a case against him so that she could expose him. It was only ever supposed to be a bit of fun, but then women like Jenna didn't have a sense of humour.

He'd seen that in the bar that night – how even with a few drinks inside her she was still wound tighter than a coiled metal spring. She needed to relax a bit, have some fun. That was all it had been for him.

He'd just wanted to warn her off, only that's not enough for her.

Not nearly enough.

He watches as the light goes off and the flat is plunged into darkness.

Unaware that she is vulnerable now.

43

JENNA

She'd been in such a hurry to get to the hospital to be with Kirsten, so caught up in her thoughts about Duncan being a victim of a hit and run, about the major life-changing surgery he was about to have, how the doctors said that he might not pull through, that the last thing she'd been expecting to see when she'd stepped outside the main door of her flat had been him, lurking around in the shadows like the creepy stalker he clearly was.

Him. The man from the bar that night. Mike.

It was really him this time.

His face lit up by the streetlamp, he makes no attempt to hide his identity from her. He wants her to see him. Wants her to know that he is here.

That he's come for her.

That is what these people do, isn't it?

According to Sharon Hargreaves and Evie Monroe, that's how these men continued to torment the victims, how they incessantly taunt them. Their actions verging on psychotic, but then any man who goes around drugging, terrorising, attacking women, raping women, is exactly that. Turning up with the intention of scaring their victim.

It is working, too.

Fight or flight, and Jenna is frozen.

Instead of screaming out loud and shouting for help, she is momentarily stupefied. She thinks about running. How if she is quick, she might be able to make it back to the safety of her flat.

How if he tries to follow her, she can slam the door shut in his face, and throw her body weight behind it to keep him out. She can barricade herself inside while she calls the police. They might get there in just a few minutes.

But what if they took longer?

If she goes now, if she's quick, she might be able to catch him unawares.

She falters suddenly.

But what if she isn't quick enough? What then?

It's too much of a risk.

These thoughts fill her head in the space of a single heartbeat as he stands there looking directly at her. His stare full of intention. His expression unhinged. As if turning up at the home of someone he recently drugged, is the most normal thing to do in the world.

She won't allow him to do this to her, to torment her like this. To make her life hell.

Like he's done to other women. No, this is on her terms now. She is in survival mode.

Running as fast as she can, without looking back.

Back inside the flat and along the back corridor, her hand inside her handbag as she grasps frantically for her keys. Her fingertips tracing the sharp edges so that she has the right one, because she knows she doesn't have long.

Twisting her key in the lock she can hear his footsteps pounding out behind her, echoing loudly, the sound getting nearer.

As the door flies open, she doesn't dare look to see how much time she has – there's no time. He'll be on her soon.

She stumbles inside and slams the door shut, pushing the weight of herself up against it.

Only to her terror it won't close and she feels the weight of him resisting it. The toe of his brown boots wedged in the gap between the door and the frame.

She wasn't quick enough.

She's led him from a busy street into the quiet solace of her flat.

'Jenna!'

She hears her name leave his mouth like a command. As if he is ordering her to listen to him. To do as he tells her.

She will not succumb to his demands. She will not succumb to him.

'I've called the police,' she lies, shouting now. Praying that someone might hear her and come to her aid. Or that he will believe her, that it will be enough of a deterrent to leave her alone.

She's going into shock, she realises as the feeling of intense fear overcomes her. Her hands start to shake as she feels him repeatedly pushing himself up against the door.

He is so much bigger than her. So much stronger than her. *If* he gets in here, no *when* he gets in here, she is going to have to fight for her life.

Scanning the kitchen, looking for something she can use as a weapon to protect herself, her eyes rest on the knife block.

The long steel inch-wide blade would do it.

But could she? She isn't sure.

Could she be brave enough to use it if she had to? Desperate enough to plunge the blade into his flesh in order to save herself.

Metal slicing through muscle, ligaments and organs, grinding against bone.

All that blood.

She thinks she could.

If there was no other way, if it was him against her. She reminds herself of what he's capable of. That this vile excuse of a man, along with Duncan, were capable of really hurting her, just as they'd done to other women. Terrorising them and getting away with it. How one of them had raped Evie Monroe and left her for dead. Mike? Duncan? She isn't certain who.

They were both caught up in this together.

If he wanted to get in here and hurt her there was nothing that would stop him.

'I know you're scared, Jenna, and you have every right to be.'

She blocks out his words, blocks out the sound of his monotonous voice and makes a run for the knife.

She is taking a leaf out of Evie Monroe's book, if she has to protect herself with it, she will.

She is certain she will.

44

EVIE

I slip into the stark, sterile private room of the neurosurgery unit and shut the door behind me, before tentatively pulling down the blinds.

Not wanting the nurses to see me and ask me what I am doing here. Because I shouldn't be in here, and I don't have long.

I stare over at him, tucked neatly beneath the crisp, white sheets of the hospital bed that sits in the centre of the room. Surrounded by a network of tubes and wires. Heart rate and blood pressure monitors bleep loudly. There's another machine monitoring his oxygen levels. A breathing tube that leads from his mouth, attaching him to a ventilator.

His head is dressed in a thick white bandage, beneath it his eyes are swollen shut, coloured with different shades of black and purple that all merge together as one.

His leg is raised, cocooned in a cast.

He looks fragile, battered and broken – but he is not dead.

Somehow, he managed to survive the accident.

Accident? Is that what you call it when it was very much intentional?

I note a handbag that has been left on a chair that sits next to his pillow, and I wonder who has been sitting at his bedside. His wife, I assume, as the door opens behind me and a woman enters the room.

Clutching a hot plastic cup of milky looking machine coffee.

'Can I help you?' she asks, looking me up and down with a wary edge of suspicion as she tries to work out who I am. 'Why are you in here with my husband?'

Her tone is guarded and full of apprehension, and I see her body physically stiffen as she stands taller. Defensive now. Suspicious.

Her face etched with worry, that is instantly replaced with confusion at the sight of me standing here, alone, with the door and the blinds shut in her husband's private room.

A crazy notion crossing my mind that tells me she thinks I'm his mistress. She thinks I'm here because I'm sleeping with her husband. I almost laugh at the absurdity of it all. Only I am not in a laughing mood. And judging by the way this woman is clenching her jaw and glaring at me, she isn't either.

'I know you from somewhere?' she says, when I don't immediately answer. Her face twisted into a look of confusion, as she is trying to pinpoint where.

'It's Evie, isn't it? Evie Monroe. I interviewed you for the *Islington Gazette* at the beginning of the year. We put out an appeal for the witnesses to come forward following your attack.' She chooses her words carefully, but she gets straight to the point.

Ever the professional, just like Jenna.

'Do you remember me? You'd just been through such an awful ordeal.'

I note the genuine sympathy in her voice, the softness there, and I nod my head. There were so many people around me after the attack that all their names and faces seem to have blurred into one indistinguishable person. The detective in charge of the case, the victim liaison officer, other police officers. Doctors, nurses, journalists.

My memory of the days that followed my attack are vague and fuzzy even now. It was as if I'd been in some kind of trance. As if I'd been forced to go inwards, hiding inside some kind of protective bubble at my core. Purposely shutting the rest of the world out, keeping everyone away from me.

But I remember her.

'An article in the local newspaper might just jog someone's memory about seeing him that night. Someone might come forward.'

'It's a warning to other young, local women out there, that there is an attacker on the loose. It's worth it for that, if nothing else.'

She'd said that.

Was it worth it?

Protecting other women, future victims, while throwing myself into the lion's den so that all those misogynistic trolls could rip me from limb to limb once the appeal went live.

I'm not so sure now. Because after the appeal had run cold and people had got on with their own lives again, they forgot all about me. I was the one left to pick up all the pieces of the broken, shattered ruins of my life.

'He's going to be okay? Your husband?' I say finally, wanting to take the focus away from me.

'Thankfully, yes. They've treated him for a bleed on the brain. They've just operated on him. He's got a badly broken leg too; he's had to have it pinned. He's stable now though.' Her words trail off as she stares at him again. As if realising the extent of his injuries.

She's still in shock. Her brain is still trying to process the trauma she's experiencing, the stress of almost losing someone she so dearly loves.

Oh, how I know that feeling myself so well.

'I'm sorry,' she says as if she's just woken up from her trance herself and realises that I'm still standing in the room with her. 'But you still haven't said why you are here. Why are you in my husband's room? Do you know him?'

'I was there.' I nod over to where Duncan lies unresponsively in the bed. 'When it happened. I went to the newsroom to see Jenna, but instead I saw him. I recognised him straight away.'

'What do you mean, you were there? Recognised him from where?' There is mild irritation rising in Kirsten's voice, though she does her best to try and disguise it.

'Your colleague, Jenna. She came to my house earlier today and showed me his photograph. Asked me if I knew him.'

'Jenna did? Why would she show you a photograph of Duncan? Why would you recognise him?' Kirsten asks, her face twisted into a look of sceptical uncertainty.

Only something else flashes there.

'She said that she was looking into the attacks again, that she was visiting the victims.'

I nod again. She is staring at my coat.

'Because she thinks that your husband is responsible for spiking women's drinks, for following them home. For raping them. For raping me.'

The confusion that was etched on her face melts away and is immediately replaced with fury, and I know that she is momentarily lost for words as she tries to take in what I've just said. She shakes her head as if trying to work out how her friend had come to that assumption, and I search her face for any traces of doubt.

But there are none.

'No,' she says point-blank, unwavering. Not even willing to entertain the idea. 'No. Duncan didn't do that. He didn't do any of those things. He's not capable. He just isn't.'

She believes in him completely, without question, the model devoted and committed wife. At least that's what she wants to portray, but I see it there.

The tiny flicker of uncertainty as it creeps in.

The unsettled feelings of doubt. The *what if*s.

Her eyes go back to my coat, and I see it. The moment that the penny drops as she works it out.

Nine months ago.

She last saw me nine months ago, just days after I was raped.

And yesterday morning. On the CCTV footage that her stupid rag of a newspaper had shared with the world. Yesterday, that's when she last saw my coat. On the CCTV footage, worn by a woman abandoning her newborn baby.

I see the way her eyes flicker towards the man in the bed, and she shifts uncomfortably on her feet as if another thing has only just occurred to her too.

That I am here now, standing in her husband's private room, after someone ploughed him down and tried to kill him.

How they'd almost done it too.

How I'd told her I had witnessed what had happened. Admitted that I was there at the scene of the crime.

'Duncan wouldn't do those things. He isn't capable of doing *those* things. He is good and kind and we have a family, we have children. We have two beautiful children. He wouldn't do this.' Her voice is becoming louder and more hysterical, and I know that if I don't calm her down quickly the room will be filled with medical staff and security.

'Oh my god, it was you, wasn't it? You did this, you ploughed into him and left him for dead?'

When she goes to grab the nurse call button, I am one step ahead. Grabbing her wrist tightly, with force, I stop her.

45

'I didn't mean to. I promise you I didn't mean to do it.'

'You didn't mean to do what? What have you done?'

Liam stands in the doorway, a confused look on his face. Having got here in record time after he'd received Jenna's almost inaudible phone call, begging for his help. Telling him that the man who had drugged her the other night had turned up unannounced at her flat. That she was scared.

'I think I've killed him, Liam. I think I've fucking killed him,' Jenna says, her legs physically shaking as she leads Liam into the lounge. Her body feels weightless now as if she's gone into shock and is outside of her body.

She stands over the lifeless man who is splayed out in the middle of her lounge. The knife from her kitchen discarded on the floor beside him.

'That's him. Mike. The man from the bar the other night. The man who drugged me. He forced his way in. I didn't mean to do it, I swear to God. I only grabbed the knife from the side in order to protect myself, to defend myself if he tried to hurt me. He was deluded, Liam, he really believed that coming here to my flat was normal. But it wasn't, was it? It was fucked up, him turning up here like that.'

Visibly shaking now, in shock, Jenna holds the man's limp wrist in her hand and holds her forefinger and middle finger over his pulse point. Moving it around in small circles as she searches for a beat, for a throb.

Desperate to find some sign of life.

'He's dead, Liam. I've killed him.'

'What did he say to you? Before this happened. Why was he here?'

'He told me he was here for my own protection. That he was checking on me, for my own safety. He believed I was in danger. He told me he was a police officer and I pretended that I believed him. That his sick, twisted games were normal. That I believed him and didn't secretly suspect him of being a threat. That it was all fine. Pretending like that. I played along. Said I'd make us both a drink so that we could talk properly. I was so scared that I wasn't really thinking, I crushed up some of my sleeping tablet and laced his tea. I was just trying to keep him subdued until I could call the police.. I just wanted to sedate him. Slow him down. So that there was no chance he would overpower me and get the upper hand. I was scared of what he might do to me. Only, I think I must have underestimated how strong the tablets are.' Jenna cries, her hand flying to her mouth as she tries and fails to suppress the sob that escapes regardless.

'Did you call the police?'

Jenna shakes her head.

'I didn't mean to kill him, you believe me, don't you?'

'Of course I do. Who else have you called? Who else knows he's here?'

'No one. Kirsten's at the hospital with Duncan. I spoke to her earlier, just before he turned up. That's where I was going when I found him lurking around outside. Christ, Liam! You don't know, do you? Duncan's been involved in a hit and run.

He's in a really bad way. Kirsten said he might not pull through. I didn't know who else to call, but you. I'm so sorry to drag you into all of this.'

The wail that escapes Jenna's mouth sounds like that of a scared, desperate animal and right now that's exactly how she feels as she collapses in a heap on the floor, folding in on herself. Distraught now at what she's done.

'Duncan? A hit and run? What? Is he going to be all right? What the fuck is going on tonight?'

She shakes her head. Beside herself because she really doesn't know.

'He's got a bleed on the brain,' she says, the reality of tonight becoming too much for her as tears escape down her cheeks.

'Shit! That's awful. God, I hope he's okay!' he says, visibly paling with shock.

'Kirsten said he might not pull through.' Jenna can hear the hysteria in her voice, but she's beyond the point of controlling it.

Liam can hear it too.

'I'm going to make us a drink, I think we could both do with one,' he says. Leaving the room.

Jenna doesn't move her gaze from the body on the floor in front of her. She is still fixated on the sight of him there, dead, in her flat when Liam returns just minutes later.

'Here, this will be good for the shock,' Liam says, his voice slicing through her thoughts as he sets both the glasses down on the coffee table in front of them.

Liam sits down. As if this is all too much for him too. This mess, this chaos. As if he is still trying to make sense of it all.

'Did they catch anyone? The hit-and-run driver, do they have any idea who did it?'

'They haven't caught them yet, but I think I know who it is, Liam, and it's all my fault.'

'How is it your fault?' He stares at her with such intensity, she wonders if he thinks she is completely mental.

She wonders too if perhaps she might be. Because that's how it looks.

How out of the two men that she'd been investigating for spiking and attacking women, one of them is now a lifeless body at her feet and the other is currently having lifesaving surgery in hospital and might not survive it.

'I think it was Evie Monroe. One of the women on Duncan's list. She'd been raped earlier this year and had reported it to the police. I think she tried to kill Duncan.'

'Evie Monroe? The name vaguely rings a bell. What? Why?'

Jenna picks up her drink and swallows it down in one, trying to gather the courage to explain. Watching as Liam does the same. And for the first time tonight, Jenna can't help but notice he looks genuinely flustered at what she's just told him.

She thinks how strange that is, that this revelation has affected him more so than the shock of knowing she has killed someone. More so than Duncan lying critical in the hospital.

'I went to see her earlier today. I know you said to leave it, to drop the story because it was too dangerous, but I had to at least try and find out if she recognised Duncan. I showed her his photo. She didn't react to it initially, at least not while I was there. Not even when I told her about the file I found on his computer. How he'd kept a record of all the attacks, how he'd boasted about what he'd done on that incel site by sharing all the links to articles about the incidents. How he taunted the women afterwards too... Even now, all these months later.

'She had looked so shocked when she'd seen me standing at her front door this morning. After the CCTV images of a woman abandoning Holly went to the press, after we printed that letter. She'd almost passed out. Her legs had almost given way beneath her. That's why she thought I was there this morning. She thought I'd found her. She's the missing mother, Liam. Evie Monroe is the woman who safely surrendered her baby.'

She shakes her head, as if she still can't believe what has happened here tonight. She can't believe what a complete disaster it all is.

'It was the photograph that did it. The one I showed her of Duncan. She got angry after she saw it and threw me out. The image must have triggered her memory. That's why she tried to kill him tonight, isn't it? He wasn't just her attacker; he was the father of her baby. We need to call the police,' she says with certainty as she grabs her phone. 'They'll be able to take Duncan's DNA. They'll have proof then of who the attacker really is.'

'Call the police?' Liam looks flustered as he rakes his fingers through handfuls of his hair, before shaking his head. 'I don't think we should be calling them yet, until we can figure out a story so that you don't get sent away for this.'

'Sent away? It was self-defence! He drugged me. He was involved with Duncan; they were attacking and terrorising women. He'd come to my flat. I was scared. He'd told me he was called Mike, but he was lying. I've got evidence of everything he posted on the incel site. He's using a fake name. Look...'

Crouching down and rummaging through Mike's pockets, Jenna finds the man's wallet, opening it up as if to prove to Liam the man came here on false pretences. That he wasn't who he said he was.

Only when she looks inside, she sees the official police badge.

His officer number and real name on it.

'Detective Constable Graham Smith?' she mouths, so quietly she's not sure any sound has come out. 'He's a police officer. I've killed a fucking police officer.'

'He wasn't lying!' Liam bristles.

'But I don't understand? He was the man at the bar the other night. He drugged me. He was with me when I started feeling funny; he led me outside for air. Told me that he'd take me somewhere quieter, I thought...' She is horrified. 'I thought he was trying to get me alone, so that he could, so that he...' She can't finish her sentence. She can't physically say the words that she thought he might have done to her.

'Police officers are capable of doing heinous shit too, Jenna. They're not immune simply because they carry a badge. You didn't report that you'd been drugged the other night, did you?' Liam asks, shaking his head. 'You let him into your flat tonight, and there is no sign of a struggle. He didn't hurt you. He hadn't physically done anything to you; he hadn't even shown evidence of being a threat. The police will say you murdered him in cold blood, you killed a police officer. You'll get life.'

Jenna is hysterical. Crying and shaking and rocking as her world comes tumbling down all around her.

As the extent of what she has done hits her with its full force.

'I was scared. He was acting deluded, saying weird stuff. Things that didn't make any sense. Making out that he'd been leading an undercover investigation about the recent spate of local spikings and sexual assaults. He said that they are close to catching the attacker. That he knew who it was. He said that he believed I was in danger.' She shakes her head and tries to process his words. 'Which is crazy, isn't it? Because it was him. *He* was at the bar the other night. *He's* the member in that forum. I've seen his posts and comments. I've seen the vile things he shares. I didn't know what else to do, so I played along. But I didn't mean to kill him, I swear, Liam. When he slumped forward from the chair, I thought he was sleeping. I thought that the tablets had just knocked him out. Only he's not breathing, he hasn't got a pulse.'

'Jenna, you need to stop crying and take a deep breath. Okay? Someone is going to hear you; your neighbours are going to hear you and they'll end up calling the police,' Liam says, taking control. 'You need to try and stay calm.

'Can you open a window. It's bloody hot in here,' he asks, pulling at the collar of his jumper as if it's digging in too tightly around his neck.

Only Jenna doesn't move.

'Sorry, you're right. I just need to calm down,' she says. 'It helps you think straight doesn't it? Serenity. It clears your head. And I've been thinking. What if Evie isn't the only one who knew about Duncan?'

'Right, but you just said...' Liam shifts uncomfortably in his seat.

'Yeah, but what if I'm wrong? What if Evie Monroe didn't go there tonight to kill Duncan? What if she went to the office to see me, she might have thought some more about the photo I showed her. About the information I'd given her. Who knows, she might have even had a change of heart and wanted to come clean about being Holly's mother.'

'Well, that's a lot of speculation and second guessing. You already said she had motive. You handed it to her.' Liam looks confused as he continues overheating. His face is puce, and he is dripping sweat.

'Is it speculation though?' she says. 'What if it's fact? What if Evie Monroe witnessed what happened tonight? What if she then went to the hospital to tell Kirsten that she saw it all. She saw the person who ploughed into Duncan. That same man's face had triggered a memory of where she'd seen him before. Her attacker. How she had recognised him immediately. What if she recorded the whole thing on her phone and she showed Kirsten and they both called the police?'

'What the fuck are you talking about.' Liam is getting angry now. 'I don't feel well,' he says, and Jenna watches as he makes an attempt to get up from where he sits, only he's lost the strength and movement in his legs.

'You're the only other person who knew about Duncan. Because I stupidly told you what I had found on his computer.

You knew that he had composed a list of all the attacks and that he'd infiltrated the incel group. You knew that he was on to the attacker. What did you do tonight? Threaten him?' She laughs bitterly. 'Or maybe you didn't say anything because that's not really your style, is it? Maybe you didn't say anything at all, and you just ploughed him down. That's more your thing, isn't it? You're more of a silent assassin. The sort of coward that slips drugs into the drinks of women to get your cheap kicks. The sort of guy that thinks it's okay to attack and rape women.' Jenna nods down to the empty glasses on the table.

'I swapped them. You were so thrown by that little gem of a nugget I'd force fed you about me thinking it was Evie Monroe who had attempted to kill Duncan, that you didn't even see me do it. You've got to be careful, Liam. Always guard your drink. Never leave it unattended, honestly you can't trust anyone these days.'

She lets out a small, bitter laugh, pleased with herself.

'I counted on you not being able to resist lacing my drink with whatever it is you used on all your other victims. I counted on you seeing me as a loose end that needed tying up. Now that the officer you suspected was investigating you is dead. And that Duncan doesn't look likely to recover from what you did to him. That's the craziest thing about all of this. You actually thought you could get away with all of this, didn't you?'

'You stupid fucking bitch. You don't know what you're talking about,' he says.

His face tells her he knows that all this time she'd been playing him.

Keeping him here and talking while the drugs he laced her drink with – the drink she swapped when he wasn't looking – took effect.

The real her was coming out now.

'They won't believe you. The police won't believe a word you say. You're a cop killer.' His words don't seem to be coming out the way he's pronouncing them. They are slow and warped, just like his vision. He does a double take. He probably thinks he's hallucinating now as the dead man on the floor makes a miraculous recovery and rolls onto his side, before slowly standing up.

'Won't they? Shall we ask them? Do you believe me, DC Graham Smith?' Jenna says smugly, seeing the look of horror spread across Liam's face. 'Kirsten and Evie believed me. That was why the detective came here tonight, Liam, only he wasn't sure just how involved I was, with the case, with you. He didn't know how much I already knew. But he'd been watching you for a while. That's why he was there at the bar that night. He suspected you of spiking my drink. You, the profile that I had invited there that night, believing it was him. He came here tonight to warn me about the danger I was in; he told me everything in the end. And you have Evie Monroe to thank for all of that.'

'You're just as manipulative and interfering as the rest of those cunts,' he manages to say, as it dawns on him, finally, what is going on here.

He's been set up.

By drugging her, he'd just given them the proof they needed to put him away for everything that she is accusing him of.

'You'd done it to Kirsten too, hadn't you? Drugged her all those years ago, when you were together. That's why you broke up. At least she suspected that you had, but when she confronted you told her that she was crazy for even thinking such a thing. You gaslit her into believing it had all been in her head before you dumped her. She never told me. Never once even hinted at what really happened between you both, but she told Duncan. Finally. Years later, when the other attacks started happening in this area. Duncan was suspicious and so he started helping DC Smith out with his investigations. They figured it out. Figured you out. They know you attacked all those other women, and they know that you were the one who ran Duncan down earlier tonight. Evie Monroe filmed it. They can prove that you are the monster who raped Evie Monroe, and then threatened her so she'd abandon her baby. With baby Holly, they can get your DNA.'

'You fucking bitch!' he manages to spit. 'You nasty, fucking bitch!'

Jenna is looking at him now, mesmerised, as he slurs his words and the drugs start to take their full effect.

'It's not nice, is it? Having a taste of your own medicine. You're probably going to start feeling a little sleepy now. Don't worry, though. We'll look after you!'

46

JENNA

'Okay then, let's see. Why do ducks have feathers?' Jenna asks with a straight face, to the two small children sitting next to her at the dinner table, staring up at her intently as they hang on her every word for her next silly punchline.

'I don't know,' Amelia says, eyes wide as if she is wracking her brain for an answer as she purses her mouth. 'To keep them warm?'

Jenna playfully shakes her head.

'To cover up their butt-quacks!'

'Butt-quacks!' Christian squeals loudly as he and Amelia fall about the table laughing hysterically at Jenna's silly joke.

Jenna grins.

She lives for these moments. Had fought her life for them.

For the nostalgic smell of roast beef as it fills the house, fighting for its space amongst the loud incessant chatter and laugher as the children giggle loudly and the adults all talk.

She is right here, at the one place where she's always felt the most at home in her life, at Kirsten and Duncan's house.

Her family.

'I may be at a disadvantage right now,' Duncan quips positively as he nods over to where the crutches he's been hobbling around with while his broken leg is healing, rest up against the wall nearest to his chair, and he places his cutlery down on his now empty plate. 'But broken leg or not, I can still make a mean roast dinner!'

'That was delicious, darling! You always make the best roasts,' Janet says, not murmuring once about how tough the meat is, or how the roast potatoes could have probably done with another five minutes – the way she would have if Kirsten had cooked. And it doesn't go unnoticed.

'Your mum is right, Duncan. You've done a great job, as always! Even though you did have a little bit of help!' She raises her wine glass, purposely not taking her mother-in-law's bait, and toasts her amazing husband. 'Thanks, Jenna!'

Winking at Jenna, Kirsten gets up and starts clearing the plates, ready for dessert.

Jenna smiles, feeling very much part of the private joke with her friend at how Duncan can never do any wrong, and very much part of this family.

Duncan's recovery is slower than the doctors had hoped. His leg is taking a little longer to heal and his memory is not as it used to be. But he is getting there and he and Kirsten look happier than ever.

Part of her hates that she ever doubted him, because she knows now that he'd kept what he had known about Liam from her and Kirsten on purpose, because he hadn't wanted to place either of them in any danger. He'd only ever been protecting them both.

Kirsten had confessed to Duncan in the past few months that during her relationship with Liam, she'd suspected that he had drugged her one night when she'd been with him.

The very last night she'd been with him.

She remembered going to bed that night and when she'd woken up, having no memory of what happened. When she had asked Liam about it, 'accused him,' he'd later claimed in anger, he had dumped her, moving on with someone else within days, purposely to humiliate her.

To show her that she, along with her crazy accusations, hadn't meant anything to him.

Kirsten didn't have proof of what Liam did to her. She'd only gone by her gut feeling, knowing that something hadn't felt right. Keeping the attack to herself, she'd never told anyone until she'd recently confessed to Duncan the real reason why she'd always hated the man.

The local attacks that had started to happen in the area had dragged Kirsten's harrowing ordeal to the forefront of her mind. She had known that she couldn't just pretend any more that it hadn't happened. Not after what she'd been through. Not when she'd learned that Jenna had been drugged too. It was too much of a coincidence, wasn't it?

That's what she and Duncan had been arguing about that night at the bar.

That's what they'd rowed about that night at the restaurant on their anniversary, as he had bought up again the fact that Kirsten was drugged, and tried to persuade her to go to the police.

Only Kirsten, convinced that they wouldn't believe her had point-blank refused to go, had refused to discuss the matter any further.

Until she'd had no choice.

She'd found out that Liam and Jenna were sleeping with each other. That Liam had somehow managed to worm his way in.

Scared for her friend, she'd told Duncan, who was already on to him by then.

Which was why Duncan had gone to the newsroom that night. Worried about Jenna's safety, he'd gone to confront Liam. Calling him out for the disgusting acts he'd committed. He'd been forced to summon every inch of willpower he possessed not to murder the man then and there with his bare hands.

Duncan was smarter than that, smarter than Liam, and he had almost gathered enough evidence to end Liam for good. Doing his own digging. As a data translator, that's what he does, that's what he's good at. Extracting data, finding patterns. Putting a file together weeks previous to this, he'd been the one to approach DC Graham Smith with all the evidence he'd managed to compile.

They'd both infiltrated the incel site and had been watching Liam closely since. It wasn't Duncan in that incel sharing articles and humiliating these women. It was Liam.

He'd given them everything they needed. The women's names, the dates that they were attacked.

Only he was doing it on a far bigger scale, publicly shaming the victims by printing articles in the newspaper, so he could share them with the group later, knowing how they would all jump on and comment. How all he had to do was lead them there and they'd do all his dirty work for him; the women would suffer endless torment.

When Mike had approached Jenna at the bar that night, he'd only wanted to check that Jenna was okay. He hadn't been the one who had drugged her. She feels stupid now that she'd refused his offer of help when he told her he would get her home safely.

Liam, realising that his game was up, stayed true to his cowardly form until the very end and had taken the gutless way out, ploughing his car into Duncan in the hope of shutting him up for good.

In the desperate hope of keeping his sordid secrets for a while longer.

Only Evie had been there too, and she had filmed the entire thing. Witnessing her attacker trying to murder a man that Jenna had shown her in the photo. Evie Monroe had finally got her justice. And, most importantly, she'd since got her baby back.

Liam had never wanted that.

He'd put the photo of Holly and the CCTV images online on purpose, deliberately to mess with Evie. It hadn't been for clickbait, or ratings or views or anything to do with the newspaper's performance, like Jenna thought. He hadn't put it out there to help find Holly's mother, liked she'd hoped.

To Liam it was all just part of his sick, twisted little game.

Another way to torment his victim.

'So, Kirsten tells me that you're going on a date tomorrow night?' Janet says, her eyes twinkling behind her new designer glasses.

Having finally gone to the doctors at her daughter-in-law's insistence, it turned out that it was Janet's eyesight that had been the root cause of her headaches and dizzy spells.

'Well, it's hardly a date,' Jenna says, shrugging Janet's notion away, while feeling her cheeks flushing as everyone looks at her now. 'I'm meeting Chris. The firefighter who found Holly that night. I'm just going to give him an update on everything.'

'An update, eh?' Janet raises her eyebrows playfully. 'Is that what you youngsters call it, in my day we called it a sh—'

'Mum!' Duncan laughs, flustered as he interrupts his mother, guessing what she's about to say.

'An "update" at a fancy Italian restaurant no less,' Kirsten adds as she comes back into the room holding a ready-made shop-bought cheesecake that is covered in a mountain of whipped cream and raspberries.

Messily thrown together: Kirsten's signature decoration to throw her mother off the scent that she hadn't made it herself.

'It will be good for you, Jenna, he seems like a nice bloke.'

'Well, we'll see. You know how I don't like to rush into things,' Jenna says humorously, hinting at the running joke that she hadn't had a serious relationship in years.

Maybe she was ready now.

Chris did seem like a nice guy, and Jenna was genuinely excited about seeing him again.

'Mmm, this cheesecake is delicious, Kirsten,' Jenna says in solidarity, hoping to change the subject and keep the heat off herself. Winking at Kirsten as everyone tucks in. 'I must get the recipe from you.'

'Of course. It's so simple, I'm sure even you could manage it,' Kirsten says, without missing a beat as she shoots her friend daggers for her attempt to throw her under the bus.

'Hmm, it's not bad, Kirsten, not bad at all,' Janet begrudgingly agrees, scraping her plate completely clean, before putting her fork down and shooting a smile in the direction of her daughter-in-law. 'For a shop bought effort! I don't miss a trick with these new specs! You just need to practice, Kirsten, and one day you'll be as good a cook as my Duncan is!'

'Oh, I can only live in hope, Janet!' Kirsten says, picking up her wine glass and draining the last dregs of her wine.

'I can only live in hope!'

47

LIAM

Sat here in the visitation room, waiting for a visit, I realise that this is the only thing I have left now, the highlight of my week. Anticipating an hour of irritating, mind-numbing conversation with my mother. My only contact outside of these prison walls for the foreseeable.

This was all Evie Monroe's fault. Me being here now.

If she'd just done what I'd told her and got rid of the kid, then none of this would have happened. I'd never have been caught.

I got too carried away, that was the trouble. Too caught up in it all, because the truth was, I'd enjoyed it.

The power I had over her.

The fear I was capable of inflicting.

I'd pushed it too far though, I realise that now.

Allowing Jenna to run all that shit in the paper just so that I could torment Evie further. The photograph of Holly, the CCTV footage, the letter. I'd been rubbing Evie's face in it all. Goading her. Tormenting her. Letting her know that if she didn't do as I said, and stay the fuck away from that child, I'd come for her and then I'd come for the kid too.

Holly.

It was weird to think that a part of me, my legacy, is out there somewhere in the world.

My kid. Because I have rights, don't I?

I hadn't thought about it like that up until now. Now that I have nothing else. Maybe it was something I could look into, something to focus on. Something to talk about with my mother other than the boring soaps she is obsessed with and regular updates on the price increase to her grocery shop.

I watch her as she walks towards me, and I see for the first time how suddenly so much smaller she seems. Frailer even. Like she has aged a decade since she last saw me.

Maybe she has.

Since she learned all the heinous things that I, her one and only son, had done to all those women.

And the strangest feeling overcomes me: *shame*. I'm awash with it. That despite everything I did she is still here. She still showed up for me. That must count as something, surely.

'Mum!' I stand up to greet her, stepping forward to hug, only she holds her hand out in front of her as if to stop me coming any closer.

'Sit,' she says sternly, her blue watery eyes look glassy.

Respectfully, I do as she asks, realising as I note her paper-thin skin how old she looks, how she might not be here when I get out. I'm not expecting it, but that saddens me.

'I'm not staying,' my mother tells me, a cold, cutting edge to her voice that I don't recognise.

'DC Graham Smith came to see me,' she starts. And I nod in understanding that, of course she is angry. She has every right to be. She knows everything now. Everything that I did.

'You did it to me too, didn't you?' A single tear leaves her eye and runs down her cheek. 'When you visited me all those times, you drugged me, didn't you? Because I haven't felt that way since you've been in here. You made me believe that I was ill. Made me believe that I was losing my mind. That I was really sick. All this time I thought I was dying.' Her voice is shaking in time with the finger she's pointing directly at me.

Like a gun to my heart as she fires out her loaded shots.

'I didn't...' I start. Wondering just how sick and twisted my mother must be thinking I am. That I was capable of doing the things to her that I did to those other women.

'It wasn't the same. I just wanted to do to you what you did to me. When I was a kid.'

I have no idea where it comes from, but suddenly I am crying. Huge wracking sobs from somewhere deep inside me take over my body and I cry loudly, inconsolably. Begging her for her forgiveness.

But she shakes her head sadly.

'I did that to keep you safe. Gave you medicine to make you sleep, so that I could keep you away from all those men that I never wanted you to grow up to be like. I did what I had to do back then to survive, so that I could pay the bills and give you a good life. God help me, Liam, I made some awful decisions back then, but I did it to protect you. But you!' She shakes her head.

'Hearing what you did to all those women. Knowing how you drugged me too. I've never been so disgusted and ashamed in all my life.'

I try to speak, try to reason with her, but she cuts me dead.

A sternness to her voice that I've never heard before. She is like a complete stranger standing before me now.

'I wanted to see you one last time. To tell you to your face. We are done. I loved you once, Liam. But not any more. You are no longer my son.'

When she walks away, I know that I'll never see her again.

I am truly on my own.

48

EVIE

I stare down at my tiny baby wrapped in the pink, fluffy blanket. A knitted yellow hat pulled down over the short tufts of mousey-brown hair like a halo. Her little scratch mittens covering her tiny hands, to stop the edges of her nails from snagging at her soft, smooth complexion.

I feel it. The first ever pinch-me moment that this is real. A small part of me still disbelieving that I'd somehow managed to get my baby back. The charity couldn't afford to deny me that privilege, knowing that the whole world was watching, cheering me on to do the right thing and claim my child back.

Holly. No. Sophia. My beautiful, perfect daughter, Sophia all warm and cosy in her car seat.

I am flooded with an indescribable, overwhelming rush of unconditional love. Filling me from the very bottom of my feet right up to the top of my head.

She is mine, finally.

Placing the envelope down on the table I stare at my handwriting that sweeps across the front.

Jenna Stone.

Because I know that she'll come looking. Wanting to check

in and see how we are doing. And she deserves some form of goodbye.

Jenna is nice like that. Genuine. Caring.

She's been through some tough times, too, in her life. We have a bond because of that. In another lifetime, I would have wanted her as a friend. A best friend maybe. A sister-figure even. But in this lifetime, for the sake of my daughter, I can't hold on to anything that links me back to him.

I just hope that she will understand.

Men like Liam get their thrills by terrorising and tormenting his victims, and no matter what happens or what I do, I will always be the victim to him.

I'm not going to stick around and wait for him to come for me again.

Legally, to kill time while he is behind bars, I have the DNA to prove that he was my attacker. I know it now means that he also has proof that he is Sophia's father, and in this sometimes twisted, messed-up world we live in, there are judges out there that I know would grant him access to his child – under the provision that every child had the right to know their biological father.

That monster.

I wasn't going to allow him to ever do that to me.

To do that to Sophia.

It's gutless of me to leave without telling Jenna all of that to her face, I know that. Leaving without properly saying goodbye. But at least I have explained. I know how important it is for her to get her answers. To find out the truth.

And who knows? Maybe this isn't goodbye forever. Maybe one day in the future, once we are settled in our new home, I'll look her up and invite her to come and visit us both at the pretty seaside village on the edge of north Wales, where I am renting a cottage. I don't have any connections there; in fact the closest I've come to even visiting the place until now is looking it up on Google and Rightmove.

But that's the point.

If I am going to do this, then I need to start again, somewhere new. Somewhere myself and Sophia can call our own. Somewhere we'll both feel safe.

Where he'll never be able to find us should he come looking.

And I suspect that he will come looking. One day, years from now.

Though I don't have to think about any of that. He's still awaiting sentencing and hopefully the judge will throw the book at him. Though I won't be waiting around for the outcome.

Either way, we are free of him now.

Hooking the car seat onto the crook of my arm, I glance around the flat once again. The prison-like cocoon, where I spent the past nine months.

'Are you ready, little one?' I ask as I close the door behind me for the very last time. A feeling of excitement bubbling in the pit of my stomach at the start of our new adventure.

It's just the two of us now, against the world.

This is it, I think as I walk towards my car.

The happy-ever-after that I'd never believed would one day belong to me.

A LETTER FROM CASEY KELLEHER

Dear reader,

I want to say a huge thank you for choosing to read The Missing Mother. This is my fifth psychological thriller, and I have to say I thoroughly enjoyed the dark, twisted turns as the lives of the two women in my story collide.

If you would like to keep up to date with all my latest releases, just sign up at the following link. Your email address will never be shared and you can unsubscribe at any time.

www.bookouture.com/casey-kelleher

As always with my books, I started the writing process with such a small seed of an idea, Evie Monroe, forced to give her child up in order to keep her safe. Jenna Stone, lead reporter at the Islington Gazette always fighting for the truth and justice.

I really hope you enjoyed it.

I'd love to hear what you thought of The Missing Mother so if you have the time, and you'd like to leave me a review on Amazon it's always appreciated. (I do make a point of reading every single one.)

I also love hearing from you, my readers – your messages and photos of the books that you tag me in on social media always make my day! And trust me, some days us authors really need that to spur us on with that dreaded daily word-count.

So, please feel free to get in touch through social media or my website.

Thank you,

Casey Kelleher

www.caseykelleher.co.uk

 facebook.com/officialcaseykelleher
 x.com/CaseyKelleher
 instagram.com/caseykelleher

ACKNOWLEDGEMENTS

Many thanks to my brilliant editor Susannah Hamilton. It's been an absolute pleasure working alongside you, on Evie and Jenna's story. As always you really helped me pull the story together so perfectly. Special thanks as always to the amazing Noelle Holten – PR extraordinaire! To Sarah Hardy, and to all of the Bookouture team. You guys really are the best! Huge thanks also to my good friend Colin Scott and for the Savvy's for all your fantastic advice and support. And to all the lovely book groups on social media. As always I'd like to thank my extremely supportive friends and family for all the encouragement that they give me along the way. The Coopers, The Kellehers, The Ellises. And to all my lovely friends. Finally, a big thank you to my husband Danny. My rock! Much love to Ben, Danny and Kyle. Not forgetting little Miska. My most favourite child. And to you, my lovely reader, I say this often, because it's true. You are the very reason I write, without you, none of this would have been possible. Casey x

PUBLISHING TEAM

Turning a manuscript into a book requires the efforts of many people. The publishing team at Bookouture would like to acknowledge everyone who contributed to this publication.

Audio
Alba Proko
Sinead O'Connor
Melissa Tran

Commercial
Lauren Morrissette
Jil Thielen
Imogen Allport

Data and analysis
Mark Alder
Mohamed Bussuri

Cover design
Aaron Munday

Editorial
Susannah Hamilton
Nadia Michael

Copyeditor
Janette Currie

Proofreader
Claire Rushbrook

Marketing
Alex Crow
Melanie Price
Occy Carr
Ciara Rosney

Operations and distribution
Marina Valles
Stephanie Straub

Production
Hannah Snetsinger
Mandy Kullar
Jen Shannon

Publicity
Kim Nash
Noelle Holten
Myrto Kalavrezou
Jess Readett
Sarah Hardy

Rights and contracts
Peta Nightingale
Richard King
Saidah Graham

Milton Keynes UK
Ingram Content Group UK Ltd.
UKHW040829300124
436892UK00004BA/187